POWER OF PEN AND VOICE

POWER OF PEN AND VOICE

A SPOKEN MAGE COMPANION NOVEL

MELANIE CELLIER

THE SPOKEN MAGE BOOK 5

POWER OF PEN AND VOICE: A SPOKEN MAGE COMPANION NOVEL

For my nephew, Reuben Allan,
in anticipation of many adventures of your own

ROYAL FAMILY OF ARDANN

King Stellan
Queen Verena
Crown Princess Lucienne
Prince Lucas

MAGE COUNCIL

Academy Head (black robe) - Duke Lorcan of Callinos
University Head (black robe) - Duchess Jessamine of
    Callinos
Head of Law Enforcement (red robe) - Duke Soren of
    Stantorn
Head of the Seekers (gray robe) - Duchess Phyllida of
    Callinos
Head of the Healers (purple robe) - Duke Dashiell of
    Callinos
Head of the Growers (green robe) - Duchess Annika of
    Devoras
Head of the Wind Workers (blue robe) - Duke Magnus of
    Ellington
Head of the Creators (orange robe) - Duke Casimir of
    Stantorn
Head of the Armed Forces (silver robe) - General Griffith of
    Devoras
Head of the Royal Guard (gold robe) - General Thaddeus of
    Stantorn

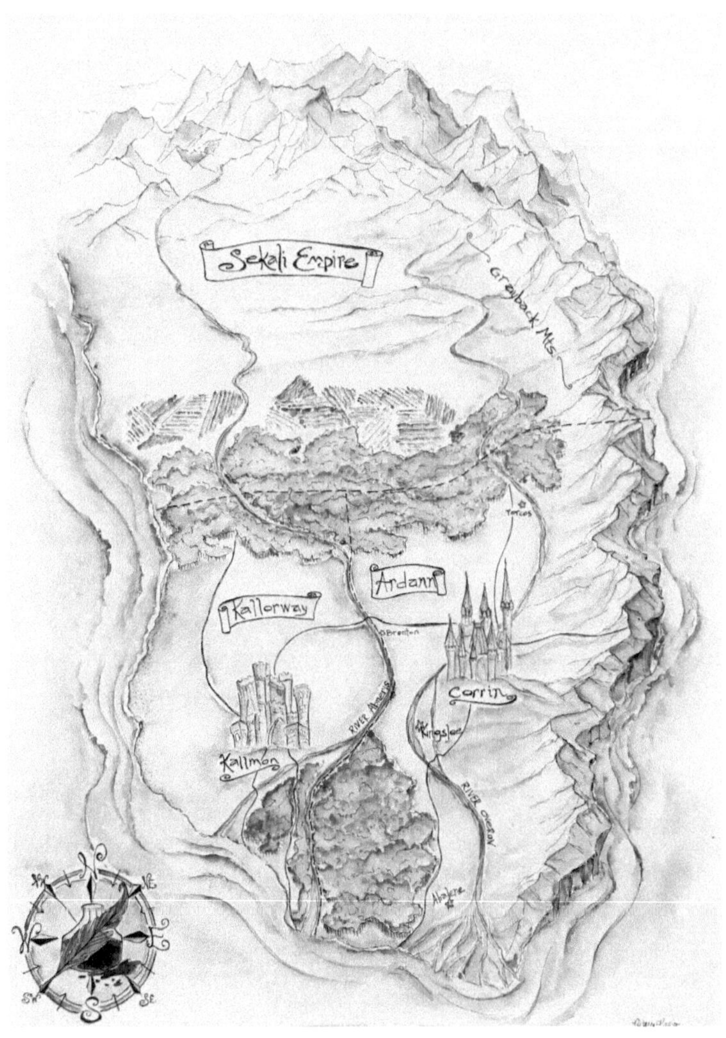

Sekali Empire
Greyback Mts.
Ardann
Kallorway
Tarcos
Brenton
Corrin
River Abahi
Kingslea
River Carfoy
Kallmon
Abalone
NW
NE
N
E
SW
S
SE

CHAPTER 1

SAFFRON

A chime rang across the glittering ballroom, silencing the music and drawing the attention of every mage present to the raised platform inside the double doors. My heart swelled with pride to see Elena standing there beside Lucas and his parents, every inch the princess. She looked almost as magnificent as the elaborate blossoms that had been placed around the door, a frame for the temporary stage and the royals who stood there.

As the one and only Spoken Mage, she had earned her place on that podium, but it was Elena as a person who had won the heart of a prince. And as one of her friends, I wasn't in the least surprised. Elena had always been impossible to ignore.

"You did an incredible job helping her choose an outfit," I whispered to Coralie who stood on the other side of my cousin Finnian. "No one would guess she wasn't born royalty herself."

"She looks almost as beautiful as you," Finnian murmured, slipping his arms around Coralie's waist.

She giggled while I rolled my eyes and turned my attention back to the betrothal announcement. As the words were spoken by King Stellan, Lucas's court mask cracked, a genuine smile spreading across his face as he looked down at his betrothed, the pride in his eyes clear from across the room.

She glanced up at him once, flushing endearingly, and then smiled at the crowd as they dutifully applauded. Finnian let out a whooping cheer, and a number of others joined him, the noise in the ballroom growing noticeably louder and more enthusiastic.

I glanced around the crowd, noting those near us who cheered most loudly and those who made only a few half-hearted claps. Finnian had once predicted that as Spoken Mage, Elena would change our world. He couldn't have been more right—and not everyone appreciated it.

"No surprises that I can see," said a quiet voice at my other side. With a start, I realized our other friend from the Academy, Araminta, had slipped up to join us.

Her eyes roved around the crowd as mine had just been doing, taking note of the various reactions.

"You would know better than I would," I said.

Since our graduation, Araminta had taken a position as a palace official, working for the Spoken Mage. I knew Elena found her assistance invaluable, especially given her knowledge of the dynamics among the minor families of the kingdom.

"It's strange to see the Ellingtons applauding so loudly," I added, my eyes dwelling on the tight clump of attendees who clustered around Duke Magnus, the head of the wind workers. "But I suppose I shouldn't be surprised."

Whatever the general mage population might think of the Spoken Mage and the changes she'd brought to our society, they viewed the Ellingtons with even greater distrust. For centuries, they had been one of the four great families, and for a long time they had been the richest of the mages, if not the strongest. But no one quite knew what to make of them now. Not after Elena and Lucas discovered a group of their members colluding with our enemies in an attempted coup.

"No one has more motivation to demonstrate their loyalty to

the Spoken Mage and the crown than the remaining Ellingtons," Araminta said, her voice dry. "Ironically, they're the least of my concerns."

My gaze caught on Duke Soren, head of law enforcement, and I shivered.

"It's shockingly cowardly of me," I admitted in a whisper, "but I'd rather find myself talking to one of those Ellingtons than Duke Soren any day. I can't quite say why, but the man has always terrified me. Whenever he looks my way, I become instantly convinced I must have committed some crime that I've since forgotten about. Do you think he ever smiles?"

Araminta laughed quietly. "Not that I've ever seen. But then I avoid him if I possibly can." She wrinkled her nose. "Of course, I tend to avoid every Stantorn that I can, just on principle."

I laughed. "You and me both." I bit my lip and then grudgingly added, "Although I'm grateful for his efforts."

One of the coup's leaders had been Duke Lennox, the head of law enforcement, and his removal had thrown the discipline into chaos, making his replacement one of King Stellan's first priorities after the Ellingtons' defeat. Duke Soren, already a senior mage in law enforcement, had the advantages both of his family's reputation for being harsh and unyielding and his close relation to General Thaddeus of the Royal Guard. With the help of Thaddeus's forces, he had brought the law enforcement discipline back into line.

I might not like him, but he had earned my respect by his single-minded focus on first dismantling and then rebuilding his discipline.

"It's certainly true that nothing—not even the general mage attitude toward commonborns—slows Soren down," Araminta said. "He might be a Stantorn, but he was the one to insist that a large number of his commonborn law enforcement guards be included among those sealed."

Many still regarded the new sealing composition—which

blocked a person's ability to access power—with suspicion. I wasn't sure what they found more threatening—that working the composition permanently stripped a mage of their ability to compose, or that it granted the commonborns it touched the freedom to read and write. After centuries without major social upheaval, suddenly a whole group of commonborns had their unstable link to power blocked and were legally permitted access to the written word.

I regarded Duke Soren from across the ballroom. Apparently the newly appointed law enforcement head didn't share this concern.

"It's admirable that he's willing to use any tool at his disposal to return his discipline to full strength and efficacy," I admitted.

Araminta nodded. "And while it may not have been his intention, his efforts have done a lot to help the crown reshape the way mages and commonborn interact. We may not like him, but Duke Soren is in great favor with the royals."

My eyes narrowed as I considered the way he hovered near the clump of Ellingtons. His placement in the crowd couldn't be a coincidence. His presence was a visible signal to the rest of the mages that they need not fear the remaining Ellingtons since he and his people remained ever vigilant.

"Perhaps he's not as single-minded as I thought," I mused to Araminta. "Maybe he knows exactly what impact his actions with his commonborn subordinates are having."

Araminta chuckled. "You think underneath—buried somewhere far, far out of sight—he's filled with compassion for the plight of the commonborn?"

I snorted, meeting her laughing eyes and starting to chuckle myself. "About as likely as Weston having such hidden depths. No, I don't think he cares about the commonborn, as such. But I'm guessing he cares a great deal about being viewed so favorably by the crown."

Araminta's chuckles faded, and she sighed. "You're likely

right. He's young for his position, and you don't get to such a rank without being a canny player. Times are changing, and he's clearly determined not to be left behind."

My eyes strayed over the broader crowd. "I heard some of the commonborn merchants actually received invitations to the ball. That must be the first time in history, surely?"

Araminta nodded. "Only the heads of the richest and most influential families, but still…"

I shook my head. "That has to have upset a few mages."

Araminta grimaced. "Of course it has. And naturally those least deserving of their own invitations are the most offended." She rolled her eyes. "But it's the gesture that matters, really. The invitations were a royal acknowledgment that the sealed commonborns, and the merchant families who employ many of them, are a rising force. Not everyone appreciates that. Not one bit."

"Did the merchants come?" I asked.

"To the last one," she said. "None of them plan to waste the opportunities they're being offered."

She fell silent and then abruptly groaned. "I have to go. Selina looks like she's about to make trouble. If I move quickly, I might be able to cut her off before she unloads whatever vitriol she has planned—most likely on someone important enough to take offense. I'm determined that nothing happen to ruin tonight for Elena and Lucas."

I waved a farewell, watching her go with a smile on my face. Elena had been right to ask our friend to join her at the palace. This Araminta bore little resemblance to the silent, nervous girl I had met in first year.

My thoughts returned to the commonborn merchants who had been included for the first time. I scanned the crowd, several unfamiliar faces catching my eye. But it was a foolish whimsy. I didn't know every mage in the kingdoms—especially those from the minor families—and you couldn't tell a commonborn apart from a mage merely by looking at them. At least not here at a ball where very few mages wore their robes and where any common-born influential enough to warrant an invitation would be just as likely as a mage to be coated in power.

Like all mages, I could only sense power once it was released through a working, and the richest of commonborns had always been able to find mages desperate enough to sell them composi-tions. And now that the new rank of sealed commonborn could actually read those compositions—instead of relying on sealed and color-coded parchments—this commonborn use of compo-sitions had only increased.

Selling compositions had never been a prestigious occupa-tion, but not all mages from minor families could afford to turn their backs on such an easy means to make money. And the top commonborn merchant families were already growing richer under the new system—allowing them to offer even more lucra-tive prices for compositions as a result. Those families had been the first to request to have members of their ranks sealed—and since many of them employed the few commonborn university graduates in existence, they had been assured of at least some of the valued places at the sealing ceremonies.

And the first thing these newly sealed merchants had done was apply to the crown for access to the written records of their mage rivals. No one questioned why the king had been more willing to approve these requests when they were made against the many Ellington merchant families. And with the recent specter of treason hanging in the air, no one with influence protested when he supported the commonborn as they sought reparation for the many inconsistencies they found in the Ellington records. It turned out that a portion at least of the Ellington wealth had been built through dishonest dealings with the commonborn merchants—merchants who until now had lacked the capacity to keep their own records.

The ease of these victories had kept the commonborn

merchants from inquiring too closely as to why the other great families seemed safe from such discoveries. Or perhaps their leaders simply knew better than to push too hard. These families had built their merchant empires over generations, under the most inequitable of circumstances, and they hadn't done it by being foolish. They must know that the crown relied on the support of the mages and that the advancement of the sealed commonborn was already straining that support.

Unable to pick out the commonborn in attendance, my attention was instead caught by a more familiar face. Duchess Annika —head of the growers. Had she personally had a part in the creation of the elaborate plants and flowers which decorated the ballroom? The hand of a mage—or more likely a number of mages, given the size of the room—was evident in their unnatural size and beauty. Many in Duchess Annika's discipline focused their attention on the kingdom's crops, but the most desirable positions were here at the palace where mages of skill and knowledge could use their abilities not only for the beauty of the royal gardens but also in the experimental beds behind the palace where growers attempted to create new and valuable species.

A sudden clamminess coated my palms, and I tried to surreptitiously wipe them on the folds of my skirt. After much consideration, I had decided to apply to join the growers—although I dared not dream of a position at the palace. Sometime before the ball ended, I would have to find the courage to cross the dance floor and speak to the duchess. Not every mage in the kingdom accepted the royal invitation to the Midsummer Ball, but every mage who wished to join a discipline did—as did all ten discipline heads. Because those heads accepted applications only once a year—at Midsummer in Corrin.

After being raised by the most powerful healing family in the kingdom, I knew many assumed I would choose to become a healer. Certainly it would have been the easy path, and I suspected my family were disappointed I couldn't do so. But I had received enough exposure to complex healings during my time at the Academy to know I didn't have the capacity for it. A healer who was liable to faint or lose the contents of their stomach at the sight of a wound was no good to anyone. I would never be able to pass healer training, and having to refuse me admittance to his discipline was a pain I would not dream of inflicting on my uncle, the head of the healers.

Ordinarily I would never have considered putting my own desires ahead of my family's expectations—not after they had given me and my mother so much. But unable to join the healers, I had tentatively suggested the discipline I truly preferred and been relieved when it met with their approval. If I was approved by the duchess, I would become a grower.

In an ordinary year, I wouldn't have felt any great concern about my chances of acceptance. My results at the Academy had been acceptable, if not noteworthy, and I was a Callinos, with connections to one of our most influential families. And, on top of all that, our year had been an unusually small one, meaning the disciplines would have far less choice than usual.

But this wasn't an ordinary year.

While there were no age limits on applicants, mages only rarely chose to request a change of discipline or to start training in a new discipline later in life. Most years, the applicants were made up of graduated mages, fresh from their two-year term with the Armed Forces.

But one of the first things the king had done after signing peace with Kallorway was to issue a royal edict ending compulsory terms for both mages and commonborn. The news had briefly united the kingdom in universal rejoicing because the mage families had been no more eager to see their children sent to war than the commonborn families. It might be rarer for mage conscripts to die, but it still happened.

The result of this mass release from conscription was that this

Midsummer, not only would the Academy graduates from two years ago be applying for entry to a discipline, but the year below them and my own year would be applying as well.

My year had done a stint at the front lines while still studying at the Academy, and I didn't believe a single one of us had any interest in returning to such a life. We had all been delighted for the freedom the end of the war granted us. Only later did it occur to me what it would mean for applying to a discipline.

As royals, Elena and Lucas would not join a discipline, although I knew Elena intended to continue her healing studies informally. Likewise, those in our year who boasted current discipline heads for fathers—Finnian and the Devoras twins, Calix, and Natalya—could be assured of their acceptance to whatever discipline they chose. And since Finnian had chosen his own father's discipline of healing—following in the footsteps of Coralie, not his father, I knew—he could also guarantee acceptance for his betrothed.

Clarence had been taken from us by the war, and Dariela had sealed herself in the infamous Battle of the Academy. Araminta had subsequently chosen to follow suit, purposefully failing her final exams as she admitted to me afterward. So that left only Weston, Lavinia, and me with any doubt as to our futures. And since Weston and Lavinia had Stantorn connections, close friendships with the Devoras twins, and were both stronger mages than I was, I couldn't imagine they were overly concerned.

Staring across the ballroom at the duchess, my stomach churning with anxiety, I could almost understand Araminta's drastic decision to sacrifice her power. As the weakest of our year —the daughter of a mage from a minor family and the common-born woman he had married—her situation would have been far more precarious than mine. I knew she had held out little hope of being accepted to a discipline even in normal circumstances, and she considered the opportunity to seal her mother more valuable than her own limited power.

Now that the moment had come, I found my certainty about my own future slipping further still. Perhaps it was a mistake to apply for only one discipline after all. My mother and aunt had assured me it wasn't necessary to make multiple applications, as those less sure of their position were wont to do. Although they were both too kind to say it directly, I knew they considered my close connection to Duke Dashiell to be enough of a guarantee.

But, unlike Finnian, who had inherited his father's strength, my blood connection with the duke was only of the most distant kind. My father had been one of the weaker Callinos mages, and it was only because Finnian's mother and my mother were sisters that I called the duke uncle and had been raised almost as his daughter. I had all the pressure of a prominent position among the great families with none of the birthright of strength that should have accompanied it.

Not that I would ever say as much to anyone. My father had died during my infancy, and my mother, an invalid since her pregnancy with me, worried about her only daughter far too much already. And nothing could be stronger than my gratitude toward my aunt and uncle, who had accepted my mother and me into their exalted household without a moment's hesitation or a single subsequent mention of their generosity.

I truly believed they loved me almost as if I were their daughter, and so I had dropped any suggestion of applying for multiple disciplines at the faintest hint that it might be seen as doubt about the duke's influence. But in my heart, I wasn't sure what I disliked more—the thought that I might not be accepted into any discipline, or the idea that I might be accepted only because the duchess believed me to have a more exalted position than I truly occupied. It would be mortifying to start my specialist training only to watch the disappointment of those around me when they realized I had nothing of Finnian's strength or control.

Lost in my own head, I had missed the rest of the king's announcements, noticing with a jolt that the royal family were already descending back onto the ballroom floor. I would have to ask Finnian and Coralie if anything unexpected had been said.

Before I could turn to them, however, the double doors flew violently open, banging back against the walls with force. The musical notes that had started to fill the air stuttered and died on a discordant tone, their echoes replaced by startled exclamations all around me.

A young woman staggered onto the platform the king and queen had so recently occupied, nothing in her appearance suggesting she had come ready to attend a ball. Her hair and clothes were dirty and disheveled, and she had a streak up one bare arm that looked horribly like dried blood, although I could see no wound on her.

A man several years her senior stumbled onto the platform beside her, pulling himself to a halt and gazing around at the crowd with astonishment. A number of footmen and guards hurried through the doors in their wake, hovering around the two as if they weren't sure whether to assist or arrest them.

"Is that Jasper?" Coralie gasped, naming Elena's commonborn brother. "I thought he was at the Sekali court."

CHAPTER 2

JULIAN

I caught Elena's friend's words from where I stood, unfortunately close behind the lovebirds. I knew my adopted sister was close to the Cygnet girl, but her name escaped me.

"That is definitely Jasper." I pushed forward to get a better view. "And he was definitely in the Sekali Empire last we heard." As Elena's adoptive brother, I had been appointed alongside her blood brother as one of the new Ardannian ambassadors to the Empire. But, unlike Jasper, I had been delayed starting my posting and had yet to leave Corrin.

"But that's not his wife Clara with him," Finnian's betrothed said, pointing out the obvious.

"She looks Sekali," Saffron said quietly, confusion in her voice.

I glanced at Finnian's cousin and then back at the girl on the platform. She was right. The newcomer might share similarities of coloring with the northern Finnian and Saffron, her skin a similar gold and her hair the same sleek black, but slight differences in feature and clothing declared her origins to be beyond the border.

As soon as I recognized it, I recognized her, biting back a curse.

"That is Princess Kalani," I breathed. "Oldest daughter of the Sekali emperor."

"What?" Coralie yelped loudly before clapping a hand over her mouth and dropping her voice to my level. "It can't be a Sekali princess!"

"I didn't recognize her at first," I said. "Not here and in such a state. But I'm almost certain."

As if to back me up, the Sekali ambassador burst through the crowd, rushing up the steps. Although the princess looked as if she was about to collapse—from injury or exhaustion, I wasn't sure—the man paused to bow low. I couldn't hear his murmured words, but it seemed clear he was waiting for permission before daring to touch an imperial princess, even to offer support.

Princess Kalani glanced at Jasper who stepped forward and exchanged several sentences with the astonished looking Chen. The ambassador's surprise turned to an expression of outrage, and he made several unusually expansive gestures with his hands.

Jasper shrugged, a helpless expression on his face as he looked back at the crowd. This time his gaze caught on our sister, however, and his expression lightened.

"Elena!"

She was up the steps to him before he'd finished calling her name, so I didn't hear whatever greetings or questions they exchanged. But they had barely spoken before King Stellan stepped forward, gesturing for the whole group to descend from their public stage.

As soon as I realized he intended to usher them into a private chamber to one side of the ballroom, I took off, pushing my way through the crowd.

"Come on! We're not missing this either," Finnian said behind me, his voice holding almost as much glee as concern.

Although I hid it better, I knew something of how he felt,

excitement coursing through me at such unexpected and dramatic happenings. I glanced over my shoulder in time to see him pull his less enthusiastic cousin along behind him. Apparently all three of them intended to join me.

I didn't hold back, elbowing my way through where necessary, the others trailing behind. We reached the entrance to the chamber just as someone attempted to close the door. I pushed my way in, projecting more confidence than I really felt. My position as a future Ardannian ambassador probably didn't give me sufficient rank to burst in on this private meeting of the king —even if the meeting did include a couple of Sekalis. But I was relying on my family connection to Elena and Jasper to cover me.

Apparently Saffron, at least, recognized that the three of them had even less excuse for pushing into the meeting because she pulled on Finnian's arm, holding him back from the door and whispering furiously in his ear. Luckily for Finnian, Elena was positioned just inside the doorway, and when I stopped the door from closing, she glanced our way. Seeing her friends lurking behind me, she called for us all to come in before shutting the door firmly against the rest of the ball.

The king glanced over, a slight crease in his brow at our uninvited presence, but he appeared too distracted to make any protest. And I could hardly blame him. Seen closer up, Princess Kalani and Jasper looked even worse than they had from afar. Visible bruises and scratches covered their exposed skin, partially hidden by the dirt that overlaid everything.

A quick glance around the room showed we weren't the only ones to have rushed to join the royals—although I suspected the others had done so with the king's sanction, at least. It looked like all the discipline heads were present, along with the surprising addition of two sealed commonborns—one of whom I recognized as the head of a large merchant family. Their presence at the ball had ruffled enough mage feathers, but their inclusion in this meeting was likely to disturb even more.

The king displayed no uncertainty about their presence, however.

I gave a lazy nod of greeting to my father, General Griffith, head of the Armed Forces, who returned it with a look of long-suffering amusement. I wasn't entirely sure if he was exasperated or proud at my managing to include myself in the meeting, but I responded with a grin.

Chen pulled up a chair, murmuring frantically for Kalani to sit down, and I expected Elena to do the same for her brother. But instead she started speaking the binding words, no doubt intending to work some sort of healing for him. She couldn't give him the energy he clearly needed—no amount of power had ever been able to do that—but she could heal him, at least. Jasper looked up quickly, shaking his head at her.

"Her Highness had a couple of powerful healing compositions on her person. I know we look bad, but I assure you we're fine." He gave his sister a wry look before amending his words. "Well, we're exhausted, but even you can't do anything about that."

The Spoken Mage might have the unprecedented ability to use her unique spoken compositions to take the energy of others, but even she couldn't gift energy. Since accessing power to craft compositions drained energy, mages had spent centuries attempting to find a way to either store their energy or share it. They had failed to do so, however. And so each mage's compositions remained limited in power and complexity to what that individual could achieve with the energy available to them. There was a reason mages studied for four years at the Academy to increase their stamina and then made careful marriages of alliance to increase the natural strength of their family lines. A composition of enough power could leave a mage flat on their back, as exhausted as if they had run a marathon or worked from dawn to dusk completing heavy labor. Without care, a composition could even drain a mage dry.

Not that composing could be the cause of Jasper's current

exhaustion. The commonborn had clearly endured some significant physical ordeal.

Elena shook her head stubbornly at her brother's words and continued. She spoke quietly, and at length, and I was inclined to think she was demonstrating wisdom in ignoring Jasper's protests. He had always been overprotective of her, but the Spoken Mage hardly had need to conserve her strength.

Her working had been finely crafted, and when she spoke the binding words, the power that flared out from her held more control than brute strength. It enveloped Jasper and the princess, who gave a soft gasp.

Their bruises and scratches disappeared, the rents in their clothing weaving seamlessly back together. The dirt and dried blood that covered both them and their garments dusted into the finest powder and slid off to sprinkle around their feet.

When the power faded, only their visible exhaustion remained to indicate anything unusual had occurred. The girl before me once again looked like the Sekali princess I had seen in her father's court, although her robe had only gold embroidery and no winking jewels on this occasion.

I gave my adoptive sister a proud look. She had come a long way from the ignorant girl she used to be. With one composition, she had restored the foreign princess's dignity, and the gratitude in Chen's expression indicated it had not been a wasted exercise.

Kalani looked across at Elena, interest on her face. "Thank you. I never got the chance to see you do a spoken working when you visited our empire, although I had an account of your abilities from my father. I am glad to have the opportunity, even if I had hoped it would be under better circumstances."

Her voice was soft but strong, and she spoke with measured tones as if she had weighed every word before uttering it. I imagined such circumspection was necessary when you grew up as the heir of a vast empire.

"We are honored to host you, Your Highness," King Stellan

said, "but we were not expecting your visit, and I must confess to grave concern about the manner of your arrival and also your physical state." His eyes slid to Jasper. "Has some misfortune befallen you in my kingdom?"

Chen had finally maneuvered chairs behind both Kalani and Jasper, the two willingly sinking into them. At the king's words, Jasper looked as if he intended to spring back to his feet, but Elena drifted over to his side and held him down with a firm hand on his shoulder.

"I apologize for bursting into the ball like that, Your Majesty," Jasper said, directing his words at King Stellan. "It's been some time since I've had any sleep, and I'm not thinking straight. When we finally arrived at the palace, the princess's identity gave us entry, but I should have been more cautious when the footman said Elena was in the ballroom." He shook his head, clearly exasperated at himself. "There could only be one reason for her to be in the ballroom, especially considering all the Midsummer celebrations we passed in the city."

"You must not blame yourself, Jasper," Kalani said gently, his name faintly accented on her lips. "We have both had such single-minded focus on reaching the palace. I'm sure I barely even noticed any celebrations."

"But what happened to you?" Elena demanded without subtlety, displaying something of her old self. Not that I had met her when she first joined the Academy. We had only crossed paths after her adoption into my family, when three years of rubbing shoulders with royalty had apparently softened some of her rough edges.

To my surprise, it was Chen who replied, turning to her and bowing low.

"Her Highness has requested I submit myself to a truth composition before she reveals any more. It is something I will gladly do to put her mind at ease. I have such compositions upon my person, but obviously I cannot be trusted to place such a working upon myself. Your brother thought perhaps you might be willing to provide assistance in this matter."

"A truth composition? On you?" Elena raised an eyebrow in Jasper's direction but returned Chen's bow. "Certainly I can do so, if it is both your and the princess's wish."

"It is," Kalani said, the previous gentle silk of her tone giving way to steel. "I must be sure of his loyalties before I progress any further."

Chen's usually impassive face bore visible lines of distress, but he seemed more concerned that his loyalty was being questioned than reluctant to be placed under a truth composition.

Duke Soren stepped forward and cleared his throat. "If a truth composition is needed, my discipline is equipped to assist. There is no need to trouble the Spoken Mage."

He spoke Elena's title with respect, as he always did. It wouldn't do for the new leader of law enforcement to display any distaste toward the mage responsible for exposing treason within his discipline.

General Thaddeus, head of the Royal Guard, and my own previous discipline head, nodded. "The Royal Guard stand just as ready to produce such a working as law enforcement."

Princess Kalani looked between the two of them before glancing back at Elena and then finally letting her loaded gaze rest on Jasper. It was the commonborn who spoke.

"I realize this is an impudence of the highest order, and I wouldn't ask unless I had sufficient reason to do so. Princess Kalani would prefer that Elena work the truth composition, and —" He took a deep breath as if bracing himself for his next words. "And we would prefer the composition be worked over the entire room."

A shocked intake of breath sounded from all around me, and a number of eyes flew to the king and queen with Crown Princess Lucienne beside them. Senior Ardannians were not as used to submitting to truth compositions as it seemed their Sekali counterparts were. Certainly I had never heard of anyone daring to suggest the royals themselves should be subjected to one.

Jasper, clearly recognizing his own daring, hurried on. "Naturally we are not asking Elena to compose a working that would compel anyone to speak—merely to reveal the truth of any words spoken. And we wish to ask only one question."

The king's heavy gaze lingered on Kalani rather than Jasper. He clearly understood it was not his commonborn subject making the request, and no one present doubted that something of import had occurred, although we had yet to receive any explanation of what it could be. But that it involved the oldest child of the emperor was enough to make clear the potential gravity of the situation.

"And what is this question?" the king asked.

"Actually, I suppose it's two questions," Jasper said. "We wish to ask if it's true that no one here was expecting our arrival, and also if anyone present in this room had any knowledge of the attack on the princess and her delegation."

The possibility of an attack must have been on everyone's mind, but there were still a number of audible indrawn breaths, and I heard one quiet mutter of, "Kallorway."

With the war so newly ended, it was inevitable that minds would leap in the direction of our old enemies. But everyone present—with the possible exception of Elena's friends—must know enough to doubt such a thing. Kallorway was still consumed with internal conflict as the newly crowned, but also sealed, King Cassius fought to hold onto his throne. It was precisely the state of affairs Ardann had desired, a situation we had orchestrated in exchange for our signing the peace agreement.

"Very well," the king said gravely. "I have no hesitation answering those questions under a truth composition, no matter who might work it." He turned to Elena. "You may proceed."

No one else in the room said anything. If the king was willing to be included in the working, no one else could possibly object. And not even a discipline head would carry enough truth compositions to work one on every person in the room. With the flexibility of her verbal compositions, and her unique ability to draw on unlimited energy, Elena was the only mage present with the capacity to complete such a working on the spot. Although I was sure Jasper's trust in her was another factor in his request.

Elena spoke slowly and clearly, using more words than I knew she needed. Obviously she wanted everyone to hear that she was crafting her working in compliance with Jasper's stated limitations. When she completed it, a glow appeared in front of her, strong and bright.

She asked each person present to state one obvious falsehood, a routine test of the working. Truth compositions usually only applied to a single person, however, so it took a great deal longer than usual, each person waiting for the glow to return to full brightness before speaking the lie that would turn it oily black.

When Elena got around to our corner of the room, she spoke the name of Finnian's betrothed first, reminding me the girl was called Coralie. Coralie spoke her falsehood with less confidence than usually filled her voice, perhaps as a result of the surprised looks being directed at our small grouping. I almost stepped away, wanting to distance myself from the rest of them, but something about Saffron's quiet dignity made me pause.

The poor girl had attempted to stop Finnian from inserting them into this meeting only to be pulled into it despite her efforts. Yet she held her ground now with calm assurance, despite being so completely outranked on every side. I respected the careful control I suspected this represented. Only a fool would truly feel no concern about being noticed in such a situation by all the most important people in the kingdom, and she had never struck me as a fool—an impression supported by the conversation I had overheard earlier between her and Elena's assistant.

But if I was honest, it was more than that. She stood closest to me, and I found myself unable to step away and leave her standing alone, exposed and vulnerable. It was an irrational impulse, but it was enough to keep my feet rooted in place.

As soon as everyone in the room had taken a turn proving the composition, the king spoke, not waiting for Jasper to repeat his questions.

"I knew nothing of any planned visit from the Sekali Empire —by Princess Kalani or anyone else. And I certainly knew nothing of any attack against Her Highness or any person traveling with her. I still have no idea what has actually occurred. If any Ardannian has offered violence toward any member of the Empire, it was done without my knowledge and is not condoned by the Ardannian crown."

Princess Kalani gave a seated half-bow in his direction. "Your words give me great reassurance, Your Majesty."

King Stellan turned to Queen Verena, and she repeated his assurances of ignorance and goodwill toward the Empire and its people. One by one, the rest of the room followed the example of their monarchs. Ambassador Chen spoke last of all, giving grave assurances that he also knew nothing of any attack or any violence offered toward his princess.

"I have also received no communication regarding any visit and was not expecting you," he added. "Just as I have heard no suggestion that your father will be anything but outraged to hear of this grave offense to the Empire." After a brief pause, he gave a bow in the direction of King Stellan. "I have also heard nothing during my posting here to suggest that Ardann would so disrespect your family or our great empire."

"Certainly not," King Stellan said, apparently seeing the diplomatic opportunity provided by the truth composition. "Ardann respects the might of the Empire and acknowledges the legitimacy of your father's position as emperor. We desire only good relations with your people, Your Highness."

She bowed again, this time more deeply. "As we desire good relations with our southern neighbors."

Silence fell for several beats, and Elena closed the working. A soft sigh sounded through the room.

The queen spoke. "Now that we have proven the innocence of both the Ardannian leadership and your own ambassador, may we at last hear the story of what has befallen you? Your words have only deepened our concern."

"Perhaps everyone should have a seat," Jasper said, his voice grim. "I'm afraid you aren't likely to be returning to the festivities any time soon."

CHAPTER 3

SAFFRON

It had taken everything in me to retain my poise and not sink into the floor as the eyes of not only the entire royal family but the full mage council rested on me. When we got out of here, I was going to wring Finnian's neck. The weight of my uncle's eyes had been worst of all as I tried to guess if disappointment lurked behind his calm expression. Did he feel we had disgraced the family? Finnian, utterly secure in his position as the duke's only child, might feel no qualms, but I felt enough for the both of us.

At Jasper's suggestion that we all be seated, I sprang into action. No servants had been permitted to enter the room, and I was clearly the lowest-ranked person present. I whisked myself across the room, pulling forward the chairs that were stored around the walls. Two of them were more elaborate than the others, and I placed these behind the king and queen. By the time I returned to the wall for more chairs, Finnian and Coralie had already joined the effort, placing a seat each for Princess Lucienne and Lucas. We soon had enough chairs pulled out for the entire group, placing them in a rough circle so that everyone had a clear view of Jasper and the Sekali princess.

When I reached General Griffith's oldest son, I found Julian had already retrieved his own chair along with a second one which he had placed between him and Finnian. I gave him a nod of thanks as I slipped into the empty place. A part of me would have preferred to take the opportunity to slip from the room, but I was concerned that doing so might attract even more attention my way. That, and I had to admit to a strong measure of curiosity. I had already endured the censure; I might as well stay to hear the answers we had all come for.

I glanced sideways at the young man beside me. As the oldest son of the head of the Armed Forces and a Devoras, he had been known to me by name all my life. But that didn't mean I knew him in any meaningful way. He was older than me by a number of years, and since his younger siblings, Calix and Natalya, had been due to enter the Academy the same year as Finnian and me, we had always been thrown together with them instead. And considering the twins liked us no better than we liked them, we had never gone out of our way to seek the association. I was sure Julian knew my name, as I knew his, but I wasn't sure he had ever spared me a thought otherwise.

I had to acknowledge now that he was good looking, in an objective sort of way. But he bore too close a resemblance to Natalya for me to feel any actual attraction. With his dark hair, he looked more like he should be her twin than the fair-haired Calix. Jasper began to speak, and I pulled my attention away from Julian to focus on his words.

"Four weeks ago, Her Imperial Highness sealed herself and an unprecedented number of commonborn children."

No one actually interrupted him, but the sense of astonishment in the room was palpable, eyebrows shooting up all around the circle. The king and queen exchanged a swift, startled look, and even Ambassador Chen's surprise broke through his usual diplomatic facade. Only Elena looked unsurprised, merely thoughtful. She must have felt the shadow over Kalani's power and been bursting with curiosity about it.

My eyes dropped to the princess's exposed wrists before I realized my foolishness. Here in Ardann we had need to mark those commonborns who were safely sealed, but in the Empire there was no need to distinguish between those who could safely read and write and those who could not since every commonborn was sealed at age two. But a princess who was sealed?

Given our own royals had marriage laws intended to ensure their line only ever grew in strength and control, I could only imagine the Sekalis pursued a similar practice. And with an entire empire at their disposal, it was no surprise that a daughter of the emperor would be capable of sealing an enormous number of commonborn. But that both she and her family would consent to such a thing seemed almost unimaginable.

I glanced at her, sympathy in my gaze. Elena and Lucas had told me a little about the culture of the Sekalis. We might be loyal to our crown and kingdom in Ardann, but they lived with a whole other level of devotion. In Sekali, bringing honor to your clan was paramount, and serving your clan and empire of far greater importance than your individual desires. It was the only way they had maintained their social structure where two entire clans remained devoted to sealing themselves for the sake of the commonborn. In exchange for their service they received great honor, but was it really enough to make up for the sacrifice?

And it was one thing for those clan members who had been raised since birth to see such service as their purpose in life. What must it have felt like to be raised as heir to the throne, only to suddenly be told you must give up your power instead?

Elena said the Sekalis greatly honored their sealed mages, though. Perhaps Kalani remained the heir? Such a thing was hard to fathom in Ardann—and we could see the chaos it was even now wreaking in Kallorway. But perhaps attitudes were different enough in the Empire. Although, the astonishment on Chen's face suggested this wasn't an ordinary royal practice, even there.

"Princess Kalani's younger sister, Princess Keiko, has now officially been named heir to the imperial throne," Jasper continued after a brief pause to let us all recover from our surprise.

So some things were the same in the Empire, after all.

"In light of her new status, the emperor named Princess Kalani as a temporary ambassador to Ardann. I volunteered to accompany her and her delegation in order to introduce her to Your Majesties and the Ardannian court." Jasper inclined his head at King Stellan and Queen Verena, and the king nodded approvingly. If an imperial princess was to descend on Ardann, then it was appropriate that she be accompanied by one of our ambassadors.

"As you know," Jasper continued, "despite the end of the war, delegations between the Empire and Ardann are continuing to travel all the way east to the Overon River before traveling south through the northern forests into Ardann."

He didn't have to explain why. Everyone present knew that while it would be more direct to travel down the Abneris River, access to Ardann through this route remained impossible. Since the Abneris was the border between Ardann and Kallorway, our side of it was well fortified with a wide stretch of jagged rocks called the Wall. Not just a physical barrier, these rocks had been strengthened by a patchwork of twenty-five years' worth of deadly compositions. No one had even begun to contemplate how it might be dismantled, and I was sure there were few in Ardann who felt certain enough of the peace to wish to see it disappear immediately anyway.

"Messengers were sent ahead to inform you of our imminent arrival, and two weeks ago our delegation set out upon this route. We made it across the Empire and some way down the river, to an unknown point within the forest, when our boat was attacked."

The king leaned forward, his brows drawn together, and his eyes keenly fastened on Jasper. "So it is unknown whether the attack happened inside the Empire or across the border in Ardann?"

"That is the case," the princess agreed with a gracious inclination of her head.

I watched her as surreptitiously as I could. How much training had it taken to maintain such poise and authority even in a situation such as this? I only wished I could achieve half her sense of control.

"Naturally the emperor had furnished his daughter with an arsenal of compositions, as well as a skilled honor guard and several mage attendants," Jasper said, resuming the story. "And yet our forces were almost immediately overwhelmed. I couldn't say what compositions they used, only that Her Highness and I experienced the same thing. Rendered unconscious early in the attack, we resumed awareness only as we were carried out through the fringes of the forest. And we were the only remaining members of the delegation. From various comments we heard, we have been forced to conclude that the others were slaughtered."

Kalani's expression didn't change, but her hand tightened around the armrest of her chair. Had she been close to anyone in the group? I didn't know if imperial princesses were allowed close friends.

"Only the two of you?" King Stellan regarded them both with measuring eyes.

Jasper shrugged uncomfortably. "We believe Her Highness was spared due to her rank—that indeed she was the target of the attack—and that I was spared due to being Ardannian. But what purpose we were intended to serve we don't know."

"So they took you the rest of the way down the river in a boat of their own?" Queen Verena asked. "They were gambling on the chance that none of our people would see them leave the forest."

Jasper shook his head. "From what we can gather, they left the river immediately after the attack and carried us east through the forest, exiting directly into the Grayback mountain range. Though clearly strong, their group was small and agile, able to travel through the forests that are largely impenetrable for a group of any size."

"They took you into the mountains?" The king frowned. "And then down south into Ardann?"

This time Jasper nodded. "Whether it was before or after the attack, we certainly crossed the Ardannian border at some point. But I can't say how far south they intended to travel. I couldn't even tell you how far they actually came."

He glanced across at the princess. "Her Highness had secreted a small number of highly powerful workings on her person in such a way that they had not been confiscated with the rest of her compositions. Using these, we were able to escape our captors and elude recapture. However, we were deep in the mountains at that point, and it took us a great deal of effort and some trial and error to find a path back out. As soon as we reached the plains, we hurried straight to Corrin, unsure who to trust and vulnerable without a single remaining composition. The one thought in my mind was to reach Elena."

She placed her hand back on his shoulder, this time giving it a gentle squeeze. I could read the pain on her face at hearing her brother had been enduring such an ordeal while she was dressing in elaborate gowns and celebrating Midsummer. But there was no way she could have known.

"Your ambassador is too modest," Princess Kalani said. "It was only through our combined efforts that we were able to escape. It is fortunate for me that Your Majesties chose to send someone of such genius to represent your kingdom. My compositions aided us, certainly, but I could not have done it alone."

Jasper flushed slightly as if uncomfortable with the praise, or perhaps with the extra attention he was now receiving from the various important personages in the room.

"Among themselves, our captors spoke in an unfamiliar tongue," he explained. "Although at least two of them were able to communicate with us using the common language."

"A different language? They spoke a different language?" Crown Princess Lucienne leaned forward, gripping both her armrests with tight fingers. "How is such a thing possible? Even the Sekali Empire, which has had its borders closed to us for generations, speaks a recognizable version of our common language."

"Recognizable, yes," Jasper said slowly, "but there are minor changes, divergences from our many years of separation. I believe the tongue spoken by our captors might more accurately be seen as a dialect than an entirely different language—although a dialect now so far removed from the original as to be entirely unintelligible."

"I could certainly make nothing of it," Princess Kalani said. "But Jasper kept his mouth shut and his ears open, and within a mere handful of days he was able to understand them, although they didn't realize it and spoke freely in front of us. It was an advantage that we used to its fullest when planning our escape."

"There were patterns and root words that were identifiable," Jasper began before cutting himself off, apparently having remembered his audience.

But from the way Lorcan and Jessamine—heads of the Academy and the University, and true academics at heart—both leaned forward with interest, I guessed they would be requiring a full explanation of this new dialect at a later point.

Elena frowned down at her brother. "But you said you don't know their purpose in abducting you and the princess?"

Jasper shrugged. "When the princess says they spoke freely, it's true. But their discussions were centered on practical matters to do with our journey. It was these details we needed to plan an escape, but they didn't inform us of their larger purpose. I can only assume they were all already familiar with it and felt no need to discuss it further."

Frowns circled the room as everyone considered this unhelpful news.

"I did manage to discover that they call themselves the Tarxi," Jasper added. "And my guess is that they're a mountain tribe dwelling in the stretch of the Graybacks that runs along the northern edge of the Empire. It's largely unexplored territory, and they certainly seemed comfortable moving among the mountains—although less than familiar with our exact route through the eastern arm of the Graybacks."

"So you escaped them somewhere in the Ardannian stretch of the Grayback Mountains," King Stellan said slowly, "meaning they may still be within my kingdom."

Jasper shifted uncomfortably. "It's entirely possible, Your Majesty."

The king glanced again at his wife, something unspoken flashing between them. Before he could speak further, however, the door to the room burst open, and a petite young woman came rushing in.

"Jasper!" she cried, her eyes flashing over those present without seeing them, not pausing until they fastened on her husband.

He jumped from his seat, and she flew forward to throw herself into his arms.

"Word came down to the city that you'd arrived at the palace half-dead." Tears clogged her voice. "I came up as fast as I could, but the guards didn't want to let me in until Araminta came along and vouched for my identity."

Jasper murmured something soothingly into her ear, casting a wary glance at the monarchs. But the queen gave him a nod, gesturing for him to take Clara over to the other side of the room. From the understanding light in her eyes, she could appreciate a wife whose sole focus was her husband in such a situation.

With Jasper's departure from the circle, a number of hushed conversations broke out. Chen and the princess, on the other side of Jasper's now-empty seat, spoke too quietly for me to hear, as did the commonborn merchant representatives who sat on the far side of Coralie and Finnian, so I limited my attention to my own neighbors.

"I thought Clara was in the Empire with Jasper," Finnian said, speaking for the first time.

"She came back a month ago," Elena replied, watching her brother across the room, now carrying on an inaudible conversation with his wife. "She wasn't there as a royal official but representing her merchant family. I understand her negotiations went well, and a couple of the Sekali clans were ready to sign trade agreements with her family. She returned to make the final arrangements on the Ardannian side."

The two merchants stirred at her words, exchanging looks.

Elena ignored them, however, giving Finnian, Coralie, and me a wry look. "I imagine the separation may be partially responsible for Jasper's eager offer to accompany Princess Kalani back to Corrin."

Finnian snorted softly and snaked an arm around Coralie's shoulders. "I'm sure it was."

"The true genius of any ambassador is getting what you want while appearing to grant a favor," Julian said in a wry voice. "Jasper was an excellent choice for the post."

"As I'm sure you will be also." Elena looked at him more warmly than I would have thought possible a year ago when she announced to us with distaste that she had joined the general's family. After everything they had been through together, she had truly come to think of him as a brother, of sorts.

She certainly viewed him more favorably than she did Calix, so there must be more to him than his unfortunate similarity in appearance to Natalya. But still my lingering mistrust remained. Who knew what lurked inside the devious mind of a Devoras?

A loud voice rose above the general low murmurings of the room, silencing every other conversation.

"I must go after these Tarxi," said Princess Kalani.

CHAPTER 4

JULIAN

*N*ot even King Stellan was able to convince the princess to remain safely in Corrin or return directly to her father. No doubt he would have liked to forbid her from pursuing a course as risky as returning to the mountains, but he had no authority to do so. In the face of her determination, assurances of Ardannian support had to be given, of course—a fact of which she must have been aware when she decided to go after her previous captors.

Only once all assurances had been given was she able to be ushered off, Chen in tow, to a guest suite which had been hastily prepared for her arrival. I wondered with a twinge of amusement who had been turfed out for her accommodation. It was Midsummer, after all, and the palace suites must be full.

Jasper and Clara had also been sent away with the instruction that he return for further debriefing as soon as he had slept his fill.

No one else left the room.

At one point, I noticed the king eyeing off our corner. But Elena stubbornly remained at our side, and after seeing the direction of his father's gaze, Lucas joined her. Since the king made no effort to evict us from the proceedings, I could only assume our removal wasn't worth conflict with his son and the Spoken Mage. I knew as far as Elena was concerned, her friends' participation in the Battle of the Academy had won them a place here.

I had thought to try for a private word with my father, but I caught him looking at me across the room. As soon as I met his eyes, he raised his brows slightly, and I nodded back at him. His eyes narrowed for a moment, and then he sighed and gave a single, ponderous nod. I turned back to those beside me with a smile. My father knew me well enough that I hadn't needed to use any words.

Within minutes, he had made his way to the king's side for a quiet word. King Stellan glanced my way once, and I met his gaze, trying to look strong and determined. When my father drifted away a few minutes later, I tried to read his expression. He looked pleased enough, so did that mean he'd had success?

When the king spoke in a loud, clear voice, everyone turned to listen, clustering closer to him rather than resuming their seats.

"As you all heard, the princess is determined to return to the mountains. She says that the insult against her family and her people cannot go unpunished, and that the responsibility to take such action lies with her. And she wishes also to be sure of the fate of the other members of her delegation. We cannot argue against such motives. And with the possibility that the attack occurred on our own soil—and an equal possibility that her attackers remain here still—we have no choice but to offer her our support."

The queen, standing close at his side, sighed. "Since with every day that passes there is less chance of catching them, we dare not insist that she return to her own kingdom and gather forces there."

"No, indeed," said Princess Lucienne. "It might be seen as a statement that Ardann does not care about an insult to the honor of the Empire."

The king nodded. "We must support her request, which means we must choose a team to accompany her."

Thaddeus and Soren exchanged glances, as if unsure which of them should be taking charge of such an endeavor. But the king shook his head in their direction.

"This is not a task for law enforcement or the Royal Guard. We can expect the party to be traveling through unfamiliar and difficult terrain, and large numbers will slow them down significantly. While I would prefer to surround the princess with several platoons, and half of our mage officers, rather than risk her safety, she has made her position clear. She wants to move at speed, and she expects anyone we send with her to be mobile. So there is no room in the mission for commonborn guards." He glanced at my father. "Or for soldiers in the traditional sense."

Lucas glanced at Elena and grimaced. "You need something more like the old breach teams."

"I think it is our most likely hope of success, yes," his father said. "And given the importance of our diplomatic relations with the Empire, it is a risk that must be taken. Especially given the resources that have been freed by the end of the war."

Breach teams, made up entirely of mages, had been commonplace in the old wars before the more modern practice of scattering mages sparsely throughout commonborn troops. In those days, mages existed in greater abundance, as they still did in the Sekali Empire. But in Ardann and Kallorway, their numbers had been squandered in war, whole family lines wiped out. This violence and loss was one of the reasons the Empire had closed its borders to the southern kingdoms.

The history books told us the teams had been made up of mages from across the disciplines. Their purpose had been not just strength but also agility, and the ability to find a way past any obstacle. They were the teams that sought to breach headquarters and assassinate leaders. But the same principle applied here. Brute force would not win the day in the untracked wilderness of the Graybacks.

"Princess Kalani has insisted she accompany the team, and Ambassador Jasper must certainly go also. Their experiences, both while captive and while fleeing, will be invaluable to the team. And Jasper's mastery of their dialect could also prove critical, if these Tarxi are successfully located."

"Will Ambassador Chen insist on accompanying her?" Thaddeus asked.

"Perhaps," the king said. "But I hope to convince him otherwise. News of these events must be imparted to the emperor as soon as possible, and I am most anxious about the disappearance of the messengers who preceded the princess's delegation. We must agree on a more direct and effective method of communication between our courts, and we must do it without delay. This incident has proven the danger to us all. If Jasper and the princess had not managed to escape, then Ardann could easily have been blamed for her disappearance."

"It is clear," the queen added, "that the princess trusts Jasper as she does not other Ardannians. That is understandable given the claim the Sekalis have made on his distant Sekali ancestry, as well as his time in her court, not to mention the inevitable bond created by their shared captivity and desperate flight. She seems to view him as she would a trusted official of her own people. We are hoping that his presence will be enough to satisfy her that she can trust the team we have assembled."

"It is also clear that she extends that trust to his sister," said the king, looking toward Elena.

"I am ready to join the team," she said quickly, her response hardly a surprise.

Elena rarely stopped to consider her own safety, especially if someone she loved was in danger. She wouldn't want to send Jasper back into the mountains without her.

Lucas took a step closer to her, whether out of an unconscious protective instinct, or a purposeful signal to his father, I wasn't sure. Either way his intentions were clear—where his betrothed went, he went also. But the king's response was swift and certain.

"I'm afraid we cannot allow you to go, Elena." He glanced at his son. "Or you, Lucas. While the two of you would be invaluable to the team, we cannot entirely rule out the possibility that this is all a Sekali stratagem."

"You think they haven't given up their hope of getting their hands on my daughter?" my father asked, taking the opportunity to stake his claim on Elena.

"We think it a less likely possibility," Queen Verena said. "But one we cannot discount. Our son and his betrothed will remain in the safety of Corrin until this situation is further explored and understood. Even if everything is exactly as claimed, we do not yet know the true power or intentions of the Tarxi. We will not send our most valuable asset straight into their hands."

Elena frowned, biting her lip. I expected her to launch into protests, but instead she glanced once at Lucas and remained silent. She had spent enough years as a tool in the mages' game of power to recognize the strength of the arguments. She had made herself too powerful to be ignored, and no one could now view her as a mere pawn. But that didn't make her free of the game. A master player guarded their queen far more carefully than their pawns.

She was learning the lesson that Lucas had learned with his mother's milk—power and responsibility created a different sort of cage from poverty and insignificance. It might taste sweeter, but it was still a cage.

"No, Jasper's sister cannot accompany the team," the king said. "But we hope a different family connection will be acceptable. Julian of Devoras has already volunteered to join Jasper and the princess, and as another of Elena's brothers, we hope he will be an acceptable choice to the Sekalis."

The queen smiled warmly at me. "Indeed we hope he will also prove a valuable member of the team. Not only has he been undertaking preparations to take up a posting in the Sekali court, but he has more experience with the mountains than most."

I suppressed a wince. It was true that my family's estate was located in the foothills of the Graybacks, but if that qualified me as an experienced member of the team, then we were all in trouble. The thought made me pause, however.

"The Devoras family stands ready to assist in any way possible," I said. "But while it is true that I grew up in the shadow of the mountains, I believe the team would benefit from a more highly skilled mountaineer than me. If Your Majesties wish it, the Devoras estate could provide an experienced tracker to join the team."

"Ah," my father said, "you are thinking of old Castus. An excellent thought. He's a commonborn, Your Majesties, but you won't find anyone in Ardann more experienced with the Graybacks. Not even he would try to track through them in the winter, but in the summer he has often completed expeditions inside their depths, seeking after lost livestock, or even the occasional strayed child."

The king inclined his head toward my father. "An excellent notion."

"An excellent notion indeed," echoed one of the commonborn merchants, speaking up for the first time. "We are glad to see the skills and experience of your commonborn subjects recognized and valued, Your Majesty. We are all Ardannians and wish to see our kingdom thrive."

He exchanged a look with his companion. "But while the Robart family acknowledge the necessary inclusion of Ambassador Jasper, we feel significant concerns about his ties to one of our biggest rivals. Already they have been given significant advantage in building connections with the Sekalis through the ambassador's wife. And this team will have unprecedented access to a member of the Sekali royal family. If Jasper is to be part of the expedition, then we request that a member of the Robart family be included as well."

A faint look of irritation slipped across the king's face, suppressed almost as soon as it appeared. He hesitated before answering, and his daughter jumped in.

"I'm sure a Robart would be a valuable addition to the team. We would request only that you choose one of your sealed members."

The merchant bowed low. "Naturally we will do so. The Robart family is more than honored by your confidence."

He stepped back to the edge of the group, his companion at his heels, as if to signal that he meant to make no more demands or difficulties. None of the discipline heads made any protest at this concession, but their eyes reflected interesting mixtures of shock and calculation. Previously, while the merchants had remained silent, it had been almost possible to forget their presence. But nothing could have more obviously demonstrated the changes taking place in Ardann than their confidence in making such a demand of the king. Unless it was that the royals had felt the need to accommodate them, even on such an important mission.

I eyed the crown princess consideringly. Had she spoken up to cover for her father's hesitation, or for her own sake? I clearly needed to pay more attention to her movements. Perhaps the princess was busy sending out a quiet message of her own—that while the older generations might be slow to embrace change, she intended to rule a new Ardann.

Unless it was a strategy between her and her father? A way to pacify both the old guard and the new, all at the same time. It was the sort of tactical maneuver I would expect from the canny royals.

But whatever the reason, the team was now stuck with three commonborns—and not one of them a soldier or guard. Castus would be worth his weight in gold once we hit the mountains. And Jasper had already proven he wouldn't be a deadweight. This new addition, however, would likely prove troublesome. And if the Robarts were influential enough to force the king's hand to include them, then it would no doubt be incumbent on the rest of us to keep him or her alive. I merely hoped they had the good sense to choose someone young and fit.

It soon became clear that particular issue would be relevant for more than the commonborn addition. While the discipline heads might prefer to send one of their most experienced members, many of the mageborn had left their days of rigorous Academy training far behind them. Those fresh from the Academy or the front lines would be most physically capable, but they lacked the discipline-specific training and the years of experience that the older mages possessed.

I stepped back a little as the debate about where exactly the line between experience and physical capacity ought to reside raged on. My inclusion was already guaranteed, and as a palace official, preparing for a diplomatic assignment, I no longer had any stake in a specific discipline.

Most palace officials were assigned to their roles from within various disciplines, often for limited terms. But just as the occasional commonborn university graduate was accepted permanently into their ranks, so were some mages. I had never aspired to be a palace official, but times had changed. Swapping out of a discipline in which you were in disgrace wasn't always the easiest task to accomplish—especially if you wished for a choice position elsewhere. But I no longer had to rely solely on my father to wield his influence on my behalf. This time I had a different family member to thank for my fortunate escape. My newest sister had advocated for me, and Thaddeus had been forced to release me from the Royal Guard when he received an official royal request.

At the back of the group, I found myself beside Saffron. Glancing down at her, I smiled, and she returned the expression somewhat guardedly. I had always thought of her as a quiet, unobtrusive child who trailed in her cousin's wake. And while it was clear she continued to possess more circumspection than her cousin, she had an air of confidence I didn't remember. Was it the influence of the Academy? Or of my irrepressible adopted sister?

And she was certainly no longer a child. With some embarrassment I realized my thoughts had drifted toward contemplation of her sculpted cheekbones and full lips. Next I would find myself soliloquizing about her sparkling eyes or some such foolishness. I gave myself an internal shake.

"She's very brave," Saffron said suddenly.

"Who? Elena?"

Saffron laughed. "I hardly think that would be news to anyone. I was thinking of Princess Kalani. She's just been through a terrible ordeal, but she wants to go straight back into the mountains again to face her attackers. I wonder if there was someone she loves among the delegation members, or if it's merely duty that drives her."

"Would duty drive you so far?" I asked.

She looked up at me, a slightly startled look in her eyes, but she seemed to give the question serious thought.

"I think duty toward those I love would drive me to do almost anything." Her brow crinkled. "Wouldn't it for you?"

I tried to give the question the same weight she had done, but I wasn't entirely sure I liked what I saw in my own heart. I forced my voice into a light-hearted tone.

"You know, I'm not sure I have such depths of duty *or* love. But thankfully self-advancement and duty to my kingdom seem to align more often than not." I winked down at her. "It's a fortunate circumstance."

A faintly disgusted look crossed her face, and she made a non-committal response before drifting sideways to join Finnian and Coralie's conversation. An unexpected surge of irritation swept over me at my joking response, although I could think of no reason to care about the opinion of Finnian's unimportant cousin.

Elena appeared at my side, forcing my mind away from the interaction with Saffron. Her eyes were fixed on the conversation around the king which seemed to finally be settling on a collection of names.

"I do wish they would let me go," she said. "But I don't need a lecture from Lucas to know there's no possibility of that." She sighed and finally glanced my way. "You'll look after Jasper, won't you, Julian?"

I smiled in my usual way. "What else is family for?"

She rolled her eyes but smiled back at me. "I still remember the first time you claimed him as your brother, although the relationship doesn't strictly apply. It meant a lot to me."

My smile broadened, although underneath I was touched at her words. "Haven't you learned by now? The Devoras family is perfectly happy to claim anyone who might be an asset to them. And Jasper has made clear just how valuable he is."

She laughed—she wasn't put off by my joking ways.

"I have had an inkling of that Devoras instinct, yes." Her tone turned serious. "But I also know there is real danger on this mission, and yet you were the first to volunteer." She turned to poke me in the chest. "You don't fool me, Julian. I've had your measure for a long time now."

"Careful, sister, you'll make me blush."

"Hush!" she said. "They're announcing their final choices."

I accepted the stricture meekly and turned my attention back to the mage council where they clustered around the king. It seemed that in the interests of keeping the already burgeoning group small, not every discipline was to be represented. I was to be joined by a captain from the Armed Forces—I remembered Captain Matthis from my term at the front and would be glad to have him at my side—a wind worker, a creator, a healer, and a captain from the Royal Guard who was going along as a bodyguard for Kalani.

I was less excited to hear that Reese had been chosen as the healer than I had been about Captain Matthis's inclusion. The Stantorn healer and I had been rivals at the Academy.

As the names were listed out, a concerned look grew on Elena's face. "But they're all men," she blurted out when the final name was pronounced.

Finnian's father, Duke Dashiell, sighed. "I'm sure you know that Beatrice would usually be my choice over Reese for any mission of importance, but she is not nearly as young. I cannot ask her to go clambering through mountain ranges."

"No, of course not," Elena said quickly. "And I'm sure all the choices are more than competent—I know from experience that Captain Matthis certainly is. But Princess Kalani is a young woman in an unfamiliar culture, and she will be going on a perilous mission forced to rely almost entirely on strangers. It might not be the most welcoming team from her perspective."

King Stellan rubbed his chin and exchanged a concerned look with his wife. "I'll admit I hadn't considered it from that perspective. It's possible the emperor might even consider it indecorous."

"The princess is to have a bodyguard," I said, without thinking, "why not a companion as well? Someone more her own age. What about Saffron of Callinos? She's a recent graduate, so her physical training is at its peak, and she hasn't committed to a discipline yet, so none of you need fear upsetting your senior mages by choosing a junior to go in their place."

Every head present swiveled around to stare at Saffron. The blank look of shock on her face was enough to bring me back to myself. What had I been thinking to suggest her in such a way?

It had been the instinct of a moment, my words spoken

without thought—something I generally tried to avoid. But it had been a selfish instinct. I had remembered the sympathy and admiration she had directed toward the princess and the derision she had aimed at me. And I had been overwhelmed by the desire to have her along so I could show her she had misjudged me.

The one person I had not thought about was Saffron herself—or I would never have volunteered her for a highly dangerous mission. All I had done was confirm that her low opinion of me was entirely valid. I could only hope the king would reject my poorly thought through suggestion.

But Duke Dashiell was the first to speak.

"I'm sure my niece would be honored to accompany the princess." He smiled proudly in her direction.

She gulped and threw him a look that seemed more terrified than honored. But a moment later she pulled herself together.

"Of course I would be more than willing to assist if Your Majesties think I could be of any use."

My heart sank into my boots. She had told me that she would do anything out of duty toward those she loved, and of course she would love an uncle who was like a father. She had given me a glimpse of her vulnerability, and I had exploited it at the first opportunity—although it had been unconsciously done.

My father would be proud. But I felt only sick.

SAFFRON

tried to keep the horror from my face as I waited breathlessly for the king's decision. Surely he would see that I was ill-equipped for such a venture beside the other members chosen for the team. But his eyes were merely thoughtful as they turned from my uncle to me.

"Saffron of Callinos," he said. "You may have just graduated, but if I remember rightly, you saw action at the front lines in your third year, and you stayed to help defend the Academy and its inhabitants when you were faced again with battle in your final year. You've proven you can be trusted in a crisis."

He nodded, decision apparently made. "We have the team, then. Eleven of you. It is a bigger group than I would have liked, but perhaps it's for the best. The hour is now late, and some of the team have yet to be informed of the situation. Discipline heads, I leave that task up to you. Please give them all the relevant information and then send them to their beds. We will need all the travelers as rested as possible. I do not think Jasper and the princess will be fit to travel tomorrow, so the day can be used for preparation and provisioning. You will leave at first light the day after."

He sent a stern look around the room. "No one is to mention a word of any of this to anyone who isn't needed for the preparations. There will be enough rumors spreading after the princess's dramatic arrival, and I don't want our true intentions added to their mix."

I forced myself to nod agreement along with everyone else, although my insides were too numb to properly process his words. What had just happened?

Most of the mage council and the royals streamed from the room, but I remained locked in place. Finnian and Coralie turned to me, almost as much shock on their faces as must be reflected in my eyes. Elena, however, turned on Julian and began upbraiding her adoptive brother in fierce tones. He seemed to take her outrage with surprising meekness, but I didn't have the focus to properly follow their conversation.

"Did that really just happen?" I asked slowly. "Am I joining some sort of breach team on a mission into the high mountains as the companion of a foreign princess?"

Finnian for once had no hint of laughter or even good humor on his face.

"This is my fault," he said. "You didn't want to be dragged into this room in the first place. Although I can't imagine what possessed Julian to suggest you." He glared across at the Devoras mage as if he wanted to go and join Elena in scolding him.

I groaned. "I should have kept my mouth shut. I made some admiring remarks about the princess to Julian, and it must have put the idea in his head that I'd be a sympathetic companion or something."

"Well, you will be," Coralie said, fierce loyalty in her voice. "You're an excellent companion. They couldn't have chosen someone better." She bit her lip. "Although it sounds rather dangerous."

She eyed Elena warily where she stood a short distance away, still in conversation with Julian. "Never mind the politics of it all, with you and Jasper both on the team, Elena is going to be a nightmare the whole time you're gone."

Finnian grimaced. "How long before we have to tie her down to stop her charging after you?"

I pulled myself together with excessive effort. "Nonsense. We're to have five experienced mages with us—six if you count Julian."

"But can you count Julian?" Finnian muttered, still glaring darkly across at the older mage.

I ignored him. "Six experienced mages plus Jasper and this mountain guide. And hopefully they won't guess we're coming for them. If Jasper and a sealed princess can get away from them alone, then our team should be safe enough."

Finnian swept me into a sudden hug. "I love you, cousin of mine. Whatever would I have done without you all these years?"

I pushed him away and rolled my eyes at Coralie. "Gotten into a great deal more trouble—which is saying something. But you have Coralie to keep you straight now, so I shan't worry about you in the least."

Coralie made a noise that almost sounded like a gulping sob and also enveloped me in a hug.

"Whoa," I said. "I'm not leaving this instant. Oh! Have you both spoken to Uncle and officially put your names down as healers? Your training will start straight after Midsummer, so you'll be far too busy to spend time worrying about me."

"We spoke to him first thing this morning," Coralie said, her voice suspiciously teary.

I grimaced. "It sounds like it was a good thing I was such a coward and put off talking to Duchess Annika until the very end of the evening. If I'd already put my name down as a grower, it might have caused her trouble with her mages. None of them are to be included in the mission."

"Or maybe it would have got you out of it," said Finnian. "I don't suppose—"

"Nonsense," I cut him off quickly. "You heard your father. It's an honor for our family to be included in such a way. I'm not going to try to weasel out of it. And you heard those merchants as well. They were right when they said it was an unprecedented opportunity to develop ties with a Sekali princess. And I'm to be her companion. Who knows what good this might bring to our family?"

Finnian let his protests drop, but I could see in his eyes he wasn't quite convinced. Ironically, given his central position in the family, he had always had less devotion to it than me. Yet another side effect of being all too secure in his place, no doubt.

I brightened a little as another thought struck me. "And now I don't have to talk to Duchess Annika at all. So it's not all bad."

Finnian let out a bark of laughter that sounded more like his normal self. "You'd rather trek through the mountains in search of dangerous criminals than apply for a discipline you actually love?"

"Well…" I grinned at him. "When the criminals reject me, it won't be nearly such a blow to my self-esteem."

"You are to stay as far away from any criminals as possible," Elena said sternly from behind me. "Leave that to the experts. You've seen Captain Matthis in action—he'll make short work of them, I'm sure. They won't be sending the princess into the thick of it, so they won't have any reason to send you, either. So don't go being heroic."

I chuckled. "Don't worry, heroism isn't exactly my defining feature."

Elena frowned at me. "Don't go underestimating yourself, Saffron. You do that too much."

I wasn't convinced she was right, but I wasn't going to argue the point either. Julian had slipped out after Elena finished with him, and the four of us were the only ones left in the now-deserted room.

"You all heard the king," I said. "I need to get to sleep." I winced. "I'll be spending my nights on the hard ground soon enough by the sound of it, so I want to enjoy the minutes I still have to spend in my soft, soft bed."

They all responded to that, ushering me out of the room at full speed. Lucas was waiting to pounce on Elena as soon as we re-entered the ballroom, meaning she had to wish us a regretful goodbye.

"Sorry, Saffron," he said. "But we've been sequestered away ever since the betrothal announcement, and everyone wants to talk to us."

I jolted. "Your betrothal! How could I have forgotten? Of course! Official congratulations to you both."

Elena waved off my words. "Never mind all that. You just go and sleep. We'll see you in the morning."

Finnian and Coralie insisted on accompanying me all the way back to the sandstone mansion that was home to Duke Dashiell's family during our stays in the capital. They wanted to stay with me, but I sternly told them to return to the ball.

"It's Midsummer, remember? There's no reason for you to miss all the festivities. I hardly need assistance sleeping. Whereas Elena might end up needing your support before the night is out."

My final argument swayed them, and they reluctantly bid me goodnight.

Coralie gave me a final hug. "I wish you could come back to the celebrations with us." She sighed. "And that you didn't have this whole thing hanging over your head. You can be sure I'll have a great deal to say to Finnian about dragging us into that meeting."

"Don't be too harsh with him," I said. "He really can't help himself sometimes. And perhaps we'll all look back on this day as a good thing. You never know."

Coralie looked unconvinced, but I shooed them both out the door and hurried into my bed. I would never admit it to them, but I felt no pull to return to the ball. I couldn't be more pleased for Finnian and Coralie, and already saw the kind Cygnet girl as family, but that didn't mean I enjoyed trailing along behind them all the time. They were still new enough in their love to do things like forget everyone else around them. And as cute as it was to watch, it wasn't entirely comfortable to be near. Not all the time, anyway.

But without Finnian at my side to remind people of my existence, I wasn't sure anyone would even think to ask me to dance. I would rather be in my bed than standing at the side of the ballroom, watching others dance.

When I woke up the next morning, it was with a start and the strangest sensation. It took a moment for me to remember why it didn't feel like an ordinary day, but when memory did return, I was surprised to discover the dread of the night before had faded. In its place was a feeling much closer to excitement.

Momentous events were happening in the kingdom and, against all odds, I was in the middle of them. It was hard not to be a little swept up in it all.

I hurried through my morning preparations, mentally cataloging my various clothes and belongings. We were not to take any servants with us which meant we would have to carry all our own gear, a prospect I hadn't properly considered the night before. I might be fit and able to fight, thanks to the Academy, but I wasn't conditioned for climbing up mountains or carrying heavy packs. I would need to choose wisely and pack lightly if I was to have any hope of keeping up.

My uncle and aunt greeted me over breakfast. My mother had remained in Torcos so was still ignorant of the upcoming expedition—a situation which was perhaps for the best. She would worry more than my friends.

"Saffron!" My aunt surrounded me in a beautifully scented embrace, the aroma a lingering effect from the night before, I assumed. "Dashiell tells me that you've been chosen for this expedition. What an honor!"

I smiled, and this morning the expression felt natural.

"I'll do all I can not to disgrace the family."

"Disgrace us?" Uncle shook his head from where he sat at the head of the table. "Of course you won't do such a thing. You've never disgraced us in your life."

My smile grew even warmer. Thankfully my uncle and aunt knew their own son well enough that I had escaped any blame for our many childish escapades. In fact, the two of them tended to give me more credit than I deserved for preventing him from getting into worse trouble.

"And you needn't worry about the growers," Aunt Helene added. "Annika was there for the whole thing, so she'll understand when you apply next Midsummer instead of this one. She won't hold it against you."

A shadow fell over my morning. I hadn't escaped my inevitable moment of reckoning, merely delayed it. But a following thought made me brighten again. Next year there would be only a single year of graduates making applications once again. And if I performed creditably on this expedition, then Duchess Annika would have reason to know my name beyond my kinship to the head of the healers.

As soon as we'd finished eating, my uncle declared he would accompany me up to the palace. "Reese will hopefully be there already, or sometime soon. I sent him straight home to his bed after I got out of that meeting. And I was glad to hear you'd done the same, Saffron. Not that I doubted it, of course!"

"And I will see to your provisions," my aunt said. "You leave it all in my hands."

I considered protesting and asking for assurances that she wouldn't go spending extravagantly on me but changed my mind.

If she felt the need to buy new supplies, it wouldn't be solely for me but also because I represented our family.

Coralie and her parents and brother were staying at the mansion for the holiday, but none of them, or Finnian, had emerged when my uncle and I left the house.

"They had a late night," Uncle said with good humor. "We'll let them sleep."

I was more than happy to do so, my mind in enough of a whirl without extra company. And I was equally happy with my uncle's decision to walk the short distance up to the palace. My body wanted to move, not sit confined in a carriage.

"I hope the princess likes me," I said abruptly, halfway up South Road. "It might be rather awkward if she doesn't."

I half expected my uncle to protest with affectionate assurances that I was universally delightful, but he took my concern seriously.

"The cultural barrier will be a difficulty, no doubt," he said. "But you're a considerate girl, Saffron. You always have been. And she's hardly an ordinary Sekali. She's a royal, raised to take the throne, even if that situation has now changed. Royalty learn young to bury their emotions deep. I can't imagine she'll allow any personal feelings to interfere with the task at hand. She'll treat you with appropriate courtesy, no doubt, and I'm sure you will treat her with all respect. That is all that can be expected of such a situation." He smiled down at me. "And there is always hope that genuine liking may grow."

It was a practical assessment of the situation, and it steadied me more than I expected. I would treat the princess with the respect and courtesy her rank demanded, and she would no doubt do the same back. And she would likely be concerned enough about the mission itself not to waste too much thought on me.

A footman must have been instructed to watch for us because we had no sooner arrived at the palace than we were ushered down a long corridor into a medium-sized receiving room. A number of people were already gathered there, including Elena and Lucas who hurried to my side immediately.

When I smiled brightly at my friends, they matched my mood, making no attempt to return to the emotions of the night before.

"I've just been explaining to the steward that you can no more be expected to carry your own shelter than the princess," Elena told me in a lowered voice. "So try not to look too muscle-bound or you'll make me into a fool."

I chuckled. "I can't say anyone has ever accused me of possessing too many muscles."

"That's the spirit," she said, with a twinkle.

"I'd apologize for her," Lucas said to me with a grin, "but I seem to remember you were friends with her before I was, so maybe you should be apologizing to me."

I dipped into a curtsy. "I'm so sorry, Your Highness, for any small part I played in brightening your life and filling your days with joy."

He barked a laugh and gave Elena a look so filled with warmth I had to look away or blush.

"You know you really aren't the same person you were in first year," I said.

"Don't worry," he said gravely. "You've already apologized for that."

I shook my head, but I couldn't keep the smile off my face. It was nice to be able to joke normally with my friends. All the tear-filled hugs the night before had made me feel as if I was being led off to my execution.

As I turned away from them, my eyes nearly met Julian's, but I quickly kept spinning, avoiding the encounter. I had expected to feel resentment when faced with him again, but I felt only mild distaste. Whatever machinations had led the Devoras to suggest my name, I would turn it to a Callinos advantage.

CHAPTER 6

Saffron was avoiding me, and I could hardly blame her. But it only served to make me more fixated on her presence. There was no reason for my thoughts to be getting so wrapped up in one of the weaker members of the Callinos family, even if she was treated like a daughter by Dashiell. But my guilt at thrusting her into our expedition seemed to give my mind excuse enough.

We weren't all gathered together until late that afternoon, Jasper and Kalani having needed a significant amount of recovery time. When they did eventually appear, Jasper a good hour before Kalani, I sidled up to Elena.

"How recovered are they?" I asked her. "Are they really up to this trip?"

Elena alone could sense a person's energy—a useful skill in a number of ways.

She frowned, her eyes lingering on them both. "They're not back up to full energy, but to be honest they're not a lot worse than all of you." She cast an accusatory look around the assembled mages. "You were all supposed to be resting, not stocking up on compositions."

I raised an eyebrow. "Can you blame us? We've all raided our stores, of course, but this is a specific and unusual situation. I'm sure every mage mind is whirling as we try to anticipate what sort of challenges we might encounter. And if the hiking is half as bad as I fear, we might not have much energy for composing as we travel."

Elena bit her lip. "Yes, of course, but that doesn't mean I like it." She glared around the room again. "I can understand you and Saffron, at least. But all those mages representing a discipline should have teams of mages prostrating themselves today to compose on their behalf, shouldn't they? They're going as representatives of their disciplines, after all."

"I'm sure they do have that support," I replied. "But no one likes relying on another mage's compositions. You don't have the same awareness of how much energy went in or what extra limitations they might have built in and forgotten to mention."

Elena frowned. "That makes sense, I suppose. I hadn't thought of it that way." Her expression changed into a grin. "I've never had other mages lining up to compose for me, strangely enough."

I tweaked her nose. "That's because you don't have any need of their services, little one. If I could save up some of your workings, I would accept them gladly."

No one else could compose with the strength of the Spoken Mage, not when she could siphon off the energy of others. Much could be accomplished with a patchwork of workings, but some things required a single working, vastly limiting their scope. There was a reason personal strength was so highly prized among mages.

She sighed. "I wish I could come. But I've told Lucas I'll try not to think of it, and I'm determined to try."

"Well, don't think of it more than once every three minutes, at any rate," I said. "You wouldn't want to be excessive, or anything."

She grinned. "We all have to start somewhere."

My eyes caught on Saffron, across the room. "Could you apologize to Saffron for me? For suggesting her. Tell her I didn't mean any harm by it; it was just the whim of a moment."

Elena gave me a look I couldn't read. "Tell her yourself."

"I would if she wasn't avoiding me."

Elena gave me an unimpressed look. "And I don't suppose you'll possibly find any chances when it's just eleven of you traipsing through the wilderness together."

I groaned. "Fine. But don't think I'll help you out next time you ask for it."

She stood up on tiptoes and kissed my cheek. "I love you, too, brother."

I didn't have a chance to talk to her privately again. A considerable amount of time was spent introducing the various members of the team to Kalani and explaining to her why each of them had been chosen. Unspoken in the air was the knowledge that we were working extra hard to compensate for not being willing to send Elena.

But despite a number of wistful glances in Elena's direction, Kalani made no overt demands that the Spoken Mage accompany us. When the princess had first surveyed the gathered company, she had drifted, almost imperceptibly, toward Saffron. I wasn't the only one to notice her movement, and the king sent an approving look in both my and Elena's directions. The mark of royal favor only increased my guilt, however. I was benefiting from Saffron's sacrifice.

As well as Captain Matthis and Reese, we were joined by Elias of the wind workers—a master of the natural elements—and Alaric of the creators—an expert manipulator of physical matter. I could imagine they would both come in useful in the mountains.

I recognized Alaric's name from the night before, since he was a Devoras and a distant cousin. But Elias caught me by surprise. He stood alone, a small radius of space around him, and now that I saw him in person, I instantly knew why. He was an Ellington.

When I remembered he was a wind worker, his selection became clearer. Duke Magnus, himself an Ellington, must be looking for every possible opportunity to bring the remaining Ellingtons back into favor.

Every Ellington who remained a mage was innocent beyond doubt. And yet, the rest of us couldn't help but regard them warily. After decades of war with Kallorway—a war fueled and fermented by the conspiracy within the Ellington family—resentment and anger still burned in their direction.

After the attack on the royal family, every Ellington—from the mighty Duke Magnus to their weakest, poorest member—had been given two choices: submit to an interrogation under a truth composition or be treated as a criminal guilty of treason against crown and kingdom. Only a few had refused. Even those who had truly been guilty had wanted the chance to argue their own particular extenuating circumstances.

It had been a chaotic period, the efforts to weed out the perpetrators hampered by the fact that the head of law enforcement himself had been one of the ringleaders. Such a widespread investigation would have strained the discipline at the best of times, but with their leader and those loyal to him removed, the entirety of law enforcement had nearly fallen apart. Only the strong leadership of Duke Soren had saved it.

For those on the fringes of the attempted rebellion, clemency had been granted. After paying heavy fines to the crown and completing a sealing composition—forever binding their access to power alongside a whole host of commonborn—they were permitted their freedom.

But those sealed Ellingtons would never be accepted in mage society. Elias and the other members of his family who had been present at the Midsummer Ball were those who had been truly ignorant of the conspiracy in their midst. And it was fortunate indeed for those Ellingtons that their number included Duke Magnus. He was the standard around which they rallied in their efforts to hold on to something of their former position and status.

On reflection, it shouldn't have been surprising at all that Magnus would leap to send an Ellington along to serve the crown. I weighed him with my eyes. Truth composition or not, did I trust him to have my back in the harsh terrain of the mountains?

He looked ordinary enough, and for a horrible moment I imagined myself in his place. No one could choose their relations —I knew that well enough—and if the other Ellingtons had left him out of their plans, it must have been for a reason. His own family had known he wouldn't betray the crown. And yet he found himself viewed with suspicion and distaste by his own society, beset on every side. With the attacks of the merchants, even those Ellingtons who hadn't received heavy sanctions were now fighting even for their wealth. And yet the irrational sense of reluctance remained as I forced myself to consider the final members of our group.

No one from law enforcement had been included on this mission. Instead our expert when it came to protection and interrogation was Captain Tabor from the Royal Guard. Officially the Stantorn had been assigned the role of bodyguard to the princess, but he was also one of our more senior members. At well over forty, he was the oldest of our group, and I hadn't crossed paths with him much in my time with the Guard. But his reputation had always been one of solid dependability and devotion to his job, and even here in the palace he lingered close to the princess, his eyes darting in all directions as if scanning for threats.

One glance at his broad shoulders and muscled arms was enough to erase any doubts that his age might slow us down, or that he might lack the capacity to throw the princess over his shoulder and sprint her to safety if it came to such drastic measures.

To my surprise, the last to join us was the Robart merchant. I had thought they would be first to arrive, over-eager at their inclusion in such exclusive circles. But perhaps there had been some difficulty in choosing the ideal candidate.

When the merchant did arrive, mine weren't the only eyebrows to shoot toward the roof. I hadn't kept any sort of close watch on who among the commonborn had been chosen for sealing, but the wealth and influence of the Robarts was great enough that I had assumed they would have any number of potential sealed members to choose from.

I certainly hadn't expected them to send a tiny girl who looked barely eighteen. She greeted us all with calm good cheer, apparently not in the least abashed by our illustrious ranks. And she carried a decent-sized pack without showing any sign of toppling over backward from its weight.

The head of the Robarts accompanied her, introducing her as Faylee. As soon as the formal introductions were over, she gravitated toward Saffron and Kalani, and the merchant choice began to make more sense. The Robarts had never claimed any particular interest in the Tarxi or their crimes. They were interested in the potential connection this trip might facilitate with the Sekali elite. Sending a girl similar in age to the princess was actually the logical choice.

The next morning, we gathered outside the eastern gate of the city, a less obtrusive place than inside the palace courtyard. The king and queen had bid us farewell the night before, but Elena and Lucas joined us outside the city for a final goodbye.

After some consultation, it had been decided that we could afford to dispense with sleeping shelters altogether. The weather would be colder the higher we went, but it was mid-summer, so it shouldn't be severe. And carrying shelters was simply too impractical, given none of us were used to long trips with heavy loads.

Everyone carried their own belongings, and most had a rolled mat attached to the bottom of their pack. Faylee carried hers, as if determined to disprove her weak appearance, but I was glad to see that Matthis and Alaric each bore an extra roll, while the princess and Saffron carried none.

Elias had an especially bulky pack which I took as a hopeful sign. He had been assigned as the team cook, and I hoped he carried spices and other flavorings as well as basic pots.

The ten of us—Kalani, Jasper, Saffron, Faylee, Captain Matthis, Reese, Captain Tabor, Elias, Alaric, and me—looked around at each other. We were missing our guide, Castus, but we would collect him at my family's estate in the foothills.

Lucas was just making a farewell speech when someone else stepped through the gate and hurried to join us. I surveyed Jocasta in surprise, especially when I noted she carried a similar pack to the rest of us, a rolled mat attached to the bottom.

Elena, however, nodded at her. "King Stellan informed us this morning of your last-minute inclusion. I'm glad you made it in time."

"It was a rush," Jocasta agreed calmly, "but I am aware there is no time to be lost." She looked around at the rest of us. "I'm Jocasta of Cygnet, Assistant Head of the Academy library."

Captain Tabor grunted. "I didn't know the Academy was to have a representative."

"They weren't, but Duke Lorcan and Duchess Jessamine convinced the king there was value in including an academic." She nodded in Jasper's direction. "You'll find me glued to the ambassador's side, trying my best to learn what I can of this new dialect."

Jasper looked pleased. "A wise decision. If something should happen to incapacitate me, it would be best if someone else could understand them." He grimaced. "I don't know how good I'll be at passing it on. But I'll do my best."

"From what I've heard and seen, your best is likely to be good enough." Jocasta glanced my way, her eyes narrowing. "Ah, and

Julian. Once again I see you've found your way to the center of the action."

I gave her a mocking half-bow. "I'm a credit to my teachers."

She snorted, and I grinned back. Jocasta had always been one of my favorite instructors at the Academy, but she had never seemed able to make up her mind whether she liked me or found me altogether too privileged and frivolous. Although now she'd spent four years with Finnian as a pupil, she could hardly accuse me again of being frivolous.

"We had best be off," Matthis said, glancing at the rising sun. "Your Highness. Spoken Mage." He gave a rough bow in Elena and Lucas's direction.

"Yes, don't delay," Elena said, but she sounded rueful.

I strode over and gave her a firm hug. "We'll be back before you know it."

She sighed. "If only that were true."

"Jocasta?" I asked softly. "That's unexpected."

She shrugged. "You know how Lorcan and Jessamine can be. And their argument does make sense. Of course, I'm sure it's no coincidence that their proposed representative was an older female from a minor family."

"Lorcan did always know how to play the game," I murmured, my mind considering these new angles and realizing again the Academy Head's genius.

With a need to choose strong mages for a small team, we had ended up with members of the four great families only. But the minor mages would be furious to learn that the commonborns had three representatives while they had none. Many of them were more incensed at the rise of sealed commonborns than the mages from the great families were.

As Natalya, of all people, had explained with a shrug: they had more to lose. The commonborns were encroaching on the territory that had traditionally been theirs—the middle ground between the commonborn masses and the powerful of the disciplines and the court. Some of them even feared they might one day be forced into a similar position to the sealed Sekali clans, their power forcibly taken away. And so they were fighting back, demanding respect and recognition from the crown.

By accepting Lorcan's proposed Academy representative, the king provided a sop for the minor families while also bolstering the female contingent, in case of the emperor's disapproval. No wonder he'd agreed.

"I'll admit I'm glad she's along," Elena said. "She's so sensible, she'll help keep you all in line."

"I thought keeping the others in line was my job," I said.

"Ha!" She pushed me gently away. "Don't get left behind."

I realized the captain was already leading the way down the road and hurried after him, throwing a final farewell over my shoulder. For all my light words, a certain dread sat deep in my middle. I hoped I would see her and Corrin again. I hoped we all would.

CHAPTER 7

SAFFRON

We were due to follow the East Road directly to the foothills, since we needed to collect our guide from Julian's family estate. There had been some discussion about riding as far as the foothills, but not everyone in the group was competent on a horse. Carriages had also been discussed, but it was felt they would be too conspicuous leaving the capital.

Personally, I suspected Captain Matthis had intervened. As the most experienced veteran among us, he had been appointed as leader, and I think he wanted to see how we all did with a full day's walk on a flat, well-kept road before leading us off-track into the mountains. And from the feel of the blisters on my feet by the end of the day, I could hardly blame him for his concern.

Given my role as companion, I had spent the day keeping close to the princess, but she had initiated no conversation, and I had ended up walking in silence or talking with Faylee who also stuck close to us. The merchant girl seemed canny and not in the least put off by the company of mages.

"I'm older than I look," she explained, although I had carefully refrained from commenting on her age. "It always catches people by surprise. It used to rile up the older boys at school because I always beat them at their work, and I looked like such a little child. For the merchant families, school is a serious business."

She grinned, looking sideways at me. "I suppose it's different for you lot. You don't go to school as children. But for us, it's all over at ten years old, unless your family has extra funds to pay for private tuition. I got a few extra years of schooling because there was some hope among the family that I might win a place at the University." She shook her head. "I'm no Jasper, though, so it all came to nothing."

"Not nothing," I said. "Your family obviously chose you to be sealed, so they must have recognized your value even without the University."

She turned to look at me fully. "Right you are. So it all paid off in the end. That's observant of you. A lot of mages don't bother to think too much about how things work among the commonborn."

I blinked, not completely sure how to respond to her forthright manner. "Times are changing," I said after a moment.

"That they are!" she said cheerfully. "Just look at me!" She crowed and held up her exposed wrist, proudly displaying the complex pattern that ringed it in what looked like ink.

The Seekers had complained, of course, when the idea of sealing commonborns was first put forward. They were the discipline tasked with the responsibility of protecting the kingdom from illicit reading and writing, and the existence of sealed commonborns greatly complicated their efforts. But Duchess Phyllida had spent hours sequestered with my uncle, and they had come up with the plan of marking the sealed commonborns. It was far from the only measure the Grays had been forced to adopt, but it was an important one.

It wasn't actually ink that stained Faylee's wrist but a darker skin pigmentation that could never be washed away. In brown-skinned commonborn, like those from Jocasta's southern town, the pigmentation produced by the healer's composition was a light beige. My uncle's healers stood by after every sealing ceremony, ready to do the workings that would permanently mark the fortunate commonborn who now had unlimited access to written words.

I caught the princess glancing surreptitiously in our direction and wondered what she made of us, particularly the open merchant girl. In Sekali, they didn't have the same distinctions between mages and commonborn, not when everyone was sealed and some commonborns could win the right to wear robes. But they still had enough of a distinction that her new sealed status had lost her the throne.

We stopped at a large inn for the night, and I sought out Jasper, Faylee, and finally Kalani. My aunt had been true to her word and packed for me, purchasing entirely new items for the occasion. The material of my three gowns was lightweight but durable, and she told me it had been crafted with the use of compositions to ensure it would dry especially quickly. In fact, everything I carried was lighter than it should have been, although it felt heavy enough by the end of the day. But none of it compared in value to the gifts I carried on my person.

My uncle had given me the stack of compositions, and it had seemed enormous. Far more than those I carried from my own supply—though I had packed every one that seemed like it could possibly be useful. He had assured me the other mages would have been provided compositions by their disciplines, if not their families, and that he and my aunt wouldn't think of sending me out into the wilderness ill-equipped. It was still hard to accept such generosity, though.

"Usually mages don't like to act in such haste," he had told me. "If planning an unusual undertaking, we would take days if not weeks to prepare, allowing time to compose a supply of workings to see us through the journey or project. But there is no time for such luxuries now."

When I had a moment to peruse them more closely, I could

see that—unsurprisingly—many of them were healing compositions, and they had been chosen wisely. But I couldn't hoard them to myself when I wasn't the only one to be forced on this trip without means to prepare or a discipline to back me up. And so I sought out the three sealed members of the group.

When I gave them each a simple composition to heal blisters and relieve sore muscles after a day's travel, they received them with gratitude. Kalani thanked me with a gracious bob of her head, accepting the offered gift without hesitation, although I couldn't read her emotions in her face. I lingered, feeling off-balance, as I tried to think how to frame my question.

"I'm sure you know, Your Highness, that I've been included in this expedition as a companion of sorts for you. And since you were unable to bring any maids or…or ladies-in-waiting, I was wondering if you would like any assistance with dressing and preparing for bed and such."

It was an awkward delivery, and I hoped the offer hadn't come across as insulting in any way. Her face continued to give nothing away, although this time the bob of her head approached somewhere toward the vicinity of a shallow bow.

"I thank you, Saffron of Callinos. However, I am able to dress and undress myself adequately, I believe."

"If you do need anything, please let me know," I said. "And just Saffron is fine."

The princess regarded me through steady eyes. "Very well, Saffron. And if I have need of any extraordinary assistance, I assure you, I shall approach you most readily."

I nodded and turned to go before hesitating. "I'm sorry that you've had to go on this trip without any of your own people around you. And so soon after your last ordeal."

"I am only sorry it was not possible to act more quickly," she replied. "I fear that even now we are too late."

"Yes, of course. Goodnight, Your Highness." I bowed hastily

and backed out of the room, nearly colliding with someone in the passage.

Righting myself, I recognized Julian and resigned myself to talking to him.

"I saw you giving that composition to Faylee earlier," he said. "That was a kind gesture."

I furrowed my brows, trying to read his eyes. As a Devoras, did he see my kindness as weakness?

"The sealed among us had no way to supply their own compositions, and no discipline to back them. It only seemed right." I paused, trying to think of a reason that might be more acceptable to a Devoras. "And they might slow the whole company down if they aren't helped."

"Yes, I suppose so," he said, his face and voice giving nothing of his true opinion away. It struck me suddenly that he also had no discipline behind him.

"What of you?" I asked. "I'm guessing you didn't have a team of mages to supply you with compositions before you left. Do you need one for blisters and muscle aches? My uncle provided me with a generous supply."

"I'm glad to hear it," he said. "I was concerned you might be exhausting yourself to provide them with your own compositions. But I imagine if you intend to continue covering four people, then your supplies might still eventually run out. I can take care of myself."

I nodded, biting my lip and looking away. I shouldn't have made the offer in the first place. A mighty Devoras wouldn't appreciate the implication that he was weak enough to need my help.

"I might not have a discipline now," he said suddenly. "But I did receive some training before I left the Royal Guard. If you find yourself in need of compositions for protection, Saffron, you can always come to me."

"Oh." I blinked at him. "Thank you." I tried to think of something else to say, failed, and fled like a coward.

CHAPTER 8

JULIAN

I watched Saffron practically running from me and wondered what it was about the girl that made me blurt out my thoughts without stopping to consider. It was truly a relief to hear she had received compositions from her uncle, but I still worried that she would run out before this was all over. And it was clear she had enough generous impulse to get herself into trouble if that happened.

None of which should have been my problem. And yet…

We gathered again the next morning to be greeted by three carriages. Apparently a single test day on the flat road had been enough, and we were now to prioritize speed. The new mode of transport meant we would reach my home before sundown—and it was one less day Saffron would need to provide compositions for her little brood.

Jocasta ushered the three girls into the first carriage, waving Jasper over to join her before following them in and closing the door behind them. I hoped Saffron was prepared for a day's worth of advanced linguistics.

I lingered, letting the others move first and only choosing a carriage once Reese had done so. I had no desire to be shut up in close confines with the uptight Stantorn all day.

As a result, I ended up with Elias and Alaric. I expected the Ellington to be subdued, but he turned out to be open and friendly, chatting about his various theories regarding the Tarxi and asking me questions about what we could expect from the mountains themselves. Apparently he had been raised in Corrin, and had never traveled as far east as my family's estate.

The time passed easily enough, but by the time the familiar view of home appeared through the windows, I was still sick of the confinement. At least walking the day before had provided some physical activity, even if it came with a burning pain in my feet.

As we stepped out of the carriage into the courtyard of my family estate, Elias yawned, covering his mouth and giving me a rueful grin.

"I probably shouldn't have stayed up half the night composing, but when I heard we were to have carriages today, it seemed like it might be my last opportunity for a while."

"We'll have comfortable beds tonight, at least," I said while inside I kicked myself. Apparently the Ellington had been better informed than me. I could have used the extra composing time.

I didn't have long to dwell on my frustration, however, given my need to play host. The twins were in Corrin for Midsummer, along with my father, which left me as the only senior representative of our family.

A large number of commonborn lived at the estate year-round, as well as a small collection of relatives who were either too old or too reclusive to travel to the capital even at Midsummer. My father had sent a message ahead, and they were prepared for our arrival, with sufficient guest rooms aired and ready. An elderly aunt greeted us, assuring us that dinner was almost ready to be served, and would be available as soon as we had freshened up. She led the princess to her room herself, commonborn servants coming forward to direct the others. I lingered behind, however, and found Matthis did the same. I didn't need to ask to know what he wanted.

"That's Castus there." I pointed at an older man who hovered at the edge of the courtyard.

Matthis examined him critically. "He's older than I was expecting."

I shrugged. "Old but hardy. He won't slow us down, if that's your concern. Unlike the rest of us, he's conditioned for the slopes and the elevation. Most likely we'll be the ones slowing him down."

Matthis nodded slowly. "That reminds me. The healers supplied Reese with enough altitude sickness compositions for the whole group. It sounds like this Castus won't need one, but I don't want anyone setting out tomorrow without working one first. We don't need anything slowing us down from here."

I gestured for Castus to come forward, and he did so, eyeing us both with curiosity.

"Welcome home, young master," he said. "I can't say we were expecting such visitors. Right surprised we were to get your father's message. Not half so surprised as when I heard I was mentioned in it by name, though. You have need of me?"

"This is Captain Matthis, he's in charge of our expedition. We've need to go into the Graybacks. And at haste."

The old man rocked back on his heels. "Into the Graybacks, you say? The lot of you? Even the princess?"

"Especially the princess." Matthis glanced around, but no one else was in ear shot. None of them wanted to risk even the appearance of eavesdropping on our conversation.

"Her Imperial Highness and Ambassador Jasper were attacked about two weeks ago on the Overon. Up in the forested section. They were carried east through the forest and into the Graybacks. They managed to escape somewhere between that point and here and to find their way down from the mountains to the capital."

A gleam leaped into the old man's eyes. "We're on a hunting expedition, then? To track down the blackguards? Now there's a journey worth the taking." He frowned and rubbed at his chin. "How many days since they descended from the mountains? And where exactly did they come out?"

"I'm hoping Jasper can help with those answers," Matthis said. "We'll meet after the meal to discuss it further. I've been waiting for your arrival to have the conversation, since I suspect you'll know better than me what questions to ask. I hear you're the expert where the mountains are concerned."

Castus regarded the captain with respect in his eyes. The tracker had never seen the front lines and didn't know some mage officers had learned to value the experience of a veteran commonborn. Castus certainly wouldn't be used to such treatment having lived his life out here on my family's estate. My mother had made my father look soft and loving, and her insistence on living out here had been one of the reasons the rest of us spent so much time in the capital. I didn't imagine many people at the estate had mourned her passing.

"I'm as much an expert as we've got," Castus said in reply. "But be warned, captain, the mountains like to keep their secrets."

Matthis looked up at the looming shadow of the closest peak. "I'm sure they do. But we've got no choice but to attempt to broach them."

"Aye," Castus said. "And I'll do my best to steer you right."

At dinner I sat at the head of the table in the seat my father usually occupied. It was a strange sensation, and one I found I didn't relish as much as I had expected. It gave me a good view of the table, but the only two close enough to speak with were the princess on my right and Matthis on my left. And both dedicated themselves to their food.

I found my eyes lingering down the other end of the table

where Saffron's chuckle kept drawing my attention. Apparently Faylee and Jocasta were more entertaining table companions than my own.

The mage-fueled lights that ran down the center of the table made the Callinos girl's golden skin glow and brought out faint mahogany notes I hadn't noticed before in her dark hair. I had to tear my eyes away before someone noticed me staring.

The servants moved efficiently and silently, just as they had been trained, and the grand room was as fit to host royalty as always. Yet I found myself regarding the whole scene with new eyes, wondering how Saffron saw it. The girl who shared her compositions with commonborns and laughed with a merchant might see it as ostentatious rather than grand. I remembered, as if from nowhere, that while Dashiell was as powerful and rich as my father, his Corrin mansion was made from red sandstone and not the palace's white marble like my father's. Saffron had grown up in my world, but she seemed to have learned different lessons from it.

Was that the influence of the healers? They had always been a soft discipline. Or was it Elena's influence? Would four years of her presence in our family work a similar effect?

When I first heard my father had gone through with adopting her, I wondered if he knew what he was doing. I now found myself pondering the same question but from a different perspective. We might none of us know ourselves when this was all over.

After the meal, Castus joined us, and Jasper imparted some good news.

"If you'd asked me in Corrin, I couldn't have told you exactly where we exited the mountains, but I recognize this estate. I didn't know what it was at the time, and we were avoiding everyone and everything, but it's definitely familiar."

Kalani nodded her agreement. "We came out slightly north of here, but in sight of the estate."

"Excellent," Matthis said. "That's where we'll start then. And do you have any idea how far you came between leaving your captors and arriving here?"

Jasper frowned, glancing at Kalani who shrugged slightly.

"Not much, I'm afraid," he said at last. "It was several days, I remember that. But we kept hitting gullies and ravines we couldn't cross and having to double back. It was anything but a straight path."

"Our best hope is that they followed us," the princess said. "If they turned straight back north instead, we'll never catch them."

Matthis sighed. "No doubt you're right, Your Highness. So I suppose it doesn't matter how far you traveled. If your path was as twisted as you say, then we can hope it's taken them some time to trace your steps. We will do our best to reverse your path and look for any signs of their passage we can find."

It wasn't much in the way of a plan, but without knowing more of our enemies' movements, there wasn't much we could do about it.

Faylee leaned over to whisper to Saffron, but I was sitting close enough to catch her words.

"That plan would never work without the aid of compositions. It's marvelous having such resources at your fingertips."

"Aye." Castus sat on the other side of the girls, also close enough to hear her words, apparently.

"Compositions are marvelous indeed, and I'm sure they'll come in right handy. But if we want to make it back out of those mountains alive, then we'll all need to rely on more than power to bring us out. Don't go getting complacent, or you'll find the mountains will eat you alive. When it comes to raw power, ain't no one who can match them."

"The commonborn has the experience, and we'd all do well to listen," Matthis said.

"As we'd all do well to get a good night's sleep while we still can," Jocasta added, heaving herself to her feet. "So if you've nothing more to share, Jasper, I'll be heading for my bed."

Jasper shook his head, and we all dispersed. Tomorrow we would face the unknown, but no one seemed inclined to linger or seek comfort from each other. We didn't know each other well enough for that.

I fell asleep more quickly than I anticipated, perhaps because of the familiarity of my own bed. I woke groggy, however, and confused, the room around me still dark.

A clanging bell filled my ears, the cause of my awakening, and it took only a moment for my tired brain to catch up. The alarm bell! We were in danger.

CHAPTER 9

SAFFRON

I staggered from my room, disoriented in the unfamiliar place. What was making that awful noise? Princess Kalani appeared from the room on one side of me and Faylee from the other. They both looked to me, but I had no answers.

Jocasta appeared on the other side of the princess, so we all turned to her instead.

"That's an alarm bell," she said in answer to our questioning looks. "But don't go asking me what's caused them to ring it."

She gave an uneasy look at the princess just as Captain Tabor appeared.

"Fire, Your Highness," he announced, all his focus on his charge. "We need to get out of this building as quickly as possible. This way."

Faylee squeaked and fell into step behind the princess. But I hesitated, glancing between their retreating backs and Jocasta, who hadn't moved.

"Where's the fire, Tabor?" she asked briskly.

"At the back of the estate," he called over his shoulder.

"They're rallying to it now. There's a servants' stair at the end of this corridor that will get you close to the kitchens."

Jocasta nodded, but I caught her eye before she could run off, glancing between the end of the hall and the disappearing princess. She hesitated for a fraction of a second before pointing at the others.

"Stay with the princess. If this is a diversion, I'd rather the captain had some back up. Especially with Faylee tagging along."

I nodded and hurried after the retreating trio. It felt wrong to run away from the fire when I might be able to assist, but she was right. The estate was in better shape than it would have been without our presence, since even without me or Tabor, we had six strong mages who could offer help. Hopefully between them all, they would have the flames doused in short order.

The alarm bell continued to ring, however, as we all fled down the main stairs and out through the elaborate entryway. I wanted to repeat Jocasta's warning to Tabor but restrained myself. If Jocasta, a librarian, had thought of the possibility of a diversion, then a trained bodyguard with decades of experience would certainly have done so.

We burst out into the estate's courtyard to find chaos all around us. Young children cried or screamed with excitement, as a handful of women attempted to herd them toward a large, clear area near the estate gates. Others headed in the same direction, assisting the elderly and infirm of the estate to reach the same place of safety. But dashing and weaving around them were able-bodied adults and older children who rushed toward the glow behind the main building.

Several of them carried stacks of buckets, or other paraphernalia I didn't recognize, and someone was carrying on a shouted conversation about water which I couldn't follow over the hubbub. A haze of smoke cloaked everything, and when I paused for the shortest moment, overwhelmed by the sudden cacophony, I nearly lost my small group.

With a start, I hurried after them. I hadn't reached them, however, when the courtyard plunged suddenly into greater darkness.

"Look!" screamed a child, pointing behind me.

I swung around to see that the bright orange glow of the fire had disappeared. With the sky no longer tinged red from the reflection in the smoke, everything looked dark and murky, made of shadows and soot.

Everyone paused in their movements, hardly daring to breathe as we waited. Seconds later the alarm bell fell silent, and a loud cheer erupted from the courtyard.

"Master Julian has it in hand," one of the women standing near me said. "We're fortunate it broke out when one of the main family was in residence."

Evidently the relatives who chose to shelter here year-round didn't have the strength of the general's immediate family. Personally, I suspected Elias—a wind worker trained in the manipulation of the elements—probably had more to do with dousing the fire than Julian, but I didn't attempt to correct the woman.

Movement started again all around me, and I realized I had once again lost track of my companions. It was harder to pick them out now, in the semi-darkness, and I spun in a full circle, trying to see their shapes.

A brief flare of light, like a small flame, made me pivot toward it, afraid of a new blaze. But it winked out almost as quickly as it had appeared. The moment of light had given me a glimpse of the princess, however, almost against the estate wall.

I hurried in her direction, trying not to trip in the darkness. I had almost reached the place where I had seen her when someone exited the mansion with a lantern—its light brighter and yellower than the fire had been. The sudden illumination revealed a violent struggle ahead of me.

Tabor lay on the ground, dead, dazed, or unconscious, I

couldn't tell. A second man I didn't recognize had Princess Kalani by the arm and was attempting to tug her in the direction of the gates.

Faylee gave a wild scream and jumped on the man's back, but for all her enthusiasm, she clearly had no training. Dropping the princess's arm, the attacker easily threw the merchant girl off. She hit the estate wall hard, groaning and not attempting to rise again.

My old instructor Thornton had trained me for such circumstances, launching surprise attacks on the trainees when we found ourselves alone, so I didn't have to think. My hand leaped directly for the front of my traveling clothes, sliding into the special pockets sewn there. These might be new garments, but every mage used such compartments, so they were always built in to our designs.

After four years at the Academy, I had perfected the placement of my most easily accessible compositions, so I knew exactly what my hand fell on. As I pulled out the roll of parchment, the man attempted to grab the princess again, but she was ready for him this time. Unlike Faylee, Kalani obviously had training, and she blocked his first lunge with ease.

But as he fell back, warier now, he drew a long knife from inside his jacket, holding it as if he knew how to use it. The princess was unarmed and now at a decided disadvantage. I wished I had taken the extra seconds to buckle on my sword when I fled from my room, but I hadn't even thought of it. I wouldn't make that mistake again.

I ripped my composition, letting the two halves fall unheeded to the ground as I pointed toward the princess. Power rushed along my arm to envelop her just as the man lunged forward. His blade encountered an invisible barrier and ricocheted back.

He snarled, cursing and spinning as he tried to find the source of the shield. His eyes fell on me, but I was already ready with my next composition. A strong, localized wind sprung up as I ripped it, rushing around the five of us and driving away the smoke that still lingered, making it hard to breathe.

Faylee groaned again, and Kalani ran to her side, my shield traveling with her. When she knelt beside the merchant girl, I breathed a small sigh of relief, knowing the shield would now be encapsulating both of them.

When the wall of air hit Tabor, he stirred, and I ripped my eyes away from him, not wanting to alert our attacker that the guard was coming back to awareness. The man's whole focus seemed to be on me, however, as he fought not to be thrown off balance by my working.

I kept expecting him to pull out a composition, either in defense or attack, but he made no move to do so. And now that I was paying attention, no sense of power surrounded him either. It made no sense that a single attacker without any compositions would attempt to take on a larger group including at least one mage, but I didn't stop to analyze the situation.

If he wasn't shielded, then I should finish this quickly. Before my hand could reach the right composition, however, he lunged. The tip of his blade would have lodged in my chest if I hadn't jumped backward so quickly. He pressed forward with a second attack, clearly wanting to prevent me from accessing another composition.

If I had a weapon of my own, I could have held him off and still found the composition I needed but, unarmed, it was taking my full attention to avoid his blade. A ripping sound from behind him distracted me for long enough that his next attack might have found its mark if something hadn't flown through the air and collided with his back.

For a moment he teetered, his blade still outstretched, before it fell from his hand and he toppled to the ground. I took a gasping breath of relief before looking for the others.

Kalani had managed to ease Faylee into a sitting position, her back resting against the wall, but the merchant girl's breathing was labored, and the princess hadn't left her side. Tabor, however, was back on his feet, his face grim as he strode forward, stuffing two fragments of torn parchment into a deep pocket.

"You'd better retrieve yours," he said, nodding toward the scraps of paper I'd let fall to the ground.

I blinked at him before remembering we weren't alone in the courtyard. Looking around, I saw a ring of commonborn watching us with varying levels of shock and awe. Stumbling forward, I snatched up my scraps of used composition and shoved them back inside my clothes. I couldn't leave written words lying around to be cleaned up by a commonborn. Such things had been easy to forget in the bubble of the Academy but were vitally important out in the wider world.

By the time I had finished retrieving my abandoned parchment, Tabor had knocked the winded attacker unconscious and slung him over his shoulder.

"We need to get the princess back inside," he told me as both of us moved toward the two girls against the wall.

"I don't think she can walk," Princess Kalani said, gesturing at Faylee, her voice level despite the excitement and danger of the past few moments.

I took a deep breath, trying to slow my own racing heart and mimic the calm of the royal. Thanks to my training at the Academy, I could fight when needed, but the shock always hit me afterward. Ever since the front lines, anyway.

"I think it's one of my ribs," Faylee wheezed.

Tabor frowned. "If it's punctured her lung, that will need a serious healing."

His eyes weighed the princess as if trying to assess how she would respond to a suggestion to leave the merchant girl and return to safety without her. But while the princess was the most important person traveling with us, Their Majesties wouldn't like it if we returned without the Robart girl either, which placed him in a difficult position.

I glanced at the princess. She continued to crouch beside Faylee, and I hoped I wasn't imagining that she looked no more ready to abandon the injured girl than I was.

"I can help," I said. "Just give me a minute." I knelt on the ground and pulled out a stack of parchments from a deeper pocket. These ones were less familiar and not arranged for immediate access, so I had to take a moment to leaf through them, looking for one I was sure I remembered seeing.

"Aha! Here it is." I pulled one from the pile and placed it on the ground as I carefully bundled the others and returned them to their pocket.

The official contributions from the healing discipline had been given to Reese, but included with the stack of compositions gifted to me by my aunt and uncle had been a small selection of powerful healing compositions. And apparently a body blow that might damage ribs and lungs was the sort of injury they had foreseen I might suffer while trekking through the mountains looking for a fight.

I hesitated, looking at Faylee. "I'm sorry, this might hurt. If I had more supplies, I'd work a pain relief composition first, but…"

She waved away my words, shaking her head.

"Just do it," she gasped. "I just want to breathe."

I nodded and ripped the parchment, flicking my fingers toward her. For a moment, she was still, her eyes drifting shut before she spasmed, her whole body shuddering as she emitted a high pitched scream.

"I'm sorry," I said again, but she had already gone still.

Opening her eyes, she took several deep, gasping breaths and then grinned at me.

"All fixed! Those healing compositions are amazing."

I stared at her. "It sounded like it hurt."

"Like you wouldn't believe," she said cheerily, "but the pain is gone now. And I can breathe again, which is the most important thing."

"Time to move," Tabor said, so I pulled Faylee to her feet.

The captain's focus was on the princess, but he glanced my way with something almost like approval in his eyes. "Looks like your shield is still functioning."

"It didn't take much of a beating," the princess said. "Once his first attack was turned away, he moved his attention to Saffron." She looked toward me. "Thank you, by the way."

"You're welcome," I said. "I'm glad I was here. And we can thank Jocasta for that. She suspected the fire might be a diversion and sent me after you all."

Tabor ushered us through the large doors back into the mansion, our attacker still unconscious across his shoulders. The guard didn't falter or appear discomposed by the weight or the awkwardness of his burden, but I could see the tightness in his face. He had nearly failed at his mission, and he must be concerned about the possibility of another attack.

We had barely made it into the entranceway when Julian appeared from the far side.

"They're here!" he shouted over his shoulder, and the rest of our team poured in after him.

Matthis took less than a second to take in the situation, striding forward to relieve Tabor of his burden. The guard instantly took up a defensive stance behind Princess Kalani, Alaric and Reese moving to join him.

I pulled the healer aside, however. "Faylee was injured. Thrown against a wall. She was having trouble breathing, and we needed to move, so I used this." I held out the two halves of my torn composition. "She seems all right now, but you'd better do some sort of diagnostic working to check if there are any more internal injuries. And that I didn't make anything worse."

Reese frowned from me to the offered slips of parchment. After a moment he took them, however, holding them together so he could scan the words written there. His brows drew together.

"This is a complex working. I didn't realize you had a proclivity toward healing or such advanced training."

I winced. Had he heard rumors of my ineptitude? The duke's own niece, prone to turn faint at the sight of blood. Even Finnian and Coralie—who would have loved me to join them in the healing discipline—had known better than to suggest it.

"It's not mine," I said. "I couldn't craft such a working."

He frowned back at the parchment. "Ah yes, I think I recognize this hand. In which case there's no need to fear any fault in the working itself. But if you didn't do any diagnosis first, then further investigation would be wise." He eyed the merchant girl before glancing back at me. "This was a valuable working to spend on her."

I frowned, but Reese was the most typical of Stantorns, so I shouldn't have expected anything else.

"We needed to move," I said, keeping back the rebuke I truly wanted to utter. "We were too exposed out there." It was easier to give explanations a Stantorn would understand.

"Very well," he said. "I'm sure Tabor was itching to be under cover. But next time, if you can, leave the healings to me. I have the experience and the supplies."

He stalked away from me without a backward glance, his focus transferred to Faylee, so I didn't have to come up with a reply. There had been criticism in his words—he had been protecting his territory as the group's healer—but also something else that might have been concern. It was almost as if he was worried I might run out of healing compositions for myself in case of dire need.

CHAPTER 10

JULIAN

"Ou know, I didn't think it was possible, but Beatrice might actually be having some small effect on our dear friend there," I said from behind Saffron.

She glanced back at me, and I stepped forward to stand beside her, not trying to hide my amusement.

"It did almost sound for a moment like he cared, didn't it?" she said. "Finnian would be shocked." She paused to consider. "Or perhaps he'd try to take the credit for himself. He did go to every possible length to bring poor Reese down to size during his year training at our estate."

I gave a bark of laughter. "I would have paid to see that. Reese versus Finnian. A worthy pairing." It would have been pure joy to see my longtime rival so exasperated. "I'm not sure even Finnian has it in him to bring Reese down to size, however."

"Well perhaps you're right and Beatrice is succeeding where Finnian failed," Saffron said. "What's the old saying about catching flies with honey?"

"I hope your uncle pays her well is all I can say," I replied. "There isn't enough gold in the kingdom to convince me to be permanently saddled with him."

"He's not that bad," she said mildly. "He did help save Abalene from the epidemic."

A strange flare of irritation filled me to hear her defending him. I glanced down into her face. Did she like the stuffed up Stantorn? But she looked more thoughtful than attracted as she watched him talking to the merchant girl. I took a deep breath. I needed to get a handle on myself.

"What happened?" I asked.

"I was about to ask you the same thing," she said. "Did Elias put out the fire?"

I nodded, anger coloring my voice. "It took longer than it should have because it wasn't a natural blaze. It had been started in multiple places and some sort of fuel was used. If we'd been even a bit slower, it would have gotten into the main building."

"It didn't, then?"

"Thankfully not. Thanks to Elias. It razed a couple of minor outbuildings and singed the back wall of the estate, but nothing that can't be rebuilt easily enough."

"And the people?" she asked, once again demonstrating her caring heart.

"A few minor burns and some smoke inhalation is the extent of it, I'm glad to say." I glared across at Reese, although as much out of habit than through any great heat. "Of course our dear healer refused to waste any of his compositions on my people. They're for the use of our team only."

Saffron made an exclamation of concern which made me soften. I didn't want her worrying about the injured.

"But we maintain a small clinic of sorts here, so they'll be looked after well enough. We're too remote to have people trekking into the nearest city to find a healing clinic."

She relaxed slightly, although her brow remained creased. "So it was definitely a diversion, then."

"Evidently." I focused my gaze on the prisoner who was now awake but being firmly restrained by Matthis, with Tabor, Alaric,

Jocasta, and Elias standing warily around in support. "We realized it must be the case once Elias determined it was definitely arson. We all hurried back inside to search for you."

I bit my tongue to keep myself from adding that I had been just as concerned for her as the princess. "I'm glad to see you were able to handle the situation yourselves," I settled on saying.

To distract myself, I stepped forward and addressed the huddled group of mages. "Shall we move to a more private location?" I gave a significant look at the now conscious prisoner. "I imagine we'll have some questions for that fine gentleman there."

Reese looked in our direction. "Yes, and about time. I need somewhere quiet to work the diagnostic composition."

Matthis nodded his agreement, so I led them all across the entranceway and down a short corridor to a generous-sized sitting room. Now that the blaze was out, my father's people were well-trained enough to handle the clean up without my supervision. And even the weakest of the extended family members who sheltered here carried Devoras blood. They weren't likely to be overset by something like a fire. In fact, the oldest of my aunts would be offended by the suggestion that she needed me hovering around getting in her way as she ordered our people about like a retired general.

At the last moment, however, I spotted Castus lingering near the front door, uncertainty in his eyes. I gestured for him to join us in the room. He might pick up on something the man said that would mean nothing to the rest of us.

Once the door was closed behind me, Matthis pushed the prisoner unceremoniously to the floor, making no effort to soften his fall. Jasper approached the man, his gaze focused on his face.

"That's one of the Tarxi," he said. "I recognize him."

The man glared up at him but said nothing.

Matthis grunted. "No surprises there. Who else would be so desperate as to attempt an attack within General Griffith's own estate?" He shook out his shoulders and frowned at the prisoner before extending the expression to all of us.

"That was poorly handled on all sides," he barked. "We have to start working more effectively as a team. From now on, we stick together and stand ready to coordinate our responses."

"At least Saffron had the sense to shadow Tabor and provide him with back up," I said, knowing enough of the Callinos girl to be sure she would never speak up for herself.

"That was Jocasta," she said hurriedly. "She wondered if it might be a diversion and sent me with Tabor and the princess."

Matthis gave a respectful nod to Jocasta. "A wise precaution since you wouldn't have done us any good at the fire, Saffron."

I bristled on her behalf but had to admit the truth of his words. I had helped direct the situation, given my familiarity with our environment, but beyond that, Elias had been the one with the knowledge and the necessary compositions on hand.

"It's a good thing she was there," Tabor said, his voice laden with disgust, although it seemed to be directed at himself. "One lone attacker, but he somehow had me incapacitated before I even knew he was there."

Saffron stepped forward. "How did he do it? I lost you all in the smoke, and when I found you again, you were already down, Captain. But you don't seem to be injured." She frowned. "He fought like a commonborn—a well-trained one, it's true, but there was no hint of power about him. And he never even attempted to go for a composition."

She looked sympathetically at Tabor. "With all the smoke and confusion and darkness, it's no wonder you didn't see him coming." She glanced at the rest of us. "It was absolute chaos in that courtyard. And without a hint of power, you wouldn't have felt him either."

"Well he must have had at least one composition on him," Tabor said. "Because he didn't lay a finger on me, but he still felled me hard and fast. It was like being hit by a brick wall of fatigue. I couldn't muster the energy to even lift my head. I think I might have passed out until Saffron's wind blew some strength back into me."

"Does he have any parchment on him?" I asked. "Torn or otherwise."

Matthis conducted a rough search of the man, who growled but made no attempt to resist. The captain found nothing. I stuck my head out into the corridor and called for the closest servant. When he came to a stop outside the door, I gave him instructions to scour the courtyard carefully for any scrap of abandoned parchment.

The young man's eyes widened, and he took off at a run. None of the commonborns wanted to risk being found with any writing in the estate outside of the prescribed areas—the library, my father's study, and each of the mage's suites. He was back soon enough to say that the courtyard was clear.

"Maybe he ate the pieces?" Jasper suggested, a note of humor in his voice.

"I didn't see him coming either," the princess said. "But he definitely didn't get close enough to make physical contact before the captain went down. I did see a brief flame near us, though, just after Captain Tabor collapsed. It's possible that was him burning a scrap of parchment." She hesitated. "But I felt no hint of power at any stage."

All the mages present exchanged uneasy glances. None of us liked the idea of a composition we couldn't sense. Nor did we like the idea of going in pursuit of an enemy who only seemed to grow more mysterious.

"One thing's clear," Tabor said. "Their goal was recapturing the princess. They haven't abandoned their hope of getting their hands on her."

His face clearly showed he considered bringing her back within their reach to be a foolhardy proceeding. The princess, however, seemed to share none of his concerns.

"Yes, indeed, this is excellent news," she said, attracting startled looks from the rest of the company. "We now know for sure we are not chasing ghosts who have long since fled. If this one is here, then the others will no doubt be somewhere near as well."

"Although why send only one to attack?" Alaric asked. "They might have succeeded if they sent a bigger team."

"I have my guesses about that," Matthis said, capturing my interest. My father had always respected the captain's grasp of strategy, so I would lay money if he was certain enough of a guess to share it, there was every likelihood he was right.

"We know they're a small group," Matthis continued, "so their resources are limited. I suspect they spread out, sending out a number of scouts to try to track the movements of the escapees. I think this one might have been watching the estate and saw us arrive. He probably concluded it was too good an opportunity to miss and so acted alone."

"That sounds plausible." Jocasta looked at the prisoner with distaste on her face. "He was probably dreaming of all the glory he would receive when he single-handedly returned with the princess."

The librarian from a minor family had never had much patience with politics or the pursuit of glory. It was hard to imagine her doing anything so foolish as attempting an attack on her own.

"We don't have anyone from law enforcement here," Reese said, rejoining the main group from where he had been examining Faylee on one of the sofas. "But surely you have some relevant compositions, Tabor. There's no need to speculate when we can get answers from the prisoner himself."

I bit back a grin to see the sour looks on the faces of the older members of our group. Good old Reese, making friends wherever he went. No one actually disputed his words, however, and Tabor began pulling rolls of parchment from inside his jacket.

Jocasta approached me while Tabor worked. "It must be past

dawn by now," she said. "It was getting close when we came back inside. Somehow I don't think any of us will be getting back to our beds, but some food wouldn't go astray."

I nodded and slipped back to the door. As the host, I should have thought of it myself. No doubt everyone would be a little less on edge with full stomachs.

This time the closest servant was an older maid I recognized. She'd been cleaning my family's mansion for more years than I'd been alive.

"Send word down to Cook to send up breakfast enough for twelve," I said. "The sooner, the better—it doesn't need to be fancy." She dipped a curtsy and began to hurry off when another thought struck me. "Oh, and have her send food to the healing clinic as well. They'll be run off their feet."

She looked a little surprised at the addition, but I felt content knowing it was the kind of thing Saffron wouldn't have overlooked.

When I re-entered the room, everyone had arranged themselves in a semi-circle around the prisoner who sat on the floor, propped against a sofa. He surveyed the group, his eyes surly and his face impassive. A glow of light emanated from a parchment in front of Tabor, but the man didn't even glance at it.

"Where is the rest of your group?" Tabor asked him.

The man said nothing.

Matthis tried next. "Why did you attempt to abduct the princess?"

Still the man said nothing.

"Who are your people?" Jasper asked in a gentler voice, going for a softer approach. "What do you want with our people?"

This time the man turned his head and spat on the carpet. I eyed the spot with distaste. I'd need to remember to mention it to one of the cleaning staff.

"This is just wasting time," Reese said with impatience. "We can all feel he's not shielded. Surely you have a composition to compel him to speak?"

Tabor glanced at Matthis who shrugged. "We knew it was likely we'd need to end up using it."

The guard picked up a second parchment which lay next to him on a small table, ready for use. Ripping it, he pointed accusingly at the Tarxi. The man looked defiantly back.

"Where are your people?" Matthis asked, this time watching the truth glow rather than bothering to watch the man. The second composition would compel him to answer, and the truth composition would assure us of the accuracy of his words.

However the silence stretched out once again. Matthis's brows lowered, and he looked from the man to Tabor before repeating his question. Again, he was met with only silence.

"Impossible," Tabor said roughly. "That one came from one of our most senior mages. And the man isn't shielded. There's no way he can resist the compulsion to speak."

"Could it be an issue of language?" Jasper asked. "I don't remember ever hearing him speak in our common tongue while we were prisoners. Perhaps the composition doesn't work if he doesn't understand the question. I'm guessing it's never been tested against someone who speaks a different language."

"That would be your area of expertise, Ambassador." Matthis gestured for Jasper to take his place in front of the prisoner.

Jasper stepped forward, hesitation in his posture. "I've been practicing with Jocasta, but I've never actually had the chance to speak it properly. I probably have the accent all wrong."

"As long as he understands you, the composition should work," Tabor said. "There's no need for fancy speeches."

Jasper nodded jerkily and spoke several words I didn't recognize. He sounded halting and awkward. The man's face changed, however, and he fastened his eyes on Jasper's face. Jasper tried again, repeating the words and adding new ones.

The prisoner's eyes narrowed, and he barked out a longer

string of words before falling silent again. Jasper tried several more times, with a variety of different word combinations, but the man did not speak again.

At last Jasper turned to the rest of us. "He seems to understand me, at least somewhat. But the composition clearly isn't working. I have no idea why."

"What did he say?" Matthis asked.

One side of Jasper's mouth quirked up. "I'm not sure of the exact translation, but I believe it was something along the lines of, 'You may be an intelligent rat, but you're still a rat.'"

Matthis grunted.

"This is a difficult composition to craft," Tabor said. "You would know that, Matthis. But I've never seen it fail. Not against someone unshielded. Have you?"

Reluctantly Matthis shook his head.

"What does that mean?" I asked.

"I wish I knew," Tabor said, his voice sour. "Just like I wish I knew how he took me out so neatly during his attack."

CHAPTER 11

SAFFRON

Jasper stepped back to stand near Jocasta and me.

"I'm sorry to say that the truth glow never faltered when he spoke," I said to him, unable to resist despite the strained mood of the room. "But I'm sure Clara will still love you, even if you are a rat."

He snorted quietly, and Julian glanced our way, looking surprised to hear me joking in such a situation. I looked back at him defiantly. We were all on edge and could do with some relief. I was used to bouncing off Finnian's irrepressible irreverence, but without him here, I felt strangely compelled to fill his place.

"There are other ways to make him talk," Tabor said slowly from the other side of the room. "But we don't usually have any need for them."

"And a good thing, too," Matthis said, "because from all accounts they're less than reliable. That's not a path we want to be wasting time on."

I was glad to detect faint relief on Tabor's face.

"That's all very well," Reese said, "but what do we do now? And how do we explain how he's resisting our compositions? We hardly want to go into battle with the rest of his people only to discover none of our compositions work on them."

Alaric frowned. "Surely such a thing is impossible."

"So is resisting a composition compelling you to speak," I said. "Or felling a trained guard without use of a composition or physical force. I, for one, would prefer more information before I go charging in."

Matthis nodded. "As would we all. And that's something the prisoner will be good for, at least. We can experiment and see which of our compositions have an effect on him."

"He might have taken the captain down in some mysterious way, but I felt no lingering traces of power around the fire," Elias said. "It's why I didn't immediately recognize it as arson. He seems to have used natural means of starting it. And from what Saffron reported, he was limited to physical weapons in their fight as well. So it's not all bad news."

"Yes, that's true," said Matthis. "And we will take what mercies we can get at this point."

"Ahhh, what's happening to him?" I asked, cutting across their conversation.

Everyone turned to me and then wheeled to follow my pointing finger to the prisoner. He had started to list to one side, slumping in place as his features grew strangely relaxed. His golden skin turned a strange shade, and his eyes drifted shut before he collapsed sideways onto the floor.

Reese bolted forward, dropping to one knee and placing his fingers against the other man's throat. After a silent moment, he looked up at us with wide eyes.

"He's dead!"

"Are you sure?" Tabor asked.

"Of course I'm sure!" Reese gave him a withering look. "I'm a healer. We don't make mistakes about such things."

"It couldn't be some sort of enchantment?" Matthis asked. "A trick?"

Reese hesitated before pulling forward a small leather case and retrieving a black pouch from inside. He drew a small parchment from the pouch and ripped it, flicking his fingers toward the dead man.

Nothing happened, and we all continued to wait. Eventually Matthis grew impatient.

"Well?" he asked.

"Nothing." Reese shrugged. "He is definitely dead, and power played no part in it. The man just keeled over and died—as we all saw."

"But that's…"

"Improbable? Yes." Reese packed the pouch back into his case, his voice now businesslike. "The odds of such a thing happening at such a moment are vanishingly small. And yet we have twelve witnesses that it did indeed happen. I'm afraid we won't be getting any chances to experiment on him."

"In a morning of impossible things, I find it impossible to believe that is a coincidence," Matthis said in a hard voice.

A knock on the door made me flinch, but Julian strode over to open it without pause. He blocked the opening with his body, however, speaking quietly to whoever was outside. I moved over to join him when my nose told me why we were being interrupted.

"Here, let me take that," I murmured, and he started, glancing back at me.

I held out my hands, and he took the first tray from the servant outside, placing it into them. Jasper appeared to take the next tray, leaving Julian free to take the final one.

"We're going to have to do something about the body," I whispered to Julian. "We can't just leave it there for your servants."

He glanced back toward the rest of the mages. "I think everyone's still in shock and half-waiting for him to suddenly revive. But don't worry, I'll warn someone about it once we're ready to move out."

I knew what he meant. In truth, I felt a little that way myself. The scene we had just witnessed was beyond eerie, and while I didn't want to say it aloud, I wondered how many of us were comparing what happened to the prisoner with what had happened to Tabor—and wondering just what, exactly, these people could do to us.

The princess, however, remained more animated than I had yet seen her, reinforcing my initial impression of her bravery. Apparently she had no concern for her own safety.

When we selected food off the trays, all the commonborn hung back respectfully, and Castus looked as if he didn't intend to take anything at all. When none of the other mages appeared to notice, I approached the guide myself and urged him to eat.

"I imagine we'll be on our way soon enough," I said to him. "And we need you strong and ready to lead us, remember."

Matthis, who happened to be nearby, looked over and nodded. "We all need to be at full capacity today. We'll have to move with far more caution than we initially anticipated."

"Perhaps it's for the best," Castus said in his gruff voice. "I always move with caution in the mountains."

"I thought you weren't a morning person," I said to Matthis, struck by a sudden memory of him at the war front. "You seem alert enough now, though."

"Alarm bells and arson have a way of doing that to you," he said, a sardonic tilt to his lips. He paused for a moment before continuing. "And while I'll admit I'm no lover of mornings, I may have overplayed it at the camp. It's a relief sometimes to be as rude as you like without consequences. And you'd be surprised what you can learn when people think you're not paying attention." One of his eyebrows quirked up, and he gave the briefest glance toward Julian before wandering away.

I stared after him. What had that meant?

"Ha!" Castus let out an amused humph. "I never had much thought to leave the mountains, but if I'd known the Armed

Forces were run by mages like him, I might have been tempted to sign up."

"They're not all like him," I murmured.

"Well, some like you would be fine, too," he said, his voice surprisingly gentle. "Not that I mean any slander on our own fine lords, of course," he said quickly, leaving me with the impression that it was precisely what he had meant.

We left the estate less than an hour later. After a short consultation between Matthis and Jocasta, Princess Kalani, Faylee, and I were given positions at the center of the group. Jocasta and Jasper walked just ahead of us, heads bent close together in frantic consultation as they attempted to increase the pace of Jocasta's learning. I had heard quite enough talk of linguistics in the carriage the day before and made no effort to intrude on their conversation, other than to call the occasional warning when they became too involved to notice major obstructions on the path.

Tabor strode close behind us, his eyes darting from side to side or straying far ahead. Alaric, Reese, and Julian brought up the rear, leaving Elias and Castus to join Matthis at the front of the group. I wasn't sure whether Matthis wanted Elias there because of his expertise or because there was enough lingering mistrust of the Ellingtons that no one wanted him at their rear.

Faylee was unusually quiet, her face paler than normal. She should have been resting after such a significant healing, but she had refused to be left behind at the estate. Her family had chosen her well. As in the case of her physical strength, her determination and mental fortitude belied her frail appearance.

I didn't mind the silence, however. My surroundings were interesting enough to hold my attention. The ground was rocky, and yet green life grew all around us. As well as boulders and patches of uneven, rough ground, we had to dodge pine trees that sprang up wherever they could find root. And when I gazed out across the seemingly sheer stretches of rock that sprouted in all directions, many of them were covered in a living green carpet. The mountains might be inhospitable to humans, but they were still full of life.

I itched to have the time and space to examine some of the plants more closely. What made these strains so hardy? They clung to life in a way that would be of great value to some of the kingdom's more delicate crops. I wished we had a grower on the team so I could ask them what studies and experiments the discipline had done into harnessing some of their traits. It was a pity I hadn't tried grower studies until my fourth year and had therefore never made it beyond beginner level study. I hadn't expected to be so drawn to the discipline. But I had discovered I loved immersing myself in the quiet peace of a garden. To be alone, working with my hands, and yet at the same time surrounded by richness, growth, and life. Growers got to create both beauty and sustenance, and what could be more rewarding?

To my surprise, it was Princess Kalani who pulled my attention back from the mountains to my companions, talking so quietly that I nearly missed her words.

"In looks, he could have been my cousin, you know. In fact, he looked a great deal like one of my distant relatives."

"The man who attacked us, you mean?" I asked after a slight pause as I scrambled to make sense of her words.

She nodded, and I tried to think what to say.

"You saw Captain Matthis did nothing to bring about his death. I assure you we were all as astonished as we appeared."

The princess glanced across at me, her brows drawing together.

"Surely you don't think I mourn his death?"

"Oh, I…" I pulled myself together. "I'm sorry, no, of course not. He attacked your delegation and took you hostage."

"Knowing he once came from the Empire only makes his actions into a betrayal," she said, more fierceness in her voice than I had ever heard from her. "My family and I have no clan because the whole of the Empire is our clan. It is a loyalty greater than any other."

"Are the Tarxi originally from the Empire then?" I asked.

"I do not know," she said. "Some of them must have been. But among the group who held us captive, not all looked as he did. Two were fairer even than Faylee, and several were brown like Jocasta. Perhaps they are the worst of us all, exiled for their crimes and banded together in their villainy."

I shivered. There was a terrifying idea. But since the princess had chosen to open up conversation, I didn't want to let the moment go.

"I'm sorry about the people from your delegation," I said. "Were you close to any of them?"

"Close?" She afforded the question far more consideration than it seemed to warrant. "Not how you mean it, I think. Sometimes I have envied the closeness allowed to your kind. But it is better this way."

"My kind?" I asked.

She looked sideways at me. "Those born without royal blood. It is an entirely different life you lead. But if I had allowed myself the sort of close friendships you possess, then no doubt I would have been tempted into including at least one of them in my delegation. And then I would carry an even greater burden than I do now, knowing they had been slaughtered because of me."

That made sense, in an awful sort of way.

"So you don't believe they may still be alive?" I asked softly.

She squeezed her eyes shut for the briefest moment. "Another luxury that royalty cannot afford is that of false hope. If any had been left alive, they would have made it down the river into Ardann by now. If you are to lead an empire, you must do so with clear vision."

"And yet, you are no longer to be allowed to lead an empire," I murmured without thinking.

She gave me an odd look, and I wished I had stayed silent. She probably didn't appreciate being reminded of her loss of status and future.

"You seem like you care, though," I said quickly, unable to entirely let the conversation drop. "About people, I mean. How do you maintain that if you always have to hold yourself apart?"

She looked genuinely surprised at the question, looking at me with a faint furrow in her brow. "Of course we care. My family is not apart from our people, we *are* our people. A shepherd who is entrusted with the care of her flock doesn't love them any less because she has no favorites among them. It is that impartiality that allows her love to remain pure."

A shadow of anger crossed her face. "And that is why any betrayal burns us so deeply. For the whole to be strong, every part must be strong. Everyone must play their part. And anyone who attempts to poison the stream must be removed without mercy."

"I would like to see the Empire one day," Faylee said suddenly, joining the conversation. "It is hard for me to imagine—so many working together for one purpose."

The princess smiled at her. "Then you must come and visit."

"I will," she said with determination, but I noticed she was carefully avoiding looking in my direction.

Ardann had been divided for so long that it was no surprise the idea of a unified society, working together for the good of all, would seem like a utopia to a commonborn like Faylee. If I was honest, I liked the sound of it myself. I had been raised among the healers, and the Sekali way aligned with the healer spirit. But I had also heard Elena's account of her time there and the emperor's attempts to force her into service to the Empire. No culture was without its dark side.

And yet I found myself almost as intrigued by the Sekalis as Faylee.

"Perhaps I will come and visit as well," I said boldly. Now that I would have another year before I could sign up for a discipline, I had no other pressing calls on my time.

"You also would be welcome." Kalani inclined her head in my direction. "But if we are to enjoy such futures, we must first root out the scourge before us."

Faylee swallowed audibly, and I sent her a sympathetic glance. The merchant had been chosen for her potential to make a connection with the princess—something she seemed to be succeeding at—not because of her skills in fighting mysterious enemies. While I was surely no one's ideal choice when forming a raiding party, I at least had four years' training at the Academy and some time at the front lines of a war. My experiences there had left me traumatized for a while—and they still sometimes woke me at night. I just hoped Faylee didn't go home with similar scars.

I glanced over my shoulder, trying to get a sense of how far we'd come, and flinched to see how close Julian was behind us. Had he been listening to our conversation? What had he made of it?

CHAPTER 12

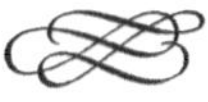

JULIAN

t first we followed the established path that ran through the foothills, the way uphill but still defined. The relative ease of the path was fortunate for Jasper and Jocasta whose attention on their feet was decidedly secondary to their linguistics conversation. Still Saffron had to intervene on several occasions to prevent one of them walking into a boulder.

Despite the potential value to our efforts of Jocasta learning the Tarxi dialect, they would have to be split up before long. We couldn't afford to lose one of them because they walked off the edge of a ravine.

Saffron and Faylee, meanwhile, seemed to be succeeding in their efforts to make some connection with the princess. She had remained aloof so far, seeming more focused on our objective than her traveling companions. But the king and queen wanted more from us than just extricating Ardann from a potentially damaging situation. They were hoping to forge stronger connections between our kingdom and the northern empire, and as a future ambassador, I should be attempting to ingratiate myself with the princess.

I could see no way to insert myself into the conversation,

however, so I contented myself with listening with interest. I had traveled to the Sekali capital the year before, an unusual opportunity to observe their empire at close quarters. But I had never had the chance to hear the mental processes of a member of their royal family.

The royal family of Ardann made use of formality as a tool in their arsenal, but it was nothing to the formality I had observed at the imperial court in the Empire. And listening to Princess Kalani, I could understand why they operated in such a way. It was a far cry from the formality I had heard spoken of in relation to Kallorway—where it was a tool of control and repression.

But Ardann had forced Kallorway to seal members of their royalty, their mage families, and their commonborns as the price of peace. So perhaps change was already underway there, as it was in Ardann.

After spending half a lifetime holding back the Kallorwegian incursion, my father relished the changes forced on our old enemies. But he seemed to gleefully anticipate a full disintegration of their society, and I sometimes wondered if it had occurred to him that similar changes were occurring in our own kingdom. Of course, we had strong leadership who were navigating the new waters with a firm hand, while Kallorway was engaged in a power struggle over their throne. But our two kingdoms were still more alike than my father would ever admit.

The great General Griffith might disapprove of anything that changed the society he had fought so hard to save, but I found my thinking diverging further and further from his. The more I studied the unfamiliar ways of the Sekalis in preparation for my posting to their court, the more the idea of change in Ardann appealed to me.

When I heard Saffron declare her intention to visit the Empire, a warmth filled me. I wasn't the only one of my generation to consider that there might be better ways than the way we had always done things.

Conversation soon died off, however, as the path upward steepened sharply. Even Jasper and Jocasta seemed to finally notice, Jocasta dropping back to walk beside Saffron while Jasper drifted all the way back to my side.

"I'm afraid life as an academic didn't prepare me for hiking up mountains," he said between audible breaths.

"You made it once before, which is more than the rest of us can say," I said.

He grimaced. "It's a strange thing, but somehow fleeing downhill from danger was easier than racing uphill toward it."

"They have a shield up in front of us," I said, suddenly realizing that as a commonborn unable to feel power, he might not be aware. "And behind us too. It's more efficient than everyone shielding themselves individually."

He threw me a thoughtful look. "That's good to know. I've been too focused to pay much attention to our strategy. I assume they've got some sort of search compositions in use as well."

I rubbed my chin which felt rough after our hurried morning dash from the estate. "That's a little more complicated. We still don't know exactly their capabilities, and we don't want to leak so much power that we lead them right to us. For now, we're letting Castus guide us. He picked up the trail of the arsonist at the estate, and we're retracing his steps."

Jasper looked startled. "I missed that entirely. We're fortunate to have his expertise."

I nodded, struck by his phrasing. A fellow mage would have complimented me or my father on Castus's inclusion since he worked for us and had been suggested by us. But Jasper didn't forget where the credit truly lay. I had been proud my family could contribute so gainfully, but his words put me in my place.

Silence fell between us for a moment.

"You were with the Tarxi for several days," I said abruptly. "Did you ever see anything like what happened to our prisoner? Or Tabor for that matter?"

Jasper shook his head. "As I already told the captains, I saw nothing of the sort. But then neither the princess nor I were conscious for most of the attack on the delegation, and our captors didn't fight among themselves."

"They were mages, though?" I asked. "You saw them doing compositions?"

"Several times when we were paused in our journey, I saw one or other of them composing," he said. "Although I saw them actually release the compositions less frequently. Of course, I can't sense power. So I had no way to tell how many compositions were being used around me that might have been worked out of my sight."

He directed his next words at the backs of the girls in front of us. "What do you remember, Your Highness? I know I asked you a number of times what power you felt around us, but only as it related to our escape plans. I never asked how many compositions they were using in general."

I noted his assumption that the princess was aware of the conversations happening around her. Given Jasper's own remarkable intelligence, I easily accepted his assessment of Kalani's perception and shrewdness. And, sure enough, she slowed her steps, joining our conversation without missing a note.

"Surprisingly few," she said. "I assumed it was to reduce how brightly they shed power. We were remote, but there was always the possibility of pursuit."

Her eyes grew distant, and for the first time I saw her stumble, her thoughts apparently too consuming to allow attention for the path. Jasper and I both reached out instinctively to steady her before quickly pulling back our hands. You didn't touch royalty without permission, especially not foreign royalty.

She regained her balance without need of assistance, her gaze turning back to us, sharper than before.

"I am a fool," she said.

"With all due respect, Your Highness," Jasper replied, "you are far from it. If you missed something, it is accounted for by the dire circumstances and our natural focus on escape."

The ghost of a smile touched her lips. "Gracious words, Ambassador, since I know you would not have missed anything within your power to perceive."

"Ah, but Jasper is a true genius," I said. "The rest of us cannot judge ourselves by his standard."

She bobbed her head. "You speak wisdom, Ambassador-Elect. It is never wise to overlook the differences in our natural giftings."

Jasper and I exchanged a short look, both eager to know what it was she felt she had overlooked, but neither wanting to risk being deemed rude by making a direct inquiry.

Faylee, however, seemed to feel no such compunction. Looking over her shoulder, she made no attempt to hide that she had also been listening to our conversation.

"What did you miss, Your Highness? Is it something that will help us capture these villains?"

"I cannot be sure about that," Kalani replied. "But it has occurred to me that while I also, on occasion, saw our captors crafting compositions, I never actually saw one of them being worked."

Jasper frowned at her. "I'm sure I saw the tall one working compositions on at least two occasions. Did you not see?"

"That is where I have knowledge that you do not," she said. "While it didn't occur to me at the time, the only compositions I actually personally witnessed being released were ones that were familiar to me. Ones, in fact, that appeared identical to those I was carrying at the time of our capture. Not all of my collection was keyed to me personally to allow others around me to assist as needed." She paused. "Naturally, however, the more deadly ones were thus limited."

"For which we can all be thankful," Jasper muttered.

I considered her words from every angle. "And you felt very little power used on you, or even around them in general? So it's possible those stolen compositions were the only ones they were working."

"It is at least possible," she agreed, "although I cannot confirm it."

"And yet you both saw them composing," Saffron said, abandoning any attempt to pretend she wasn't also listening with interest. "Another mystery then."

"But one that strikes me as a great deal more favorable than the others," I said. "If they are limited in some way and unable to do workings in the same way we can, that gives us a significant advantage."

"At this point we need one," Jocasta muttered from ahead of us, though she didn't actually turn to join the conversation.

"You may relay this new insight to Captain Matthis," the princess said to us all.

"I'll talk to him," Jocasta said, immediately increasing her pace.

The princess seemed satisfied with this response, stepping forward to resume her original place with Saffron and Faylee. From the beginning she had accepted the captain's leadership over the expedition—perhaps because of his combat experience or because she respected King Stellan's right to put an Ardannian in charge—but it was clear she had no hesitation in issuing orders to the rest of us despite our kingdom of origin. If it came to a matter of enough importance, would she attempt to override the captain?

"There!" Castus's voice sounded loudly enough to be heard down our straggling line, and we all picked up the pace, eager to see what he had discovered.

We had been traveling for most of the day now, and the path had almost disappeared, no more than a goat track at this point. The tracker pointed off to one side where a misshapen tree nearly hid an offshoot of the trail. The small stretch of slightly trampled dirt skirted around a large boulder before ending at a small section of level ground.

"That was his camp," Castus said, certainty in his voice.

I looked around the space, noticing what could be the scattered remains of a small fire. A couple of boot prints showed clearly enough to support his claim.

"I feel no power here," Matthis said. "But it could have faded by now."

"Or the princess is right, and it was never shielded at all," Jocasta added.

"A possibility," Matthis conceded, although it was clear he found it hard to imagine someone undertaking the sort of endeavor attempted by this abduction party without ready access to power.

"It is a good place for a camp," Alaric said, "and he will not be returning to it. If we stop here for the night ourselves, we will have opportunity to conduct a few experiments, and see what traces of power might reveal themselves."

"Aye, it's as good a spot as any," Castus agreed. "And better than many. My ears aren't as sharp as they once were, but I can hear a stream around here somewhere."

I was assigned to join Castus in locating the water, and we had no trouble doing so. It flowed slightly higher up than the flat ground of our camp site, but the path to it was easily accessible. The old tracker pointed to another clear boot print in the mud beside the stream.

"Knew what he was doing, that Tarxi," he said. "I wonder how long he was using this as a base."

"Do you see signs he had anyone else here with him at any point?" I asked, unease gripping me.

But he replied with confidence. "Nothing at all. I'd have spoken up if I'd seen anything like that, My Lord."

"Of course," I muttered, feeling foolish.

A tiny, crackling fire greeted us on our return to the camp

site, its warmth and cheer welcome in the inhospitable surroundings. Saffron seemed to find the small mountain clearing fascinating, however. She was oblivious to the rest of us, crouched over a small clump of hardy mountain flowers that appeared to be growing out of solid rock.

When I crossed over to stand beside her, she glanced up, her mind still clearly on the plants.

"Aren't they amazing? Who would expect to find such resilience alongside such beauty?"

I looked from the delicate flower to her shining eyes and barely bit back my response. She didn't seem to notice my silence.

"I can't wait to learn how they grow with so little soil and purchase. I would love to try some of the compositions I learned at the Academy on them, but I didn't bring any with me, and I know we can't afford to waste energy on such things right now."

"If you like," I said, without thinking, "when this is all over, you could come back for a visit to my family's estate. I'm sure Castus would be happy to take us on some day trips up into the mountains so you can examine the plants as much as you like."

She looked at me with such surprise that I quickly added, "I'm sure Finnian can weasel his way out of training long enough to join us for a short trip. Although I suppose it's too much to dream that Elena could extract herself from court for a mere pleasure outing. We'll have to come up with some compelling excuse for her."

When Saffron still looked confused, I grinned at her, trying to cover my own discomfort at making such a rash suggestion. "How else will we show them the site of our great heroics?"

She snorted at that before her attention was thankfully claimed by a grinding sound a short way to our right. When we both turned to look, we found Alaric, surveying an enormous boulder that now blocked the only path into the little clearing.

He glanced our way, giving a nod of satisfaction as he placed two torn scraps of parchment inside one of his pockets. "We'll shield ourselves, of course. But we may as well make use of some physical barriers as well."

His words seemed to remind Saffron that we were standing idly by while others prepared our camp for the night, and she moved quickly away. I gave a final glance at the flowers that had so captured her. It's true they were lovely, although I doubted I would have noticed them if she hadn't pointed them out.

It didn't surprise me Saffron felt an affinity with the growers. I had heard she wasn't well suited to healing, but among the growers she could still bring life—just life of a different sort. Her considerate, observant nature made it easy to picture her in a garden, nurturing growing things.

When Matthis strode past, deep in conversation with Castus, I shook off my thoughts and joined them. We had more pressing matters that needed our attention.

By the time we were all sitting down to a hot evening meal, Tabor, Matthis, and Jocasta had agreed that there was no sign of any previous use of compositions in the area.

"The arsonist was definitely here, however," Jocasta said. "And he came and went a number of times. Unfortunately, there's no clear trail higher up to show where he came from, and we don't have the compositions available to fully recreate days' worth of his movements."

"So are his people waiting for him to return, or will they be making their way here at some point?" Elias mused aloud.

"If we had more people, I'd leave a group here, just in case," Matthis said. "But we can't afford to go splitting up." His eyes lingered on the princess, and I knew he felt the same weight of pressure we all did. How were we going to capture her attackers while still ensuring her safety? Our relationship with the Empire might well hinge equally on both outcomes.

Perhaps it was this concern, weighing on all our minds, that led us to take a cautious approach the next day. Castus and

Matthis took multiple short trips out from our camp, surveying possible paths to take, while Tabor remained behind to guard the princess. The rest of us were asked to do what we could to produce tracking compositions.

A flat mood already hung over the camp, likely the result of a night spent on thin bedrolls. I had thought the cots at the front lines were bad, but the discomfort of our current trip was far worse. And that was despite the fact I wasn't the only one to have used compositions to ease my pains after the previous day's exertions. I had definitely seen Saffron handing out parchments to all three of the sealed members of our group.

Without the distraction of physical exertion, the day seemed to stretch endlessly before me. I had little desire to sit around uselessly, so I was almost glad for Matthis's request for compositions—even if it was the sort of repetitive drudgery I had always despised. I had no experience with the kind of compositions required, but they were unlikely to present any particular challenge.

"Didn't you ever do tracking compositions in your two years at the front?" Saffron asked, frowning down at the blank parchment in front of her.

"You're forgetting I was a lowly lieutenant," I said. "Good for following orders and using long-established procedures. Procedures put in place by those brave souls like Matthis who actually selected the armed forces discipline."

"Yes." She rolled her eyes. "A lowly lieutenant who just happened to be the oldest son of the general."

I grinned. "I'm not denying the position came with some advantages, but being asked to come up with experimental compositions on the run wasn't one of them."

She sighed. "No, I suppose not." She gave me a curious look. "Did you see much action? Or was that one of the advantages of being the general's son?"

I snorted. "You have met my father, haven't you? A Devoras is expected to be strong and courageous." I deepened my voice. "We don't cower in safety like other mages."

"Yes, I can imagine him saying that. And he sent Calix and Natalya out with the rest of us, now that I think about it." She paused. "What is it like having General Griffith as your father?"

"What's it like having Duke Dashiell as yours?" I countered.

She turned away, hiding her face. "He's not my father," she said, her voice muffled, and I wanted to kick myself. Her father was dead, and here I was making jokes. I tried to retrieve the situation by answering her question properly.

"Considering the war began before I was even born, it has mostly consisted of not having a father around at all. On the occasions when he was at the estate, or in Corrin, it tended to involve reminders of family duty and questions about why I wasn't as dedicated to the family interests as Calix."

I said it without heat. I had long since accepted the dynamics of our family. I was the oldest, set to inherit, and Natalya was the only daughter. Calix had to distinguish himself somehow, and if obedience and filial duty was his chosen route, then I wished him joy of it. It had never held much appeal for me.

Saffron's face, however, was full of pity—although, from what I knew, her own family situation was less than ideal.

"So you spent most of your time with your mother, then," she said, her voice gentle.

I laughed. "As little as I could. Mother wasn't exactly the nurturing sort."

She looked startled, and I tried to bring up a memory of her own mother. She rarely attended social functions, but she had seemed to dote on Saffron from the occasional times I had seen her. Between her and Helene, Finnian's mother, Saffron must have spent her childhood swimming in the sort of warmth my own had lacked.

"Don't go feeling sorry for me, though," I said lightly. "You're a Callinos, so you know what it's like to be part of an enormous extended family. There were always aunts and cousins enough on hand to keep us in line and provide company if we desired it."

She looked like she wanted to argue but refrained from doing so.

"Besides, I learned early enough how to successfully deal with my father," I said. "We have what you might call a transactional relationship. I do my duty by the family and, in exchange, he exerts the family's influence on my behalf. It's a system that works well enough for all involved."

Saffron wrinkled her nose but didn't voice any disagreement aloud. Instead she continued to survey me as if I were an unfamiliar object worthy of curiosity.

"And what did your father think when you helped Elena in the Empire? The king can't have been pleased that you assisted his son to set off alone into Kallorway."

"Ah, but Elena is family, so assisting her was assisting family. And since my father was the one to bring her into the family in the first place—I was initially against her adoption, you know— he couldn't blame me for being obliged to offer her my help."

"How did that argument work on your father?" she asked, a wry note in her voice.

I chuckled. "About as well as it seems to have worked on you." I let my voice drop. "But helping her was the right thing to do."

"Careful," she said, a teasing note in her voice that I liked. "You're starting to sound less and less like a Devoras."

"Oh, but look how well it worked out for me! A Devoras must always play the long game. Now, I'm willing to admit that if things had gone differently in Kallorway, I might have lived to regret it. But who could blame me for helping Lucas and Elena infiltrate our enemy's kingdom when doing so helped us win the war?"

"I'm guessing General Thaddeus found it within his power," she said, the amusement still in her voice.

"That," I said with a sigh, "is all too true. And consequently my advancement within the Royal Guard came to an abrupt halt. But once again you see my true genius. I helped my adopted sister dearest, and in return, she helped me. Thus you see me now—no longer a royal guard but instead a valued official of the crown, a central part of helping to forge a new world."

"So a true Devoras, after all," she murmured, and the joking note was gone.

I tried to think how to bring it back, but Elias interrupted us.

"The captain left an example composition I've been copying, if you'd like to make use of it. I think I've about used up all the energy I can safely exert, given our situation."

I assumed since Elias had been chosen for the expedition that he was a mage of some power and skill. He had probably managed a significant number of compositions before the effort of controlling the power had drained his energy too low to continue.

"Thank you!" Relief sounded in Saffron's voice. "I had no idea where to start."

"It's simple enough because they want us to make as many as possible," he said. "We don't know how often we'll have to use them. He said not to put too much power into each one, since we don't want to be wasteful. If the composition runs out too soon, we can always work another one."

I placed the parchment on the flat rock Saffron and I were both using as a table. She leaned in close to read it, and her hair fell forward like a veil between us. The scent hit me, not floral like some of the ladies at court favored, but a clean, soapy smell. It was honest and appealing—just like Saffron herself—and I had to lean back to stop myself from burying my face in it.

I jumped up. "I'm going to refill my water skin," I said quickly before hurrying away. I needed to clear my head. If I wasn't careful, I was going to forget we were on a deadly mission with consequences for the entire kingdom. I needed to start focusing and produce some compositions.

CHAPTER 13

SAFFRON

*J*ulian left strangely quickly, and I carefully didn't watch him go. I needed the space. Talking to him was far more natural than I would have expected, and I had nearly forgotten he was a Devoras. Just like he seemed to have forgotten I wasn't actually Finnian's sister. He laughed and joked with me like an equal because he thought I was one. I would do well not to forget it wasn't actually the truth. I might be from one of the great families, the same as him, but I didn't have his strength.

Our current task reminded me of that fact all too clearly. The composition that was needed was simple enough, and I suspected the captain had written it out in far more detail than he would normally have done for the sake of the rest of us. The limitations were detailed and explicit.

When worked, it would highlight the path most recently taken by a set of human feet and nothing more. The power would stay only a few yards in front of us, rather than ranging out and potentially giving away our approach.

When Julian returned, he sat slightly further around the rock than he had before, asking politely before he took the parchment to study it himself.

"Well that seems simple enough." He glanced at me, something in his eyes I couldn't quite read. "Just remember not to push yourself too far. You'll need to leave yourself enough energy for the climb."

I nodded but said nothing, my focus now on the composition. I wrote the binding words quickly at the top of the parchment, the familiar swell of power building around me. As I completed them, the power simmered, no longer straining to break free, and I turned my attention to shaping it as I poured it into the words taking form beneath my pen. I was careful not to draw on more power and not to shape it beyond the explicit words on the page. When it came to an unfamiliar and detailed working, I preferred to err on the side of too little than too much, especially after Elias's instructions.

It was a familiar process since I had just completed four years of training focused on how to control the amount and shape of the power that I released with my written words. But the effort took concentration, the phrasing unfamiliar and the composition long. At one point I felt the power trying to build and tamped down on it, refusing to draw any more.

As soon as I'd finished the last words, I wrote *End binding*. The sensation of power cut off completely, but a wave of tiredness washed over me, and I had to refrain from rubbing my eyes. I never noticed the drain of energy while I was absorbed in controlling the power, it always hit when the composition was complete.

A moment later I had recovered, though, and was ready to start again. I wasn't close to true exhaustion, not after a single relatively minor composition. But when I sat back after my fifth composition, massaging my cramping hand, I had to admit it would be foolish to push myself any further.

I stood up silently, gathering my small collection of parchments and slipping them into an internal pocket. I would give them to the captain as soon as he returned. I tried not to look at Julian who seemed as oblivious to the clearing around him as I had been while composing. He was already working on his eighth composition and showed no signs of flagging.

Had he noticed how few I had managed, or was he too absorbed in his own efforts?

Now that I was paying attention, I could smell hot food, a welcome aroma, and I gravitated to the small fire. Faylee, unable to compose like us or to assist Jasper and Jocasta in their studies, had assigned herself the task of fetching the rest of us water and aiding with the cooking. My nose suggested she was suited to her self-appointed role.

I must have been working for longer than I realized because Castus and Matthis already sat beside the flames, bowls of simple stew in their hands. I crossed over to them immediately and presented my day's efforts to Matthis.

He thanked me, looking over them briefly and nodding his approval. I let out a silent breath of relief. Nothing in his words or face indicated he thought their number pitifully small, although I was sure I must have produced the least of everyone.

Faylee popped up, a grin on her face and a bowl of stew held out to me. Seeing her reminded me that some among us couldn't contribute any compositions at all, and I immediately felt guilty for allowing myself to wallow in self-pity.

"Thank you." I tried to make the words as heartfelt as I could, and her smile grew impossibly larger.

"I think I might have a talent," she said. "I never cooked at home because my family employs a chef. Maybe I've missed my calling."

"That's fortunate for us," I said. "Because I'm not sure Elias has much talent in that direction."

Faylee laughed. "I've already officially volunteered to take over from him. As long as he's willing to continue carrying the supplies."

"I imagine he was willing to take such an exchange."

She winked at me. "You should have seen the weight lift off the poor man's shoulders. Metaphorically, of course. I'm not volunteering to take the actual weight—my pack is quite heavy enough."

A gentle throat-clearing behind me made me turn away from Faylee who moved back toward the bubbling pots. To my surprise, it was the princess who was seeking my attention.

"Your Highness, how can I help you?" I asked.

"I would like to wash in the stream while there's still daylight. I have suggested to Tabor that you would be a more acceptable companion than him for such a venture."

I glanced at the bodyguard who stood several steps behind the princess, looking uncomfortable.

"Oh, of course." I searched around for somewhere to put down my bowl.

"Please finish your food first," she said. "You have been composing. I well remember how exhausting it can be, and I wouldn't wish for you to collapse halfway through the wash."

Pity for the princess surged through me again, as well as renewed frustration at myself for wasting time and energy feeling sorry for myself when she had been forced to seal her power away forever.

"I won't be long," I said and proceeded to wolf the stew down so fast that I burned my tongue.

The princess watched me do it, although no hint of impatience crossed her face, and as soon as I stood up again, she joined me. Turning to Tabor she instructed him to remain behind.

"We will only be behind that rock ledge," she said, pointing toward the out-of-view stream.

I looked toward the bodyguard. "Thornton took his training seriously. I can have a shield composition out in record time."

He nodded at me. "You were quick enough to shield her last time. That's why I picked you."

I gave him an awkward nod in return before hurrying away with the princess. It warmed me to know the burly bodyguard considered me a worthy replacement, even for such a simple exercise.

As we approached the water, it occurred to me that I might join the princess in taking a wash. It was still warm enough to make the water appealing, and we had all been hurried unceremoniously out of our beds the previous morning without time for anything like washing.

I glanced at Kalani, wondering if she would consider it to be a dereliction of my duty to join her in the water or whether she would think it demonstrated true dedication. It was hard to guess what someone was thinking when they'd been trained their whole life to keep their emotions hidden from an entire court.

Even the way she had phrased her request for me to join her… It had actually been a command, with no hint of question, but phrased in such a way I had barely noticed. And she had made it sound like I was her choice rather than the truth revealed by Tabor's words—I was being foisted on her by her overzealous bodyguard. Kalani might be a similar age to me, but it was easy to imagine her holding her own in court.

She turned and looked directly at me, silently acknowledging my scrutiny. I flushed and looked away, wondering if I'd violated some sort of royal protocol.

"Will you wash as well?" she asked.

I laughed. "If you don't think it will get me in trouble with the captain."

"I'm sure he would commend you for keeping within arm's reach of me at all times," she said gravely.

I grinned. "Yes, precisely."

I stripped off my outer garments, laying them carefully over the cleanest-looking boulder I could find. I left on only my shift but hesitated before stepping toward the water. The shift had no pockets, and I couldn't very well carry a roll of parchment into the water in my hand. But neither did I feel comfortable leaving all of my compositions behind.

After a moment's indecision, I twisted my hair onto my head, securing it with a short length of leather. Choosing two shielding compositions, I thrust them into the rolls of hair. I wouldn't be able to wash my hair, but I would feel better with the rest of me clean at least.

By the time I was ready to step toward the stream, Kalani was already dipping her toes in. She gave a soft gasp but didn't pull them back.

"It's cold." She took another step in, up to her knees now.

I followed, moving carefully. It wasn't an especially deep or wide stream, but it moved swiftly, and the bottom was covered with mossy rocks that provided a slippery foothold.

"Best we not go in too far," I said. I wouldn't want to lose my balance while up to my waist in the fast-moving water.

Kalani nodded her agreement, and there was silence for a few moments, except for the burbling steam and our own splashes.

"I think perhaps you have the wrong idea about me," Kalani said, taking me by surprise.

"The wrong idea, Your Highness?"

"I could see that the news of my sealing greatly shocked your people, and you seem to be avoiding the topic with me."

"I…I'm sorry, Your Highness. I didn't wish to give offense or cause you pain."

She nodded once as if my words confirmed her thoughts.

"Precisely," she said. "I think perhaps you imagine that my family forced me to make a great sacrifice. But it is I who made the suggestion."

I stopped splashing myself, staring at her with an open mouth. "You suggested that you seal yourself? And give up the throne?"

"Certainly." She calmly continued to wash. "It was the best way I could serve my empire."

"But…why?" I asked, still too shocked to be diplomatic.

"With my greater levels of power, I was able to seal so many, you see." She explained patiently, as if to a child. "It is not how we have done things in the past, but it has helped relieve the immediate pressure of so many commonborn children. You already know that it doesn't prevent my passing my strength on to my children, of course. So it does nothing to dilute the royal bloodline."

I slowly resumed washing myself, my mind turning over the things she wasn't saying. We knew the Empire was straining not just because of a recent increase in the commonborn population but also because of rumblings of discontent among some in the two sealed clans. I could only imagine that the example set by their crown princess would have a significant impact on those clans. If they had started to doubt the honor and importance of their sacrifice, they could doubt no longer.

It still seemed like an immense sacrifice for Kalani, however. And yet she seemed genuinely impassive about it, although it was possible that was a court mask.

"If I may say so," she said, "it was an inspired notion on my part. My father is very pleased with me." She glanced across the short stretch of stream between us. "I have been curious for some time to visit our southern neighbors, and now I am free to do so as I was not free before. And my next sister becomes the heir. She is far more suited to the role than I. I will serve my empire as a diplomat, and she will serve as ruler. We must all offer our best to our people."

I slowly shook my head as the whole situation finally became clear. Kalani had sacrificed something she valued less to win what she truly wanted. And she had helped both her family and her empire in the process. It truly was an inspired move.

I had thought that for Kalani—not only a Sekali but also a princess—there was no room for individuality or personal choice. I had thought that to serve her family and empire she had to let them subsume everything of herself as an individual. But now, with this explanation, I understood better what she had said the day before. She could best honor and serve her family by living to her strengths. It might require some sacrifices, but life always did—at least if you wanted other people in that life.

Something hovered on the edge of my mind, something life-changing, but before I could grasp it, Kalani spoke again.

"Perhaps you—" But she got no further. Adjusting her weight, she lost her footing and fell into the water, dousing me with the splash.

I spluttered, my body flinching from the shock of the sudden cold. My eyes closed for only a second, but when they opened again, she was fully submerged in the water and already swept out of my reach.

She came up for air, gasping, her fingers stretching uselessly toward me. I could see her legs scrabbling to find purchase, but the stones beneath her were too slippery, and the current pulled her along too fast.

My eyes flew ahead of her path, and I realized too late that some way beyond us the stream fell over the edge of a small lip of rock, plunging into a waterfall of unknown height. And I hadn't even thought to ask Kalani if she could swim.

With no time to think, I threw myself forward full-length into the water. I gasped at the temperature but forced myself not to lose focus, keeping my eyes fixed on the flailing princess. Thankful for the many afternoons Finnian and I had spent in the water near his family's estate, I propelled myself forward, working with the current to push me closer to Kalani.

She saw me coming and stretched her fingers for me again,

only to bounce off a large rock just before I reached her. The sudden impact sent her spinning away from me, but I lunged, grabbing at the hem of her shift.

I locked my fingers on to the material, holding us together, but I had now lost my fragile balance in the water, and it took everything I had to keep my head above the stream. My knees and shins knocked painfully against the stones of the bottom, and my legs reacted instinctively, trying to find somewhere to stand. But the effort only further unbalanced us both as the current continued to sweep us forward.

We were going to go over the edge, and there was nothing I could do to stop it.

My free hand flew to my hair as I frantically tried to remember what limitations I had written into my shields. I certainly hadn't been thinking of a situation like this.

As we had been taught at the Academy, I carried two separate shields. I didn't have the strength to craft a shield that would both protect against all types of attack and last for any length of time. One of the ones I carried was designed to protect against attacks from other mages using raw power—the kinds of attack that might seek to control and bind my limbs or render me unconscious. A shield like that would do no good against rocks and water.

But the other had been crafted to protect against physical attack of all kinds. And in the Academy's arena, those attacks could come using more than just a sword. If my enemy chose attack compositions that utilized physical objects, such as rocks, then a shield against power would do nothing to protect me. In the panic of the moment, I couldn't recall composing this specific working, but surely I had written in full protections against all kinds of physical danger. Surely...

There was no time to distinguish between the two workings. Whipping them from my hair, I stuffed both into my mouth, gripping down hard on whatever scraps of parchment made it between my teeth. The material in my other hand was nearly wrenched from my grip as the full weight of the princess dropped away. But a half-second later, the pressure eased as I fell also.

Violently pulling the pieces of parchment away from my mouth, I heard the familiar sound of tearing paper. Power exploded out around me, catching the princess within its radius, just as we crashed into the foaming water below.

CHAPTER 14

JULIAN

I stood up and stretched, easing the sore muscles in my back that protested spending so long cramped over a boulder. Ten compositions would have to satisfy Matthis because I wasn't pushing myself any further. Not in such an uncertain situation.

I delivered them to the captain, telling myself that I was just regaining my bearings and not scanning the clearing for Saffron. She was nowhere in view, but then neither was the princess.

Matthis accepted my stack of parchments with a grunt of thanks, but Castus grinned up at me with a look that was far more knowing than I would have liked.

"If you're wondering where the princess has disappeared to, young master," he said, "she's gone for a wash in the stream with that Callinos gal."

I nodded once but didn't say anything, not used to being so easily discomfited. Why did I feel sure he knew it wasn't the princess I had been searching for?

I nearly decided to go refill my water bottle, telling myself it was a natural thing to do after composing for so long, but remembered at the last moment that Castus had said the girls were washing. A flush crept up my neck, and I had to fight to keep it down. No matter how much I might want to, I couldn't possibly go down to the river in that case.

With great difficulty I tried to refocus on the pot of stew Faylee was stirring. I hadn't succeeded when a blossom of power burst to life beyond the bounds of our camp.

My feet were moving before my mind caught up. It had come from the direction of the stream. Startled exclamations sounded from behind me, and a figure appeared to my right, keeping pace with my headlong dash. Tabor. No doubt he had been just as focused on the absent girls as me, although for different reasons. His royal charge had already nearly been abducted once this trip —letting her out of his sight must have put him on edge.

We nearly ended up in the water ourselves as we sped at full pace to the side of the stream. Looking wildly around, I could see the discarded clothing, but neither Saffron nor Kalani was in sight.

The power was fading but still discernible, coming from our right, and we both took off down the bank. Tabor, ahead of me now, came to a sudden stop. I collided with his back, nearly sending us both over the edge of a small drop. We recovered just in time, staggering backward as we fought to regain our balance despite the uneven stones beneath our feet.

"There!" the guard said, his focus holding steady.

I peered over the edge and saw two struggling white shapes in the water below, arms and legs flailing in all directions. They had nearly made it out of the violent foam at the base of the small waterfall, but they kept bouncing strangely off a collection of jagged rocks that protruded from the water. And every time they did, the sense of power around them faded a little more.

"They're shielded, but it won't last much longer," I said, but Tabor had already launched himself off the edge.

It wasn't a sheer cliff face, the steep drop offering jutting sections of rock to use for hands and feet. But the captain was taking it at a perilously fast pace, and I didn't have the years of physical training he did. If I fell and ended up in the water as well, it would do no one any good.

Thrusting my hand into my jacket, my fingers skimmed over the complicated pattern of tiny pockets. I needed barely a flicker of conscious thought for the action, most of my attention focused on the girls still being battered by the water below.

Ripping the parchment I retrieved, I pointed with a finger at a clear spot on the very edge of the water below, the same spot Saffron seemed to be trying to drag Kalani toward.

A hubbub of voices sounded behind me as power swirled beneath my feet. With a jolting sensation, I lifted into the air, carried on an invisible platform of pure power.

I floated over the edge of the rocks and lowered gently toward the designated patch of ground, feeling as if I moved impossibly slowly. But it could only have been seconds before my feet touched solid dirt and the sense of power dissipated.

Tabor vaulted the final distance to land at the base of the waterfall a half-second later, and we both plunged forward into the water. The girls had made it a significant way to the edge of the small pool, so the water was only mid-thigh when my grasping hands managed to grab one of Saffron's arms.

Tabor got a firm grip on the princess, drawing her gently out of the water, moving slowly and carefully on the slippery rocks. As soon as Kalani was tugged from her hold, Saffron slumped, letting my hold on her prevent her from being sucked back into the waterfall's maelstrom.

"Come on," I said gently. "Not far now." I braced myself, strengthening my stance. "See if you can get your feet under you."

It took her some effort, slipping and sliding, but by clinging to both my arms, she managed to get a firm purchase on the stones under our feet.

"It's only a few steps and there's a short stretch of sand," I said. "Just keep hold of me."

Tabor had somehow already managed to get Kalani up onto the shore, but Saffron and I continued to take our time, feeling each step carefully on the slippery bottom. As soon as we had our feet on the surer purchase of the sand, we paused, both letting out a slow breath.

She looked up at me, her hair wet and bedraggled and her eyes huge in her dripping face.

"Thank you," she said, panting slightly. "My physical strength and my shield were both starting to give out."

I shook my head. "And no wonder when you just spent so long composing. You must be utterly exhausted."

She grimaced and nodded.

It struck me suddenly that she was standing close to me, both hands gripping my arms, and wearing nothing but a wet shift. I could feel the warmth building at the base of my neck again and looked quickly over at Tabor and Kalani.

Someone on the higher ground had run back for blankets, and Elias was in the process of throwing them down to Tabor. I took a steadying breath and looked back at Saffron. How had I always thought her quiet and insignificant? She was breathtaking and far too attractive for my peace of mind.

I cleared my throat. "What happened?"

She groaned. "It was such a simple thing. The princess lost her footing on the moss on the streambed. I was standing right by her, but it all happened so fast, I couldn't get hold of her. So there was nothing to do but throw myself in too."

My brows drew together. "That was putting yourself in danger as well."

She shrugged as if that didn't matter. "I didn't know if she could swim or not. Or what might be at the base of the waterfall. Thankfully I'd retained enough sense to keep two shielding compositions on me, but they were written to shield me, not someone else. I needed to be close if they were going to protect us both."

I shook my head. "It was still brave."

"In truth there wasn't time for bravery, just reacting."

A small grin tugged at my lips as I looked down into her dark, shining eyes. "What do you think bravery is?"

She laughed a little, the sound shaky. "I suppose so. I'm just glad you and the captain turned up." She paused, looking away almost shyly and then dropping her hands from my arms. "Thank you for rescuing me." She bit her lip. "I saw you coming down the cliff. That must have been a valuable composition."

"Think nothing of it," I said quickly, suddenly afraid for her to guess how little thought I had given to the matter.

"Oh, well…thank you," she said again before wading out of the water.

She wrung out her hair as she went, and I tried not to let my eyes linger on her movement. Her words clung to me, however. Vaguely I registered the freezing feel of the water against my legs, but I couldn't seem to move.

She was right, it had been a valuable composition. But I hadn't hesitated for even a moment, despite knowing Tabor was on his way down to help them. And I couldn't lie to myself and say it had been the same general selfless instinct that had driven Saffron to throw herself after the princess. I couldn't even pretend I had been thinking of the princess herself and her importance to Ardann.

My mind had been solely focused on Saffron and the fact she was in danger. And no expenditure of effort or resources had seemed too great. I had known Tabor's efforts would center on Kalani, and even the slimmest danger to Saffron had inspired me to act. My compositions, however powerful or complex, could be replaced. She could not.

The thought coursed through me, taking root everywhere it went and changing me in ways I couldn't yet fathom. Saffron was important in my life. She couldn't be replaced. I had known her for years—or was it only days?—but I saw her clearly now. Her kindness, her compassion, her loyalty, the thoughtful consideration she applied to everything she did. Her qualities might not be flashy and dramatic like those of my adopted sister, but they called to something deep inside me.

All my life something in my core had resisted my father's view of the world, the way he immersed himself in the mage obsession with strength and power. But only my time in the Sekali Empire, coupled with Elena and the changes she represented, had allowed me to see inside my own heart. I shared my father's desire for importance—I was still his son—but he yearned for power and influence within the existing system. He didn't see that in fifty years' time, his name would be forgotten. I wanted future generations to remember me because I helped change the world for the better.

But Saffron...I watched her accept a blanket, wrapping it around her shoulders and shivering slightly as she asked Kalani something I couldn't hear, concern on her face. Saffron wanted to help change the world because she truly cared about people. She wanted to do it because it was the right thing to do. I could see the conflict within her. She was one of those who were starting to see our world differently, but she still felt the pull of loyalty to her family, and she hadn't lost her desire to honor and please them.

Even when she conflicted with herself, both sides were fueled by love. She made my own idle defiances of the past seem petty and juvenile. Saffron cared about the opinion of those she loved, not about being remembered by history.

And suddenly I could understand something of that emotion because I realized that I would sacrifice any reputation among future generations to win her approval in my own lifetime.

"Julian?" Jasper's concerned voice, calling from the top of the rocks, brought me back to reality.

Saffron swung around at the sound of my name, her brow

creasing at the sight of me still in the water. I strode forward, trying to cover my lapse with action.

Thankfully a diversion arrived in the form of Jocasta and Castus who came around a clump of trees, on the same level as us.

"We've found a less perilous way down," Jocasta said matter-of-factly. "And although it's summer, the day is already starting to cool. I recommend we get you all back to the fire and some dry clothes as soon as possible."

Tabor lost no time in ushering the princess after Castus, who had already turned to lead the way back. Jocasta gestured for Saffron to follow them, walking close beside the girl and asking the same questions I had done in the water.

I trailed in the rear of the group, glad to escape further scrutiny. My whole world had just changed, and I needed time to assimilate my new reality.

SAFFRON

My concerns that I would suffer some sort of official reprimand or unofficial censure for the accident proved unnecessary. Instead Julian spread a highly favorable version of events that highlighted my quick thinking and disregard for my own safety. It wasn't quite how I remembered events unfolding, but I couldn't actually dispute any of the specific points.

Tabor even thanked me for my efforts to protect the princess, as did Kalani herself. She explained that she could swim but had taken in a mouthful of water when she first slipped, putting her off-balance as she struggled to breathe.

Her bodyguard might not see me as culpable, but he had issued stern instructions that there was to be no more bathing. The princess would have to content herself with splashing water on her face for the rest of the trip.

I had expected to find it hard to sleep after the shock of our misadventure, but I underestimated the extent of my exhaustion. Thankfully I woke refreshed enough to face the coming hike without too much trepidation.

With our new collection of compositions, and a way forward

determined by Matthis and Castus from their investigations of the local area, we were soon continuing up the mountain. We arranged ourselves in the same order as before, but now we had to move single file with no easy opportunity for conversation.

The mountains rose steeply above us now, both impressive and intimidating in their grandeur. At their tips, still far distant from where we trekked, white snow clung despite the time of year. The air tasted cleaner and crisper than any I had breathed before, and the unfamiliar scent of pine—so different from the warm smells of the forest near my home—filled my nostrils.

It was hard work, clambering over and around rocks, and up steep, sometimes slippery inclines. I had little breath left for talking, even if it had been feasible to attempt it. But somehow, no matter how impossible the way ahead appeared on first surveillance, we always found a path that allowed enough purchase to continue forward.

When we found an area broad and flat enough to stop for the midday meal, Castus shook his head, his face full of respect. "Whatever else these Tarxi might be, they're mountain dwellers, that's for sure. I don't think I would have been able to find that path if we hadn't been following those glowing steps."

"It's for the best," Matthis said. "Our group is too inexperienced. With the footsteps to follow, it leaves you alert to watch for dangers and pitfalls we wouldn't see coming."

When we finished the cold meal and prepared to begin again, I had the chance to see the working for myself. Matthis ripped one of the parchments, and a glow appeared on the ground in front of us. Apparently the arsonist had stopped in this spot as well because his glowing footsteps appeared all around the clearing, shining under our feet. A small opening between two rocks also blazed brightly, and I could see where his prints had squeezed through the gap.

The benefits of these glowing markers must have balanced our lack of experience, because we arrived at a suitable spot for a cramped camp at around nightfall. The glow that lit up the small space made it clear we weren't the first to use this area for the purpose. In a day we had made the same progress as the arsonist had in the opposite direction. How long ago had he come through here? Three days? Seven?

Julian appeared at my side and offered to fill my water skin for me.

"There's a creek, but it's a little hard to access." He smiled, his eyes lingering on my face.

I raised an eyebrow. "Afraid I'll fall in?"

"Even you couldn't manage that here." He winked. "It's more of a trickle than anything, it's just awkwardly located."

"Thank you." I handed him my water skin, not completely sure how to respond to the warmth of his manner.

My eyes followed him as he moved away from me, gifting his easy smile to everyone he passed. Likely I was reading too much into it. He might be a Devoras, but he was still incredibly attractive, and I was responding like a foolish first year. Any minute now I was going to start giggling. The looks he gave me had no extra meaning just because they came from the most attractive gray eyes I'd ever seen.

But when I went to retrieve and roll out my sleeping mat, I found Julian already doing it for me. He placed it in the same position I had occupied in our previous camp, between Kalani and Faylee, and he offered no explanation for his efforts—just the same warm smile that seemed to hint at something more.

When he approached me by the fire that evening, holding out a bowl of stew, my fingers brushed against his. Instantly my heart betrayed me, beating faster in spite of myself. I tried to watch closely as he handed the next bowl to Kalani and then moved back to Faylee, instructing her not to forget to eat herself. Had his hand or eyes lingered with either of them? My head said one thing and my heart another, and I went to bed unsatisfied.

When I woke in the middle of the night, my mental debate

struck me in a different light. I had spent half my evening trying to decide if I had seen any difference in his manner between the three of us. All my focus had been on whether he felt the same spark I did at our touch, and my observations had led to no sure conclusion. I hadn't stopped to think how strange it was to see a powerful member of the Devoras family treating a princess, a commonborn merchant, and me, a Callinos, so equitably.

The next morning he was there, standing ready to help me put on my pack while he inquired in a friendly way about my sleep. I mumbled my answer, not willing to admit it had been disturbed by thoughts of him. How many hearts had been broken by the general's oldest son? He was destined for a marriage of alliance, and I had no interest in a hot-headed, power-hungry Devoras.

So why couldn't I stop thinking about him? And why did my eyes leap toward his figure whenever he came into view? Our continued trek up into the mountains left all too much time for these considerations to weigh on my mind.

That night he sat beside me at the fire, volunteering stories about his childish adventures in the foothills around his family estate. In spite of myself, I responded with stories about Finnian's escapades, and my constant attempts to extricate us both from them.

He laughed in all the right places and even confessed as the fire died down that he might have more sympathy for Finnian than he had ever imagined. "I'll admit to having had some confusion in the past about why you and Elena are so attached to him."

"I won't say he's not infuriating because he very frequently is," I admitted. "But he's also extremely hard to dislike. Even Calix and Natalya don't dislike him, exactly, and that's saying something—everything considered." I looked at him sideways, wondering how he would take my comments about his siblings.

But he merely chuckled. "I suppose if I thought of Finnian at all, I thought of him as the Reese of Calix's year. But clearly I've done him a disservice."

Reese, who happened to be moving past on his way to fill up his water skin, heard this remark and replied with such a foul insult that he earned a reprimand from Jocasta who still sat on the other side of the fire.

The healer regarded the Academy representative resentfully. "I'm not a trainee any longer, Jocasta."

"No." The Cygnet stared him down, not budging an inch. "That is true. You're no longer a child and cannot be afforded the extra grace of one." She looked significantly toward the cluster of sleeping mats where Kalani already lay. "We all represent Ardann here, and there is no need to be throwing around words which may carry even greater offense in the Empire than they do here. Circumspection is what is called for, Reese."

Reese muttered something inaudible and hurried away at top speed.

"Ha!" Julian muttered to me. "Look at him run."

"You sound altogether too pleased with yourself." I got up, brushing myself off. "And I, for one, am heading for bed. I'm sure tomorrow will be just as exhausting as today."

Physically speaking, I was right. The next day followed the first almost identically, with merely the brief excitement caused late in the afternoon by the tracks doubling back on themselves. After a short consultation, Castus hurried ahead, returning to report that the previous traveler had encountered an impassable ravine and been forced to seek another way around. We avoided the section of doubled footprints, taking the single way that branched off them, and made camp shortly after.

But the day had been even more emotionally fraught than it had been physically exhausting. Somehow Julian had engineered an adjustment in our walking order, and he shadowed close behind me, always ready with a helping hand whenever I needed to scramble over a particularly awkward stretch of ground. It was sweet, and I could think of no reason to refuse his assistance. But every time our fingers touched, my own skin warmed and my heart began to beat at an unnatural rhythm.

At least I could blame the path itself for my shortness of breath and the speed of my pulse.

I could no longer deny that Julian was giving me special attention. But our conversation from the night before, so enjoyable at the time, had taken on a new significance during my daylight reflections. Julian had once misspoken and called Uncle Dashiell my father. And nothing in my stories of my shared childhood with Finnian had dispelled that false notion.

I had reminded myself only recently that a Devoras of his rank would make a marriage of alliance. Perhaps his father was already seeking one on his behalf, part of their endless exchange of favors. Did the general's son think my rank and strength was of a level with Finnian—equal to himself? For Julian to be showing so much interest in me, he must have misunderstood my position.

Of course, he would find out the truth eventually, and no harm was done in the meantime by my accepting his assistance over a slippery patch of stone—if only my heart would behave. But the faster it beat, the more I knew I couldn't risk spending time with this surprising member of the Devoras family. He had said he was confused about Elena's affection toward my cousin, but I had been equally confused about her affection toward her adoptive brother. It seemed we had both been wrong, but it didn't change the realities of our birthrights.

After a day of his constant presence, I tossed and turned for half the night, unable to get comfortable. When I realized we weren't preparing to leave the next morning, dread filled me. Had Matthis run out of tracking compositions? Buried halfway down the line, I had no idea how quickly they were needing to be refreshed. If he wanted us to spend the day composing, I could have done with a much better sleep.

But Julian appeared at my and Kalani's side to update us on the situation, and it turned out to be a more significant concern than a lack of compositions.

"I should have seen the inconsistency last night," he said. "But I was distracted." He glanced at me while I pretended not to notice his gaze. "We've been tracing the most recent traveler in the area, assuming it was the arsonist and hoping if we reversed his path, it would lead us to their main camp. But the back-tracking we saw at the ravine makes no sense unless the traveler was moving in the same direction as us."

I raised an eyebrow. "You mean at some point we inadvertently picked up more recent tracks than those of the arsonist? Tracks left by someone who was coming this way and moving up the mountain instead of down?"

"It would appear so," Julian agreed. "Which means the situation has changed. The most likely interpretation is that we're approaching their camp. If there's enough activity around here, we may have just crossed with a new path by chance. Or else someone has taken this trek from the estate before us—with news of the arsonist's death, perhaps—and whatever route they took up the mountain has now merged with the original path down taken by the arsonist. Either way, we're not going to keep blindly stumbling forward."

Jasper came over to join us, nodding as he overheard the last part of Julian's words. "I'm hopeful we're near the camp. Parts of our route yesterday looked familiar, although it's hard to be sure, even with my memory." He grimaced ruefully. "So much of these mountains look the same."

Kalani nodded. She had been somewhat subdued since our close encounter with the waterfall, but news that we might be nearing our target had brought the fire back into her eyes.

"I have been staring around me until my eyes water," she said, "but I cannot be sure if any of our surroundings are familiar."

"It makes sense it would have taken us much longer to find a path down than it has coming up," Jasper said. "We had no guide to follow and were exhausted beside."

"The real wonder is that you weren't caught." Julian shook his head. "These Tarxi seem to be the experts in the mountains."

"Yes, I was too grateful at the time, and too focused on moving forward, to spend much time wondering why," Jasper agreed. "But I've given it considerable thought since our conversation the other day. I believe it must be true that there is some limit to the Tarxi's access to compositions. I don't understand what it might be, but if they could have produced such easy ways to track our progress as we have been utilizing against them now, we would never have escaped."

"So what is the plan, then?" I asked.

"We're sending out a smaller team to scout the situation," Julian said. "They'll move forward with a great deal more caution and bring back word of what they find."

CHAPTER 16

JULIAN

I had presented the situation as if the purpose of splitting up was to allow the scout team greater speed and mobility. But I could see in Saffron's eyes that she saw through that excuse. If it was obvious to Saffron, no doubt it was also obvious to Kalani, but neither of them questioned it. And as long as the princess wasn't demanding to be included, Matthis was content.

He had no idea what we might find and had no desire to bring the princess any nearer to her previous captors—especially given the interest they had shown in reclaiming her. Her own enthusiasm for the prospect of apprehending the group of Tarxi only deepened his unease. He had been appointed to lead our group, but the princess far outranked all of us, and I knew he hoped to avoid any crisis of authority.

But I still hated to walk away from the burning questions in Saffron's eyes. My heart wanted to believe it was concern for me that shadowed her, but the stakes were too high for me to put any stock in such a notion. She had plenty of room for concern without reference to me.

Given we still didn't understand the death of our prisoner or the strange attack on Tabor, Matthis left only Tabor and Saffron to guard the princess. They had Jocasta with them as well, however, along with Faylee. I had wondered if the librarian might protest her lack of inclusion, but she had accepted it in silence. She was to remain behind as our second language expert in case anything went wrong during the scouting mission and we lost Jasper. It was a pragmatic consideration that turned my stomach, and I positioned myself directly behind the academic as we filed out of camp. Elena expected me to bring her common-born brother home alive.

Matthis himself had written the composition we now followed, demonstrating far more skill than had been on display from the workings contributed by the rest of us. Only he could see the bright path we followed now, and the whisper of power it produced was so minimal that it would be easy to miss if the Tarxi had any sort of shielding compositions around their camp, filling the air with a sense of power.

I knew I wasn't the only one straining my senses forward, trying to detect any hint of power ahead of us. But I felt nothing. Matthis led us, with Castus close behind, followed by Alaric, Elias, Reese, Jasper, and finally me.

We moved slowly for some time, focusing more on silence than speed, before Matthis held up a fist signaling for us to stop. A whisper passed down the line, and Jasper wormed his way forward. The trail had turned into a tangle of tracks, and Matthis now wanted his interpreter up front, despite Jasper's vulnerability in a fight.

The area around us had leveled out somewhat, more of a small mountain plateau than a valley, and the trees clustered more thickly, the scent of their green needles pungently filling the air. It was an ideal place to make a more long-term camp.

As we inched forward, Matthis indicated for us to spread out, abandoning our single file line. I wove through the group, placing myself back near Jasper, every muscle and nerve taut with tension.

Bird calls sounded around us, along with the rustling of something small in the undergrowth between the trees. Plants clustered thickly here, taking advantage of the soil that had built up on this plateau, so much more hospitable than the unwelcoming stone of the harsher cliff faces.

Nothing—not sight or sound or smell—suggested the presence of any humans other than ourselves. And I could sense no power anywhere close. Despite myself, my tension relaxed slightly, my body unable to remain on the knife edge without any indication of actual danger.

I remained alert enough, however, to whisper a warning to Jasper when I realized he was moving more quickly than the rest of us, inching ahead of our slowly advancing line. He turned to look back at me just as he took another step forward.

His foot brushed against something—a wire, perhaps—and the trees around us erupted. Birds took wing, screeching and cawing their protest, as thick logs swung down from nearby trees, hurtling toward us from all directions.

I flung myself forward, tackling Jasper to the ground as the closest log hurtled over the top of where he had been standing, swinging by two lengths of rope. Power whooshed to life around us, repelling the next log which came so low it would have nearly skimmed the ground if the shield had not blocked its way. Someone further back had found time to work a composition.

Neither Jasper nor I moved for a long moment after silence fell. It was a true silence this time, the wildlife around us startled from their normal activities by the threat. But gradually noises resumed.

I rolled into a sitting position and thrust my hand into my jacket, reaching for a further shielding composition as well as a powerful attack. But when I scanned between the trees, I saw no sign of the Tarxi rushing to respond to our triggering of their primitive trap.

Another moment passed and another. Still nothing. I looked around at the rest of our group. Elias and Reese were closest to Jasper and me, and both also sheltered on the ground. Logs hung between us, some dangling awkwardly, one end against the ground where they had slipped free from their binding. Every mage in our group gripped compositions in his hands, and by now we were all shielded. No one had launched any attacks, though, because there was no sign of any target.

"Any hope of surprise is now gone," Matthis said, matter-of-factly. Drawing out a new composition, he ripped it. Power raced away from him in a thin veil, filling the air in every direction. He scanned between the trees, as if watching for his power's return. I felt it when it came, although I saw nothing.

Matthis, however, turned to us, a guarded expression on his face. "We are the only humans anywhere near."

"They've already moved on then? Without their man?" Alaric sounded disgusted. "Does that mean they've been watching us? Or that they had a hand in his death?"

"Perhaps," Matthis said, refusing to be drawn into speculation. "We must see if we can find any sign of their camp."

The presence of the trap made us certain of finding something, but our solitude had convinced me we were looking for subtle signs of an old camp. I wasn't prepared to stumble into an arrangement far more established than the one we had slept in ourselves the night before.

"Over here!" I called, and the others came running, all except Jasper who hadn't left my side since nearly being caught by the swinging logs.

A number of simple tents stood in a rough circle, a fire pit at their center. I pulled back the flap of the closest one and peered in confusion at a leather pack inside. Matthis strode into the center of the camp and kicked the still smoldering logs at the bottom of the fire pit.

"Someone was here recently," he said.

"Aye, the smell would confirm that." Castus joined us, pointing over his shoulder. "They've dug themselves a shallow latrine back that way."

"Then where are they?" Jasper asked, voicing the obvious question.

His face was pale, his eyes skimming over the tents and the surrounding trees.

"Do you recognize it?" I asked.

"Yes and no," he said slowly. "I don't recognize this site specifically, but I recognize their tents and the set-up of their camp. There's no doubt it's them."

"You told us there were only seven of them," Matthis said, "and the size of the camp seems to support such a number."

"Only six now," Reese muttered.

"If they sent out several scouts like the one we encountered, they may have only left a couple of people behind to hold the camp," Matthis continued. "They could be out hunting right now. Or collecting water. Even bathing."

"And they could have found our camp," I said, my breath hitching.

Matthis hesitated for only a moment. "We head back. And never mind sound—this time we're going for speed."

I didn't resume my position at the rear of our small column, instead staying close behind the captain as we rushed back the way we had come. No one spoke, our focus on moving quickly through the treacherous domain. But I couldn't have been the only one with nightmarish visions dancing around my mind, spurring me forward, because we made record time.

When we burst into the clearing, startled exclamations greeted us, along with a swell of power. Matthis grimaced.

"Sorry, Tabor, that's a wasted shield."

The royal guard grunted. "Better a wasted shield than an injured royal." It was a line I remembered from my own time among the Royal Guard.

We all looked around the camp, our heads swiveling in every direction, although there was no sign of any disturbance.

"There's been no sign of anyone here, then?" Alaric asked. "Because we found their camp, but it was deserted."

"Deserted?" Tabor narrowed his eyes.

"Recently," Matthis expanded. "With clear indication they intend to come back."

"Well, then," Kalani said briskly, "that sounds like an opportunity."

CHAPTER 17

SAFFRON

$\mathcal{I}$ examined Julian as surreptitiously as I could. He didn't appear hurt, although he was covered in fresh dirt.

"What exactly happened to you?" I asked Jasper when I noticed he wore a layer of the same dirt.

"The trail led us to a sort of small plateau covered in trees." He winced. "We were *trying* to approach quietly when I triggered a trap. Swinging logs, if you can believe it. Nothing sophisticated, but I blundered right in."

"A trap?" My eyes widened, and I gave him a closer look. "Are you all right?"

"Thanks to Julian. He tackled me to the ground about half a second before I got flattened. And then someone else got a shield up, I presume."

My gaze flew to Julian. "Neither of you were hurt?"

Jasper shook his head. "Shaken up for me, at least, but unhurt beyond a couple of bruises. I should have been paying more attention."

"Nothing about these Tarxi operates in a normal way," I said. "You can't blame yourself."

Matthis called for Jasper, and he moved to join the main

conversation which was occupied with planning our next move. But I remained where I was, my eyes now locked on Julian.

I could see him standing there, unhurt, and yet my heart continued to beat frantically from Jasper's tale. Julian had praised my bravery and apparent selflessness in risking myself to protect Kalani, and yet he had done the exact same thing to save Jasper—a commonborn. I had made unfair assumptions about him from the beginning. Despite a lifetime of Finnian as an example, and more recently Lucas, I had believed that the disengaged, self-centered mask Julian wore represented his true self. I should have known better. At our level of society, everyone required a mask.

With a jolt, I wondered what mine was. I was the quiet, dutiful niece, following meekly in Finnian's wake, afraid to disturb the waters. But was that really a mask?

Perhaps, in my case, it wasn't a mask so much as a layer. It was one part of me—the part I chose to let people see. Only around my family and close friends did I feel free to reveal the deeper parts of myself. But was that because I was a private person, or was it fear that drove me? Was I afraid that if I let others see my true self, I would end up disgracing the family? Or was I afraid of taking advantage of the position I had been given—the one I had never done anything to deserve?

I put my hand up to my suddenly pounding head. Why did getting to know Julian create such chaos in my mind? Why did it make me question every part of myself?

The answer came with blinding clarity. Because I wasn't just getting to know Julian. I had fallen in love with him.

It seemed impossible and strange, but I also knew it was true. It didn't matter, though. Julian might not be the typical Devoras son I first thought him, but he still had the wrong idea about me. And I didn't dare assume the preference he had shown for my company represented anything deep enough that he would consider fighting his family when he realized the truth.

He looked up at that moment, meeting my eyes across the distance. Everything else fell away, and I wished I could rush over to him and reassure myself he was really unharmed. He seemed to pick up something in my gaze, cocking his head slightly to the side, his face taking on a quizzical look.

Anxiety suddenly gripped me. Could he read something of my new realization in my face? Could everyone? A Callinos had too much pride to pine after a Devoras, even one out of her reach. I forced myself to look away, using thoughts of my family to spur me on. What would Finnian think if I came home and told him I had fallen in love with Julian, of all people?

He would be pleased for you, once he got to know him, a tiny voice whispered, but I thrust it aside. Finnian would never get that chance, and I wasn't encouraging my wayward heart by pinning my hopes on an impossible dream.

"That's decided, then," Matthis said, breaking through to me. "We'll go at first light. The same group that went today."

Matthis paused as if waiting for the princess to object. I examined her face, noting the way her eyes narrowed slightly, but she said nothing. I had been amazed at Elena's acceptance that she couldn't come with us, and I saw the same thing in Kalani now. When you were royalty, you knew you wouldn't be allowed to lead the charge, no matter how much you wished to do so.

Finally paying attention, I gradually picked up that a decision had been made to catch whoever was staying at the camp unaware the next morning. By now everyone seemed convinced they had little to no access to compositions, and Matthis was hoping they might think an animal had inadvertently sprung their trap. But even if they arrived to find the Tarxi alert, they hoped their superior numbers would be enough to overwhelm them.

After the way they had catapulted back into camp today, I imagined the captain would have liked to leave more people behind to help guard the princess. But already the chosen attackers only outnumbered the potential Tarxi by one. The best way to protect Kalani was to make sure this ambush was a success and none of the Tarxi had the chance to get anywhere near our camp.

Kalani's only stipulation was that a message be sent back to us as soon as they had all been safely apprehended. I hated the idea of Julian, and even Jasper, marching off to face unknown danger, but I had to admit to being grateful no one suggested I come. I had seen enough battle to last a lifetime.

CHAPTER 18

JULIAN

A tense atmosphere filled the camp as we sat around our tiny, smokeless fire that evening. I suspected I wasn't the only one who would have preferred to launch into action immediately, but I couldn't deny that in this terrain the Tarxi had the advantage. We would be the ones at a weakness if we tried to launch an attack in the darkness.

Which meant we had to wait.

I positioned myself next to Saffron again, although she seemed more guarded than she had the night before. I tried to get a good look at her face, hoping to read her emotions there, but she kept it averted.

Was she resentful at being left behind to babysit the princess? It didn't seem like her—she wasn't the bloodthirsty sort. And, personally, I was relieved to hear she wouldn't be with us. The day's events had shown I couldn't afford even a momentary lapse in concentration, and Saffron's presence had a tendency to drive all other thought from my mind.

I searched around for a topic of conversation that might engage her.

"Do you miss Torcos when you're in the capital?" I asked. "Or do you prefer Corrin?"

"I like both places," she said after a moment's thought. "But I always miss my mother when I'm away from home. And you? Do you prefer your estate or the city?"

I leaned back, frowning. "I always thought I preferred Corrin. But being out here, in the mountains?" I tipped my head right back and breathed deeply. "It smells like home, and I didn't realize I'd missed that."

"There's always something special about home," she said softly.

"Admittedly in my case it means escape," I said. "I'm more likely to see my family in Corrin."

She wrinkled her nose. "I might feel the same way if I had Calix and Natalya for siblings."

I laughed. "They're really not that bad, you know."

She looked at me skeptically. "I did live with them for four years, remember."

"Ah, but that's the thing about the twins," I said. "They're a great deal easier to like when you're *not* living with them. We've gotten on quite well ever since I left for my first year at the Academy."

"I can't quite imagine you at the Academy."

"Oh, that's easy enough. Just imagine Reese trying to be top at everything, and me always beating him."

She laughed and shoved me lightly in the shoulder. "You're secretly a brat, Julian of Devoras. How have I known you my whole life and not known that?"

"Oh, certainly," I agreed with easy-going calm. "The best part was pretending that I didn't really care about being first and wasn't trying hard."

She laughed again, and I grinned too, happy to have cheered her out of whatever dark mood had come over her.

"You know, I think you and Finnian really would get on," she said. "Once you finished whatever male posturing you thought was necessary."

"Does Julian ever stop male posturing?" Jocasta muttered from my other side.

I clapped a hand to my heart. "Now why would you say something like that about your favorite student?"

"I wouldn't," she said.

I chuckled. I had always liked Jocasta—certainly much more than Walden, although I had never suspected him of treachery.

"How are things at the Academy now?" I asked. "Have they repaired all the damage and picked a new library head?" A somber note entered my voice. "I know they assigned a new combat instructor right away."

I had respected Thornton—an extremely distant cousin— even if I didn't exactly like him, and his training had kept me alive during my two years at the front. I had been grieved but not surprised to hear he had given his life in defense of his beloved Academy and the royal family.

Jocasta and Saffron were silent for a moment, reflecting, perhaps, in their own ways, on the old combat instructor.

"Thornton was nothing if not thorough," Jocasta said after a minute had passed. "He was already training his successor, which made it easy. And given the new instructor is yet another Devoras, I'm not surprised that's the one detail you remember."

She gave me a long-suffering look. "As you well know, repairing the building is the work of a day when you have the creators to draw on. That was done last year—as you would have seen if you'd bothered to attend your siblings' graduation."

"You're forgetting that was back in the dark era when I was still with the Royal Guard under Thaddeus—and in the general's black books. Thaddeus doesn't believe in rewarding recalcitrant members of his discipline with time off for celebrations of any sort."

Jocasta gave a snort, her face expressing her opinion of the old general. That was one of the things I'd always liked about Jocasta. She didn't revere power in the same way everyone else around me had always done.

"But what of the library head?" I repeated. "You haven't told us what they've decided there. You can't exactly end up with a worse head than Walden turned out to be. Although at least he chose a jovial facade to hide behind all those years."

A strange look came over her face. "I believe they're to announce their choice when we return."

Saffron, who had been staring at her suspiciously, sat up straight. "Jocasta! Is it you? Are they making you head of the Academy library?"

Her look of discomfort grew even deeper, and she didn't attempt to deny it. Both my eyebrows shot up.

"They're making you head? How very well-deserved."

"Yes, indeed." Saffron clapped her hands with excitement. "Congratulations! How marvelous."

"What a coup for the Cygnets," I said thoughtfully.

Library head was a senior discipline position. I didn't think such a senior position had been held by a mage from a minor family before—in any discipline.

"I don't need to tell the two of you that times are changing," she said. "And it seems—for the moment, at least—that loyalty is being regarded more highly than strength."

"Or maybe they're just recognizing there are different types of strength," Saffron said with stubbornness in her voice. "You've earned this position, Jocasta. I'm so glad they've recognized that."

Jocasta smiled at her with more fondness than she usually displayed for students.

"Yours was certainly an exciting year, Saffron. I hope you won't take it the wrong way if I say I sincerely hope we never see such a cohort again."

Saffron laughed. "I can well imagine. How we upended everything! But for the better in this case. You'll make an excellent library head."

"I shall certainly endeavor to do so," she said. "And I do appreciate your vote of confidence. I haven't been entirely sure how much I could thank my own merits and how much I could thank my cousin. Not," she said with a twinkle in her eye, "that I intend to question the matter too closely. Never look a gift horse in the mouth and all that."

"So she's managed to talk them down, then?" I asked.

Jocasta nodded. "Only just, but the fire is quenched for now."

Saffron looked between us. "Who? Did what?"

"I'm sure you know that Coralie's mother is a distant cousin of Jocasta," I said. "Did Coralie mention that her mother has come out of retirement to rejoin the Grays?"

Saffron nodded. "She did say something about her mother taking her old position with the Seekers again…something about the happenings in the kingdom being too momentous to just watch from the sidelines down in Abalene."

"In actual fact," I said, lowering my voice slightly, "Queen Verena herself requested her return."

Saffron's eyes widened.

"The Seekers have been the discipline hardest hit by all the changes," I explained. "They've needed creative thinking to find ways to manage the new reality. It isn't a simple thing to allow some commonborn access to words while still keeping reading safely locked away from the rest of the population."

"Coralie inherited her flexibility of thinking from her mother," Jocasta said. "My cousin was always a shining light in our small and unimportant family. She was a rising star among the Grays back in the day. If she hadn't retired, I might not now be the highest achieving member of our family."

"And more than that," I added. "The monarchs wanted her at court because she was always well-liked. A group of minor families had banded together and were intending to bring formal demands to the king that he cease the practice of sealing commonborns."

Saffron stared at me. "I knew some in the minor families weren't happy—that they felt the growing population of sealed was a threat to their position, and possibly even their power…I didn't realize it had gone so far, though."

"It hasn't, thankfully," Jocasta said. "Because they were talked out of it. And, thus, here I stand—the recipient of royal favor on behalf of the Cygnet family."

I raised an eyebrow and surveyed our meager camp. "You would think a king and queen could come up with a better reward than trekking up mountains and sleeping on the hard ground."

Saffron elbowed me. "She means her new position." She looked across at the librarian. "Although I suppose being included on this mission is also a sign of royal favor."

"Undoubtedly," Jocasta said dryly. "Although I'm inclined to agree with Julian on this one."

"See," I whispered loudly to Saffron. "I told you I was her favorite."

Jocasta stood up, giving me a look of long-suffering. "Don't stay up too long, children. It's a big day tomorrow."

I laughed. "If that was supposed to be an imitation of my mother, you need a great deal more disdain in your voice."

Jocasta waved a hand in my direction, not deigning to waste any more words on me, and wandered away toward her bedroll.

"I'm sorry you didn't have a better relationship with your mother," Saffron said, a sad look in her eyes as they rested on me.

I shrugged. "I've never known anything but what I had. You needn't go feeling sorry for me."

I watched her face soften and could guess where her thoughts had turned.

"Your mother never seems to travel into Corrin," I said,

seizing my courage in my hands. "But I'd like to meet her one day."

Saffron's whole body clenched, her startled eyes flying to mine. I carefully kept my face impassive as I tried to puzzle out her extreme response.

"She's an invalid," she said quietly. "The journey would be excessively tiring for her, and she wouldn't be able to go about the city anyway. It's better if she stays at home."

"And is home your Uncle Dashiell's estate?" I asked, keeping my voice as neutral as I could.

Her startled gaze returned, this time paired with a crinkle between her brows.

What would she do if I reached out and smoothed it away with my finger?

"We have our own home in Torcos," she said. "But we spend much of the year with my uncle and aunt, yes. They have always been everything that is loving and generous."

"It must be hard for her. To be an invalid always surrounded by healers."

Her face softened, although the surprise still lingered, as if she hadn't expected me to consider such a point.

"She never mentions it," she said softly, "but it must be hard. And hard for my uncle, too. He has dedicated his life to the pursuit of health for as many as possible, but he can't heal her."

"She has the energy sickness, then?" I asked.

It was the only explanation for her continued ill-health, given her closeness to the head of the healers. No mages—healers or otherwise—could replenish energy. And that was as true for those poor few afflicted with the mysterious energy sickness— which plagued them with excessive fatigue—as it was for a healthy mage who exhausted themselves on a complex composition.

Saffron nodded, her face drooping.

I had only ever met one healer who might have a chance of

helping such a patient. And I was fairly sure Saffron was one of the few people alive who knew of his existence. But I also knew she would never even consider asking Declan for such a thing. The eccentric mage was the last of his family for a reason—when they used their own energy to perform miraculous feats of healing, that portion of energy was gone for good. Their unique ability—which had created both Elena and Jasper with their different gifts—had led the rest of Declan's relatives into an early grave. Saffron was too compassionate to ask someone else to risk their life to restore her mother's strength, although I felt sure she would have done it herself if she stood in Declan's place.

"My mother is Aunt Helene's sister," Saffron said, seeming to gather herself. "They're both Ellingtons by birth, you know. They even had to submit to truth compositions after the attempted rebellion."

"Naturally they wouldn't have had anything to do with that business," I said. "They've been part of the Callinos family for decades."

I couldn't remember if I'd known Finnian's and Saffron's mothers were Ellingtons, although I had known they were sisters, of course. Everyone knew Finnian and Saffron were cousins.

She drew another deep breath, looking at me sideways with a guarded expression. "It's all the more generous of Uncle to accept us into his household given he was only the most distant of relations with my Callinos father."

"I'm sure he considers his wife's family his own," I said. "Dashiell has always struck me as one of the most likable discipline heads. Perhaps it's on account of his being a healer."

"Perhaps," she said, looking almost deflated, as if she had expected some other reaction from me.

I tried to read her face and formulate a question in my confused mind, but Tabor strode past the fire and frowned at us both.

"It will be an early start in the morning," he said.

I was the one going as part of the attack, but his eyes lingered on Saffron. Was he thinking about her role as back up bodyguard for the princess? Whatever his motivation, the message was clear —the time for talking was over.

Reluctantly I stood and offered my hand to help Saffron rise. Once she was on her feet, I let the light grip of her fingers go even more reluctantly. But important events pressed around us. Figuring out her mysteries would have to wait for later, more certain, times.

"Goodnight, Saffron," I said, letting her hand fall.

"Goodnight, Julian," she replied, almost fleeing from me in the direction of her mat.

I lay down to my own sleep more slowly as I puzzled over her responses, both spoken and unspoken. What had she been trying to say? And what reaction had she expected? It had almost been as if she anticipated surprise from me at the details of her family situation. All that talk of Ellingtons and of Callinos relations...

It hit me with such suddenness that I nearly sat bolt upright. She had been trying to warn me she wasn't a close relation of the duke—not by blood, at any rate. She had naturally assumed that such a thing would matter greatly to a son of General Griffith.

So much of her previous unexplainable behavior now made sense. If I could get her talking, get her to forget our positions, she was relaxed and seemed to enjoy my company. But the clearer I had made my feelings, the more she had retreated into those unexpected guarded moments. She thought I didn't know the realities of her family tree.

Despite myself, a smile crept over my face. How like her to try to warn me so gently. She had no doubt thought to save us both a painful conversation later.

But a second later the smile disappeared. Did she really think so little of me? Did she think the only part of her I cared about was her bloodline?

I wanted to dash across our small camp and call her back out of her bed. I burned to assure her that such considerations didn't weigh with me beside all her obvious qualities. I couldn't bear to think she was lying on her mat right now, thinking she wasn't good enough.

But too many people lay between us, and our strange, cramped situation didn't lend itself to such confessions. However much they strained and protested, my feelings would have to restrain themselves for now.

As soon as I had a chance, however, I would make her see that none of that mattered. My thoughts sputtered and slowed. Her control of power and her pedigree made no difference to me, it was true. But I couldn't say the same for my family—and certainly not for my father. If I survived the next day and came home to declare Saffron as my choice of bride, what would my father say?

I didn't care what he might say to me, I had long ago ceased caring overly much about that. But I cared what he might say to Saffron. Or about her. How could I blame her for thinking so little of me when he was everything she pictured a Devoras being —and more?

Calix would side with him, of course. And Natty. The only family member I could be sure to have on my side was Elena. No doubt their reactions would enrage her. But for all that the sprawling members of the Devoras clan loved to claim the Spoken Mage publicly, she was still viewed as an outsider within the family.

But on further consideration, I thought the healers in the family might be supportive. Healers in general had always been something of a breed apart, and their discipline seemed to respect Dashiell without exception. There was a reason the only Ellington healer who knew about the conspiracy was Acacia at the Academy—and she had only discovered it by accident.

I considered the matter further. There was a reason Saffron

was concerned I might have misunderstood her position. She truly was treated like a daughter by the duke. She had always moved in the same social circles as the twins and me, and I had never seen anything but acceptance for her there, although she never drew attention to herself. That was an angle I could use with my father.

Saffron might not have raw strength, but she had influence—and outside the usual Devoras circles. Her close friendship with both Elena and Lucas would have to be worth something as well.

The more I rolled it around in my mind, the more certain I became that I could win my father over to my cause. Saffron had even saved the princess twice now, and although the Sekali was as difficult to read as our own royalty, I thought she showed a preference for Saffron. I knew all too well that the girl had a gift for worming her way into your heart despite your intentions.

First I had to convince Saffron, and then I would convince my father. And when it came to him, my best plan was to start with Elena. She would no doubt be overjoyed and make some ridiculous claim about having planned it all along. If we approached my father with the news together, it would be a lot more difficult for him to make a scene. He knew how close Elena was to Saffron.

I forced myself to stop planning the future. Saffron had just warned me away, in her considerate way. It was far too soon to be celebrating victory in my mind. For all I knew, she found the idea of being connected to a Devoras as distasteful as my father would have found being bound to someone from a minor family.

Which was actually another argument in my favor. I could point out Finnian's choice of wife and remind my father that I could have presented him with a more painful daughter-in-law than a well-connected Callinos.

I clamped down again on those thoughts and told myself sternly that it was time for sleep. It was a long time actually coming, however.

CHAPTER 19

SAFFRON

The members of the attack party filed out of camp almost silently in the pre-dawn gloom. Those of us who were to remain behind watched them go in equal silence. Faylee had been the first one up, handing a simple breakfast to each of us as we arose. Had any of them found it as hard to choke down the mouthfuls as I did?

Julian had seemed nonchalant the night before when I reminded him of my true position within the Callinos family, and even that tiny seed of hope made it harder to watch him march away now. Kalani, on the other hand, watched them go with a burning look. I knew that unlike me she wasn't wishing them back but wishing herself with them.

As soon as they were out of sight, Tabor set us to work. Faylee doused the fire, which still smoldered from the night before, and packed up the food supplies. Jocasta and I rolled up all twelve of the bedrolls, strapping them to the full packs which we lined neatly along one side of the clearing.

I was eager to have something to do with my hands, but there was all too little work to be done. When we stood back and surveyed the line of packs, I grimaced at Jocasta.

"We're all going to go out of our minds if we're now to sit in the middle of an empty clearing and twiddle our thumbs until we get word from the others."

"I made some notes from my conversations with Jasper," she said. "I was going to study them."

I groaned. "Of course you would have something useful to do. I'm almost desperate enough to ask if I can join you."

"I wasn't planning on offering," she said in a dry voice. "Unless you've discovered a true love of linguistics since we all spent the day cooped up in a carriage together. I won't get anything done if I'm to listen to your sighs all morning."

"Jocasta! I'm not that bad!" I flushed.

She grinned at me. "I'm not blind and neither am I deaf, Saffron. And I spend my days working with young people. I know far better than to attempt to occupy someone whose thoughts are far away—with someone else."

Before I could respond to this decisive sally, she turned and walked away.

"She scares me a little, sometimes," Faylee said, appearing at my elbow.

"Who, Jocasta?"

Faylee grinned at me. "You needn't sound so surprised. I know I can be blunt myself, but blunt people don't necessarily appreciate the same quality in others, you know." She delivered the critique of herself in the same way she might have remarked on the weather, or the beauty of the mountains.

The merchant girl was a different breed of commonborn from those Elena had grown up alongside. Despite hailing from a small town, Jasper's studies had given Elena an expanded world-view from the limited one she should by rights have possessed. But even then she hadn't matched the manner of Faylee, clearly raised in the capital in the upper echelons of commonborn society. To us mages, the commonborns might look like one homogenous whole, but the reality was far different. And such nuances were becoming more and more important as the commonborns claimed a greater role in our more layered society.

Faylee dropped her voice low. "The princess scares me far more, though."

I was even more surprised by this confession. "Whatever for? No one could accuse her of being blunt."

Faylee sighed despairingly. "Exactly! I can't read her at all. And my family is relying on me to make some sort of lasting connection with her."

I sighed. "Welcome to the world of royalty. You never quite know where you stand with them—not for sure. I think they do it on purpose to keep us on our toes."

Faylee's eyes widened. "I should have let my cousin come, after all."

When I looked at her curiously, she continued. "She was desperate to be the one chosen. She thinks I get special treatment because my father is head of the family. But all my uncles and aunts made the decision together. They debated the matter forever but eventually decided I was the more personable option." She gave me a comical look of dismay. "Can you imagine the pressure of such a statement?"

I shuddered. "All too vividly."

Thankfully, growing up beside Finnian meant I had never been in danger of being labeled in such a way.

"Well, if it makes you feel better," I said, "just remember you could have been the one to be born a princess. And then you would have had to guard and measure every word you ever spoke and learn how to keep every emotion hidden away behind a careful mask. So it could be worse."

Faylee blanched. "Next time I feel intimidated by the princess, I'll feel sorry for her instead. What a life!"

"Well, don't entirely forget that intimidated feeling," I cautioned. "She is part of a family who rules an entire empire.

And one who isn't altogether predisposed to like us southerners much."

Faylee gave a soft wail. "I thought you were supposed to be reassuring me!"

"One part reassurance, one part caution," I said. "You'll thank me eventually."

"Thank goodness they sent you along, Saffron of Callinos," she said. "At least I'm not the only one here to keep the princess company. And you have a great deal more experience at such things than me."

I thought of my own earlier musings. Maybe I did have more experience of court and wearing a mask than I had ever given myself credit for. Should I be pitied for it as well? Was it a cage that trapped my true self away?

Before I came on this journey, I would have said no. I would have said that loyalty and duty to my family were more important than anything else—that it *was* my true self. But I hadn't forgotten Kalani's words in the stream, despite the near-death experience straight after.

Maybe stifling myself wasn't a way to protect my family but instead served to limit me so that I couldn't serve them to my fullest capacity? Maybe the best way to honor the Callinos family was to be the best possible person I could—even if that meant I couldn't be a healer or I expressed opinions that some people disagreed with. Because at the end of the day, I was a Callinos, even if I was a weaker one. And being the best person I could be meant being the best Callinos I could be. Was there room after all for me to be an individual without rejecting my family identity or the love they showered on me?

I glanced around the now-clear camp site, wishing I could discuss the question with Julian. He understood my world better than anyone. He knew about the burden of family responsibility, and yet he never seemed to wear it as the heavy weight I had always done.

Julian wasn't here, however. And even Faylee had wandered away—off to brave the intimidating Jocasta in order to investigate what she was doing with her small notebook. How recently had the merchant been sealed? Written words must still be a source of fascination to her.

In her place, Kalani drifted toward me, Tabor shadowing close behind. I could feel the power hovering around them both. Clearly the captain had decided to have a precautionary shield in place this time rather than relying on his reaction times. I suspected he had a shield against power in place, aware as he must be of the strange way they had taken him down without a physical attack at Julian's estate.

"The captain thinks we would be better off finding some nearby cover," the princess said.

"It's an exposed spot." Tabor's eyes darted around us. "And we've been established here awhile now. I don't like it."

I stiffened, my own eyes racing after his. "Do you hear something? Or sense something?"

He shook his head. "But then, I didn't last time, either."

"Surely that was different, though? It was nighttime in a crowded courtyard with a fire raging nearby."

"Chaos is dangerous, there's no denying that," he said. "But being open and exposed is dangerous as well. Especially when you don't have the measure of your enemy."

"Very well," I said. "You're the expert. Should we leave the packs?"

He nodded. "Leave everything. If all goes smoothly, we'll be back for it. If it doesn't, I don't want us weighted down."

"I'll get Jocasta and Faylee." I took two steps toward them before catching movement in my peripheral vision.

I spun back around in time to see the captain's arms drop to his sides. He swayed, his face going slack, and fell hard.

I screamed and reversed direction, leaping over Tabor's collapsed body to grab at Kalani's arm. But as I turned to tug her toward Jocasta, people streamed into the clearing. Every one of them ran toward me and the princess, and I could see no clear route to Jocasta.

"Run!" I screamed in the librarian's direction. "Get out! Get help!"

There was no point trying to draw my sword. With Kalani taking up one hand, I needed my free hand for compositions. I thrust it into my pocket, reaching for my first shield, only to remember I hadn't had a chance to replenish it since the waterfall. My fingers flashed sideways, going for one of my secondary shields, but the mistake had cost me precious seconds.

At the last moment, my hand stilled, my mind whirling. I had almost forgotten the layer of power that already coated Kalani. Tabor's shield was still burning strong. Whatever attack had felled him hadn't burned the shield out in order to reach him, it had gone straight through it.

I needed an attack composition. I ran desperately through all the options in my mind. Why hadn't I been more prepared for something like this? My fingers latched on to a wind working. I had reasonable skill with those and always carried several on me.

The attackers had circled us now, approaching warily as if aware of the shield and unsure of its limitations. Unfortunately I had no more idea on that front than they did.

I used my teeth to rip the parchment I pulled out, and a wind swept the clearing. Kalani and I stood unmoved at the center of it, but it hit Jocasta and Faylee with as much force as our attackers, sending all of them staggering.

"What do we do?" I gasped at Kalani, trying to think how to use the small window of time my composition had given us.

"Do you have a way to bind them?" she asked.

"Only one at a time," I groaned, but I was already reaching for the composition. Even if it only evened the odds, it would still be worth it.

The Tarxi were regaining their balance, calling to each other in unfamiliar words I couldn't comprehend. Jocasta was also back on her feet now, and her eyes darted between them, her brow furrowed. Her eyes reached me and stopped, her gaze locking with mine across the distance of the clearing.

Run, I mouthed, but she stood her ground, shaking off Faylee who was trying to cling to her and reaching for a composition.

But one of the Tarxi had been blown back far enough to place him near the two of them. He saw the parchment in Jocasta's hands and lunged for them both. Jocasta jumped out of his reach, somehow managing to drag Faylee with her. When the man tried to charge them again, she kicked him in the stomach, and he staggered back, wheezing.

She locked eyes with me again.

"Energy," she yelled at me. "They were talking about your shield, and they said something about energy."

The man in front of her snarled and came at her again, and this time she pulled Faylee with her all the way out of the clearing. The Tarxi ran after them.

I ripped my composition, pointing randomly at one of our attackers. I felt the power of it race in his direction and hover around him, but nothing happened. The working should have locked his arms and legs to his side, immobilizing him completely. And yet he retained use of his limbs, the attack not slowing him in the least.

"It didn't work!" I cried to Kalani. "But he's not shielded! I can't feel any power around him. It should have worked."

She started to say something, but her entire body went slack, cutting off her words. I tried to stop her crashing to the ground, but my single grip on her arm wasn't enough. She slumped down onto her knees, her body tipping forward until her head thunked against the ground.

The remaining Tarxi—only three, I now realized, although it had initially seemed more in the confined space—closed the circle around us. One of them dropped what looked like two ripped pieces of parchment to the ground. The same one, perhaps emboldened by the princess's collapse, strode into the circle of our shield.

It did nothing to stop him.

When he reached down to snatch up Kalani, I kicked him hard enough to send him sprawling. I stepped forward, meaning to follow up my attack, but hands grabbed me from behind. The remaining two had followed their leader's example and breached the shield, both converging on me.

Either the shield had only ever protected against attacks of power, or it was yet another working that had no effect on the Tarxi.

One of them, a giant of a man, lifted me off the ground, keeping both my arms restrained with a single one of his. I kicked wildly and ineffectually, unable to wrench myself free.

The second one, a woman, produced a length of rope. Within seconds I was bound hand and foot and hanging over the giant's back. Meanwhile the leader had similarly scooped up the princess who now lay limp across his shoulder.

They lost no time in hurrying away from our camp, the giant who carried me bringing up the rear. The last thing I saw was the still form of the captain, lying where he had fallen.

CHAPTER 20

JULIAN

Moving through the partial darkness took concentration, a welcome distraction from the unknown ahead of us. I was once again relegated to the rear, and for a while my world narrowed to the ground beneath me and Reese's feet in front of me.

As the sky lightened, the journey grew easier, and it seemed no time at all before our narrow path flattened and was overtaken with trees. No one spoke because our strategy had been determined in advance. Separating, we spread out through the trees, moving to place ourselves in a wide circle around the location of their camp site.

I moved carefully, eyes alert and testing each step before I took it. If we set off another trap, we would lose our element of surprise.

But I found nothing unusual among the litter of plant matter at my feet. And though my progress felt agonizingly slow, I knew it was necessary to ensure we all reached our positions at the same time.

The occasional flash of movement through the trees showed me Jasper, some way to my right. With our numbers so low,

Matthis had entrusted him with a selection of compositions, allowing him to operate as one of us today. Our unusual situation called for extreme measures, but I couldn't banish the thought that this might one day seem a normal way to proceed.

How many mages had died at the front because they had neither the temperament nor the physical capacity to respond to an attack? And how many commonborn had died because their training and capability couldn't match the power of the enemy's compositions? Maybe one day we would see pairs of mages and sealed commonborn, working together to utilize their different strengths. For a moment my mind wanted to track the thought, expanding it and considering all the other ways such an approach could be useful outside of battle. But I pulled my thoughts back into line. If I wanted to see such a future, I had to survive today.

The tents came into view ahead of me. I stopped, attempting to peer through the trees to see if the others were in position. A flash of color all the way on the other side of the tents might be Matthis, but I couldn't be sure.

So far we had used no compositions, not wanting the power to give away our approach. I had my sword in one hand and two parchments in the other, however, ready to go as soon as Matthis gave the signal. We had decided to go for a brute force approach, unsure what would work against the mysterious Tarxi.

My nerves stretched tight, ready to launch into action, but still the signal didn't come. I readjusted my grip on my sword, my ears straining.

A sudden, strangled scream reverberated through the trees. My taut body flinched, spinning instinctively left, in the direction of the sound.

"Go!" Matthis shouted, and noise and movement erupted around me.

For a second, I hesitated. I should be attacking with the others —I could already see Jasper charging into the open space around the tents. But the scream had been one of extreme pain. It was hard to judge distances in these woods, but it had sounded near me. And if it had been Reese, positioned to my left, I was the closest one to him.

I gave another glance toward Jasper, but he had already disappeared from sight, cut off by the trees. I let slip a curse and took off to my left. I bounced off the trunk of a tree, moving too fast to keep a steady course. My mind reminded me that such haste was dangerous, but I didn't slow down. I had heard nothing since the initial scream, and the silence was more unnerving than further screams would have been.

I nearly missed him, lying on the forest floor. He wore natural browns, rather than healer purple, designed to blend in to our environment. I adjusted my course, barely slowing my pace enough not to overshoot him.

Letting my sword fall to the ground, I dropped to both knees beside him. My attack compositions, more valuable than my weapon, I stuffed roughly inside my jacket. They would do no good here.

He lay still, eyes closed and face pale. Both of his hands pressed against his stomach around the staff of a thin spear protruding from his middle. Blood pooled between his fingers and dribbled down his sides.

It was a crude weapon, not a true spear but rather a stick whittled into the shape of one. I could see no sign of any Tarxi so could only assume it was another trap.

My hands floated uselessly above his stomach. I had no practical nursing experience, and with little training in healing, I carried no compositions powerful enough to mend such a wound. If it wasn't already too late for such workings.

If our roles were reversed, Reese would have known what to do, but I wasn't even sure if I should pull out the spear. Would it do more harm than good?

While I was still hesitating, Reese's eyes fluttered open. He let out a string of weak curses that would have earned him further reprimand from Jocasta if we had still been at camp.

I rocked back on my heels, a surprisingly strong swell of relief filling me. I might not like Reese, but I didn't want him to die. Especially not like this.

"What do I do?" I asked. "Should I pull it out?"

"No!" His weak exclamation, delivered with a grimace of pain, still managed to convey his opinion that I was a fool of the highest order. "Composition…I need a composition."

"I don't have one. Not one that will do for this."

He gave me a withering glare, the pain in his eyes enhancing the expression. "My…case."

Of course. I should have known he'd bring it with him. I cast around in the detritus on the rough ground around us. For a moment I was distracted by the sounds of fighting from the direction of the tents. I glanced back that way and heard someone shout, "It didn't do anything!"

But I shook my head and returned to my search. If I didn't focus, Reese was going to die.

I found the case against the base of a tree, a short distance away from us, where it must have been flung when he was struck. I scrambled over to retrieve it, hurrying back even as I ripped it open.

"Yellow pouch," he said, sounding weaker than before.

I eyed him with concern but didn't stop what I was doing. Fumbling through the contents inside, I pushed past a red pouch and a green one before my fingers fastened on one dyed yellow.

I pulled it out and upended its contents on the ground.

Reese growled another curse. Apparently the violation of his sacred case prompted a reaction even as he lay at death's door. I ignored him.

Grabbing up one parchment after another, I scanned their contents, discarding each one hastily to snatch up another.

Reese made another attempt to speak, but it came out more

like a gargle. I didn't dare even look at him, afraid to waste any precious seconds.

Peering at a new one, I saw the word *stomach* and paused, reading it more closely. I made it through two paragraphs before deciding it was close enough.

I went to tear it, but a wordless exclamation from Reese made me freeze. When I looked in his direction, he was attempting to shake his head.

I shuffled back over to his side.

"Pull...out," he managed to whisper. "Then tear. Fool."

I shook my head. Only Reese would waste his dying breaths insulting me. He was right, though. The composition couldn't do its work while a giant stick of wood still pierced his stomach.

I gripped the wood with my right hand.

"This is going to hurt," I said, but I didn't pause to let him brace. There was no time.

Ripping the spear upward and out, I brought the parchment to my teeth with my left hand and ripped. I flicked my fingers toward his now gushing wound, as I had seen healers do countless times.

Power flowed over him, sinking into his stomach. The flow of blood slowed and then stopped. Seconds ticked by.

"Should it be taking this long?" I asked.

"It's a complex working." The increased strength in Reese's voice indicated the healing was already taking effect. "Stomach wounds are difficult, and I was near death."

Was that...*pride* in his voice? At being strong enough to carry such a composition in his healing case?

I rolled my eyes. "You're welcome."

"I suppose you did well enough," he said grudgingly.

I considered replying, but the tight look on his face made me pause. Healers usually worked pain relief compositions in conjunction with the workings to repair the damage. There had been no time for such niceties here, so how much pain was he suppressing?

The clang of two swords made me forget the healer. I jumped to my feet, moving toward the tents before remembering I had discarded both my sword and my attack compositions.

I caught a glimpse of Jasper. He seemed to be hanging back from the sword fight raging between an unfamiliar man and woman and Matthis, Elias, and Alaric.

The untrained commonborn hesitated, looking at the combatants and then down at a number of compositions still in his hand. Even at this distance I could see his frown. But a moment later, he squared his shoulders and ripped two of the parchments.

"Get down!" he shouted, dropping to lie flat himself.

Matthis and Alaric responded instantly, Elias several beats behind. Rocks rose from the fallen pine needles around Jasper and flung themselves across the open space around the tent. One raced in my direction, only to ricochet off a tree trunk and collide with the ground.

The two Tarxi were hit hard. The woman took a rock to the back of the head and collapsed. The man took one to his sword arm and a second to the leg, letting out a string of words I didn't recognize but had no trouble interpreting as curses.

Matthis was back on his feet faster than seemed possible, wrestling the sword from the injured man and forcing him to the ground. I stepped toward them and then hesitated, glancing back toward Reese.

Castus knelt on one knee beside him, helping ease the healer into a sitting position. The tracker looked in my direction and waved me away.

"I'm no good with a sword, young master. I'll take care of His Lordship."

Reese looked awful, his clothing torn and blood streaking him all over, but from his sour manner his body underneath must have recovered. He was already eyeing the havoc I had made with his healing case, muttering inaudibly to himself.

I abandoned them both and raced to the tents.

Matthis glanced at me as I arrived, his eyes dropping to the blood all over my hands.

"Reese?"

"Healed by one of his own compositions," I said. "But it was a near thing. I think he must have triggered a trap."

Matthis nodded and returned to directing the others to bind the two prisoners. The woman had already woken, and I caught Jasper eyeing her with relief on his face. He had returned his remaining compositions to some internal pocket, and he kept glancing down at his hands with a wary expression in his eyes. How had it felt to release power for the first time? Clearly he was glad not to have used it to kill.

"What happened?" I asked the group in general.

Elias glanced my way. He was rubbing a spot on one shoulder where he had taken a hit from a rock.

"Our compositions didn't seem to do anything. They came charging out of two of the tents, swords drawn, so we had to fight."

I looked at Jasper. "Your composition worked."

He frowned, his eyes fixed on the two prisoners. "The swords worked on them, so I thought maybe stones would as well."

Matthis grunted. "Quick thinking. Everyone, take note. They may be immune to many of our compositions, but they can still be injured by physical objects. Choose your attacks accordingly."

His words reminded me that it wasn't over yet. As far as we knew there were still six of them.

"Are there any signs of anyone else here?" I asked.

Alaric, who had been inspecting the inside of each tent, rejoined us and shook his head. "All empty. Looks like you were right, Captain, and the rest must be off on scouting missions like our arsonist."

The injured man said something quietly to the woman bound beside him, what sounded like amusement in his tone. She replied with a short, irritated phrase that I could have sworn was a command to shut up.

Jasper stepped forward, eyes fastened on the man. "What did you say?"

The woman repeated the short command, more urgently this time, and the man looked sullenly back at Jasper, saying nothing.

"What did he say?" Matthis asked him.

Jasper swallowed. "I can't be sure, but I think he called us fools. Captain, I think he said we've been set up, and the true ambush is happening back at our own camp."

CHAPTER 21

SAFFRON

I bounced along on the giant's muscled shoulder, mentally screaming every insult I could think of. Aloud I said nothing, though. I didn't want to inspire them to stop and gag me.

In my position at the back of the short column, I had no way to check on Kalani and could only trust that they still wanted her alive as they had seemed to do in the past. We had been fools to think we could hide our presence from experienced mountaineers, over-confident from our conclusion that they weren't using compositions.

But apparently they hadn't needed compositions to find us and plan an effective ambush when the majority of our fighters were gone. My mind briefly flickered to Julian. Had they been ambushed first? I could only hope the Tarxi had bypassed the others completely.

And not just for Julian's sake. If Jocasta managed to escape and find the rest of our team, then we had some hope of rescue.

My spirits briefly lifted when the fourth Tarxi appeared behind us. He was alone and looked frustrated and angry. He barked something to his companions, and one of them issued a caustic-sounding reply. While I couldn't understand the actual words, it didn't sound as if he had managed to catch Jocasta and Faylee to me.

But the further we traveled, the lower my mood dropped. Where were they taking us? And what did they intend to do with us when they got there?

They hadn't stripped me of my compositions yet, but I had no doubt they would do so as soon as they judged us far enough away to safely stop. I wished I had taken some time to come up with creative hiding places for a couple of my more powerful compositions, but it had never occurred to me that anyone would be interested in abducting me.

When my mind circled around to yet another horrible future, I forced myself to stop imagining what might be coming and instead analyze the attack. If we were to have any hope of escape, then I needed to work out why neither our shield nor my second attack had worked. How were the Tarxi immune to our compositions?

They had proved to be unaffected by Tabor's shield, and yet they had hung back at first, seeming worried about it. Which suggested they *could* be affected by one. So perhaps it mattered what type of shield?

I tried to push aside my fear to think clearly. Tabor had trusted in his physical strength—his great fear had been the unheralded attack in the courtyard. So what if I was right in my earlier guess, and he had only activated a shield against an attack using pure power? That would require no special ability of the Tarxi for them to just walk through it.

But neither had the shield stopped their attack on either Tabor or Kalani. What was it Jocasta had managed to translate from their words? Something about shields and energy. I had seen both the guard and the princess go down, but I had felt no composition at work, no hint of power in the clearing outside our shield. And yet I had seen the torn pieces of a composition dropping from one of their hands. They had done a working, even if I hadn't felt it.

So either they had found a way to shield the sensation of power from their workings, or their composition hadn't used power at all. It made no sense, but I didn't stop to try to work out how such a thing was possible. I just needed to know what would and wouldn't work against them.

If I assumed that they somehow used energy directly in their workings, rather than power, it might explain how they had caused two people to collapse. They could have simply drained them of energy. Elena was capable of sucking someone's energy away, although in her case she used power to achieve it. But she was utterly unique, so there was no reason to assume the abilities of the Tarxi had to work exactly the same way hers did. If their working didn't use power at all, but instead operated with pure energy, it would also explain how their working was unaffected by a shield crafted to block power.

What it didn't explain was why compositions didn't work against them. But, no, that wasn't quite right. My first composition, the wind one, had pushed them all back just as it had Jocasta and Faylee. And a similar wind had worked against the arsonist in the Devoras estate courtyard.

But that hadn't been a direct attack on them. I had created a wind, and it had then interacted with them as a real wind would have done. I needed to focus on physical attacks then, whether from my own blows or from compositions.

I began to catalog the compositions I still had on me. If I could just find a way to get my hands on a couple of them…

The bouncing stopped, and I was slung to the ground, catching myself with one elbow before my head hit the ground. To my relief, when I maneuvered myself into a sitting position, I immediately saw Kalani beside me.

She lay on the ground, still unbound, but her eyes fluttered open and met mine. I tried surreptitiously to move closer to her. Her hands were still free, and if she could get hold of any of my compositions before they stripped me, we might have a chance.

"They haven't taken my compositions yet," I whispered. "And they seem to be affected by attacks from physical objects—wind and I'm guessing fire, stones, things like that. Do you have any compositions? Or can you get any of mine?"

I wasn't sure if the palace had supplied her with a new selection to replace the ones the Tarxi had already stolen from her, but I suspected if they had, they would have focused on defensive compositions not attack ones.

"A physical shield might work, too," I whispered. "I'm not sure about that one, though."

She nodded slightly and snaked a hand toward me. I twisted in her direction, trying to give her access to my pockets, but a rough hand grabbed my shoulder and spun me back.

"None of that now," the female Tarxi said. She called over her shoulder. "Someone bind the princess. And check them both for compositions."

She spoke in the common language, so she obviously wanted us to know what she was saying. She wanted us to know we were to be given no opportunity to escape.

As she methodically checked every one of my pockets, slowly stripping away months of stored effort, my mind flew to Julian. Was he still alive and well? Had he discovered our abduction? And would he be able to find us?

I had to hold on to hope that the answers were all yes.

"Captain Tabor will come after us when he wakes up," Kalani whispered after we had both been divested of all compositions and left sitting against a broad tree trunk, tightly bound. Clearly she was trying to cheer me. "He seems highly dedicated to his role."

I bit my lip and looked away, unable to bring myself to meet her eyes. She had seen Tabor go down, as he had gone down back at the Devoras estate and as she herself had then done. But she hadn't seen him as I had when I was carried out of the clearing—unnaturally still, eyes wide and blank. I didn't think the captain would be protecting anyone ever again.

CHAPTER 22

JULIAN

I raced back toward our camp along with Matthis, Castus, and Alaric. Elias had been left to watch the prisoners along with a still-weak Reese and Jasper—who had been instructed to see if he could convince the man to start talking again. From the looks on the two prisoners' faces, I didn't expect him to have much success.

Elias had made no complaint at being left behind. Perhaps he had been conscious of the same thought that briefly passed through my mind. Whatever we had all thought of him when we left Corrin, the Ellington had earned our trust. No one hesitated for a moment to leave him in charge of the prisoners.

But my thoughts had room for little else but Saffron. Her face filled my mind and made it hard not to urge the others to move faster. But we were already moving as quickly as we dared in the difficult terrain.

We had been seven against two and had still encountered difficulties. They were five against four and likely caught by surprise. I tried to pin my hope to Tabor's experience and wary nature, but the Tarxi had taken us by surprise too many times for me to place much assurance in anything.

The trip to the tree-filled plateau had gone quickly, although we had moved carefully and quietly. The return trip seemed to drag on impossibly long. I had thought our previous race back after first discovering the Tarxi camp had been tense, but it was nothing to the terror I felt now when we had more than vague suspicion to fuel our fear.

When we finally burst into the small clearing, for a blank moment I thought it was empty. But my eyes quickly caught on the neat row of our packs, lined up along one side.

Matthis uttered a quiet curse, pulling my attention to a prone figure sprawled awkwardly to one side of the space. The captain knelt beside Tabor's large body before looking up at all of us.

I didn't need the shake of his head to tell me there was no life left in this clearing. I swallowed and turned away, trying to wrestle down the emotions that wanted to take over. There was no time for grief or regret now. Such things would have to wait. And I was ashamed at the tiny seed of relief that it was not Saffron's body lying discarded in the clearing.

"They were definitely here, then," said Alaric, his voice grim. "And it looks like they got the princess."

"But what of the others?" I asked. "Would they have taken all four of them?"

Matthis closed Tabor's eyes, his fingers uncharacteristically gentle.

"With only four Tarxi, it would have slowed them down considerably to take four prisoners, but I don't see any sign of other bodies." He frowned around the deserted camp. "And there's no sign of any wound on Tabor. It looks like they got him in the same way they got our prisoner back at the estate."

"So you think they did that?" I asked. "It wasn't something he initiated himself?"

"We can't know for sure," Matthis said. "But this lot certainly seem to have been expecting us. If they didn't kill their man, then they somehow knew he had died, and that we were on their trail."

I kicked at one of the packs, sending it rolling across the clearing as I vented my frustration. We had made so many mistakes. All those generations of ingrained arrogance had been our undoing. And even now Saffron might be paying the price.

I went to kick another one, but Alaric's hand on my arm stopped me.

"Easy now," he said quietly. "There's every reason to think they're alive. We'll find them."

"Aye," said Castus. "They kept the princess alive last time, didn't they? And our ambassador with her."

I forced my breathing to slow, and my mind to think rationally. Yes, there was still hope. And if there was hope, then Saffron needed me to be thinking sharply and clearly, not giving in to fear.

"What's that? There?" Castus spoke sharply, pointing at something on the far side of the clearing.

The three of us mages all drew our swords, but it was Jocasta who limped into sight, half-carrying a pale Faylee who cradled one arm against her chest.

"Jocasta!" Matthis sheathed his sword and rushed over to take the burden of the injured Faylee from her. "What happened here?"

Jocasta took in the situation in a glance, a shadow crossing her face when her eyes fell on Tabor's body.

"Oh," she said heavily. "I was hoping..." She looked back at Matthis. "What of Jasper and Reese and Elias?"

"Guarding our prisoners at the Tarxi camp," he replied.

She nodded wearily. "It could be worse, then."

"It's bad enough," Matthis said. "We were played like fools. We wouldn't have even known you were in trouble if one of them hadn't spoken incautiously, thinking we couldn't understand."

"Well I'm glad to find you here," Jocasta said. "But I would rather have found Reese. I don't have a composition that will heal

Faylee's arm, and she's not going to make it much further without a healing."

"Your ankle seems to be injured as well," I said.

She shrugged, clearly thinking this of less importance.

"Reese was nearly killed by another one of their traps," I explained. "He was healed in time, but he's weak. We didn't want anything slowing us down."

"He thrust a selection of compositions at me as we were leaving, though," Alaric said. "Let me see what I have."

I helped Jocasta lower herself to the ground while the creator leafed through the stack of parchments. Matthis had already eased Faylee down, and the merchant girl was lying flat on her back, her eyes closed.

"Is it just a break?" Alaric asked Jocasta, indicating Faylee with his head.

She nodded. "A complex one, but yes. My ankle is just a sprain, I think."

"I would rather have Reese here to run some diagnostic workings," Matthis said, "but we'll have to do the best we can with whatever he sent. I don't want us hanging around here for long."

"This one's for a break," Alaric said, selecting a composition at last. "No way to tell how much power is in it, but hopefully it will be enough."

"Are there any pain relief ones?" I asked hastily, remembering Reese's recent experience.

"Yes, several." Alaric withdrew a second composition and tore it first, flicking his fingers toward Faylee. "Would you like one Jocasta?"

She shook her head. "We should conserve our supplies."

He shrugged and tore the original composition he had selected, flicking his fingers toward the merchant girl once again. Within a minute, her color had returned, and she sat up and swung her arm around experimentally.

"That was a lot better than the last one." Her voice sounded strong, although her manner remained subdued. She glanced once at Tabor and then quickly away.

"There's nothing in here for a sprain, and that was the only one for a break, I'm afraid." Alaric gave Jocasta an apologetic look. "You're going to have to keep hobbling until we can get you back to Reese."

"I can make a rough splint, if you'd like one," Castus offered.

"Thank you," Jocasta said. "I think that would be for the best."

The tracker moved away, scanning the ground and muttering to himself, presumably looking for a stick of the right proportions.

"What happened?" Matthis repeated his original question now the immediate needs of the injuries had been met.

"They ambushed us," Jocasta replied. "We didn't hear or feel them coming. Tabor had a shield up around him and the princess, but he went down before we realized they were here. He never even had a chance to fight."

Her shoulders slumped, and she took a moment to clear her throat.

"I tried to help, although it was hard to know how when they seem unaffected by most of our compositions. Saffron and Kalani were together when they attacked, and Faylee was with me. They got between us, and once they started attacking the two of us as well, we couldn't do anything but run."

"Saffron told us to run," Faylee said quietly. "I think she was hoping we could get to you and bring back help. There were too many of them for us once the captain was down." She looked ashamed. "But we didn't even manage that, thanks to me."

Some of Jocasta's usual brisk tone returned as she spoke bracingly to the younger woman. "If you hadn't slipped and sent us both off that ledge, we likely wouldn't have gotten away at all. So there's no need for any self-recrimination."

"But what of Saffron? And the princess," I added as an afterthought.

"The last we saw of them, they were surrounded," Jocasta said. "I suppose it's possible they managed to run like us, but I doubt it. We only had one attacking us while they had three."

"So we must assume the princess and Saffron are both prisoners," Matthis said. "Given these Tarxi know so much more than we do about the mountains, there's no time to be lost in going after them. I still have a number of tracking compositions, so we shouldn't have any trouble tracing their path. And now we know what types of attack to focus on, we have a good chance against them."

Jocasta gave him a sharp look. "You've worked out their secret, then?"

"Hardly that." I sighed. "We've worked out by trial and error that we need to limit our attacks to the purely physical. And if I remember rightly, Saffron's physical shield also worked against the Tarxi back at my estate, so presumably that would stop them. But we know no more than that."

"They were talking to each other," Jocasta said. "I'm not as good with their dialect as Jasper yet, but I'm sure they said something about energy. I think that must be the key to their strange abilities, but I don't understand how."

"Yes, that's right," said an unfamiliar accented voice. "It is the energy."

We all jumped, whirling around as Jasper strode into the clearing, pushing a young man ahead of him. The stranger's arms were twisted up behind his back, held firmly by Jasper, but he showed no sign of resisting. His brown skin was coated in a faint sheen of sweat, as if he had recently completed some significant exertion, but he had no visible injury to indicate how Jasper might have subdued him.

"What's this?" asked Matthis sharply.

"I couldn't convince the prisoners to say a single word to me," Jasper said. "We even tried a truth composition that Elias had on him, but it didn't work any better on them than it did on the arsonist. So, since Elias and Reese didn't need my help guarding them, I decided to come after you." He looked a little sheepish, as if he knew he had gone against orders but hadn't been able to resist finding out what was going on back here.

He gave his new prisoner a slight shake. "This is one of the Tarxi. I recognize him from when I was their captive. He was heading this direction—and he claims he was coming to surrender."

"Surrender?" Matthis sounded skeptical, but it would explain why the Tarxi was submitting so meekly to Jasper who was hardly a trained fighter.

"I need to speak to you," the Tarxi said. "Who is your leader?"

"I am." Matthis stepped forward threateningly, his movement revealing Tabor's body behind him.

Jasper drew in a startled breath, and a regretful look crossed over the newcomer's face.

"I am sorry about your friend," he said. "There was nothing I could do to stop it."

"And why should we believe you care?" Matthis asked. "You and your people killed the princess's delegation and held her and our ambassador captive for days. And now you've attacked us again."

"He says they have the princess and Saffron as prisoners," Jasper quickly added. "He claims to have left the group that captured them at the first opportunity and run all the way back here."

My heart lifted at this confirmation that Saffron was still alive. But I had to restrain myself from jumping in and demanding that this Tarxi lead us to her immediately.

"Do they intend to harm either of them?" I asked, unable to entirely prevent myself from speaking.

The young man looked at me for the first time. "The princess is too valuable to them to be harmed. They hope she is their key to the Empire. And they will keep the other girl as leverage against Ardann and the princess. They are safe for now."

"Key to the Empire?" Jocasta asked. "So it's the Sekalis who are their enemies?"

The Tarxi sighed. "It is more complicated than that. I think I will need to explain it all from the beginning."

"This could all be a ploy to keep us here for a second ambush," Matthis said. "I'm not listening to any stories until we've moved out."

"I know a place," Castus said. "About halfway between here and their camp. I noticed it on our way past this morning. There's less flat ground, but it's more protected—rocks on all sides and no trees."

"Perfect." Matthis nodded. "Let's move."

After a short consultation, Alaric used a composition to carve a deep hole in the solid rock beneath the clearing. He lowered Tabor's body in and used further compositions to cover him with dirt and rocks. It felt wrong not to linger or speak some words over him, but we didn't have the luxury of time.

Somehow we managed to carry all the packs between us as well as assist Jocasta to hobble along the difficult, uphill path. When we reached the space Castus had noticed we all piled in with relief.

Alaric suggested he fetch Reese and Elias along with their prisoners, but the Tarxi protested. "If the people we left behind to distract you are still alive, then please wait until you have heard my story. I have come to ask for your assistance, and if you will not assist me, I would rather my fellow Tarxi not know of my plea. They would consider it a betrayal."

"Isn't it?" I asked.

He met my gaze firmly. "It is they who betray the rest of our people."

"I think we should let him start at the beginning." Jocasta

sounded weary after her climb. "And young man, perhaps you could start with your name."

He nodded, slipping into a cross-legged position with fluid grace. "My name is Amias, and my people are the Tarxi. And most of us wish you no harm."

"But some of you clearly do." Matthis watched Amias with folded arms and a closed expression, giving no indication he intended to sit.

I, however, folded myself onto the ground with somewhat less grace than the Tarxi. I was curious to hear his story, and my feet were sore enough already.

Amias nodded toward Jocasta. "You asked if the Sekalis are our enemy, but I suspect they do not even remember we exist. I don't think anyone does. We are the forgotten people—though once we were your cousins. And we would like to be remembered again."

"Abducting a princess will help with that," Alaric muttered.

"You claim to have come from Ardann?" Matthis sounded unimpressed.

"We came from everywhere," Amias replied. "Ardann, Kallorway, the Empire. Our distant ancestors were driven from their homes, and with nowhere else to turn for refuge, we made the mountains our own. But it is a hard life, eking out an existence on the mountain slopes. Our children meet with accident and disease, and our elderly have far too few years to grace them. Long we have dreamed of being welcomed back to the flatlands. But each generation passed down the warnings of the ones before—if we were discovered on the flatlands, we would be feared and slaughtered. And so we have remained, trapped and bound by our fear."

"You didn't seem fearful when you attacked our delegation," Jasper said, his face impassive as he watched Amias closely.

"There are some among us who have chosen to channel their hardship into anger," he said. "I do not attempt to deny it. And that faction—though they are small in number—have seized control of my people. Over the years, some have suggested rejecting our gifts altogether and attempting to hide among you as commonborn. But those who rule us now say we are mages, and that we will not live as giftless servants, subservient to those who wronged us. Those who follow them in their anger have long watched the flatlands, waiting for an opportunity to strike."

"And they saw Princess Kalani venturing out of the Empire as such an opportunity?" I asked.

Amias nodded. "Precisely. But the rest of us saw an opportunity as well. We have watched and waited for as long as they have, although we watched for a different sign. And in anticipation of such a day, I was assigned to echo their talk and win their trust."

"You're telling us you were basically an intelligencer from within your own people?" Jocasta sounded fascinated.

Amias nodded. "I believe that is the word you would use. When the news came from Ardann, it created great excitement among our people."

"What news from Ardann?" I asked, although I already had a suspicion.

"News that there was one among you who could manipulate the energy of those around you. And that this girl, this Spoken Mage as you call her, is to be accepted as a princess."

He leaned forward, his eyes lighting up. "Is it true?"

"It is true," said Jasper warily. "She is my sister."

"Your sister?" Amias turned an astonished face to Jasper. "Then that would explain why you…"

"What of the Spoken Mage?" Matthis's harsh voice cut across Amias's words. "What relevance does she have to you?"

"We are mages," Amias explained, "although not like you. Just as some in the flatlands pass down the ability to control power and some do not, so we pass down certain abilities in our bloodlines. Unlike all of you, we cannot access power—controlled or uncontrolled. But when we write—if we use the right words—we can create compositions that will manipulate energy."

"You mean you can take the energy of others? Like Elena?" Jocasta asked, her voice eager, her manner almost reminding me of Lorcan when he discovered something new. "But you say you don't use power to do it. So what? You compose with energy directly? That's why you can only manipulate energy itself?"

"That is impossible," Alaric said slowly. "Since the Battle of the Academy it has been known that the Spoken Mage can take the energy of others, but she does so with power, just like she works any other composition. And a shield to protect against power will block her attempt."

Amias frowned, absorbing his words. "So she is not quite like us then, this Spoken Mage. It did seem too good to be true." He brightened slightly. "But perhaps it is enough."

Jasper and I exchanged a glance. We knew something Jocasta did not, a secret Elena had shared only with her family and closest friends. Elena was not the only one in the "flatlands", as Amias called them, who could manipulate energy. Declan's miraculous ability to heal injuries and illnesses past the reach of any regular mage came because he worked his healings by directly gifting a part of his own energy. And it was an ability that had been long passed down in his family, although he was now the last left.

Elena and Lucas had met him in Kallorway where he was part of the rebel conspiracy against the old king. And they had maintained contact ever since. Elena viewed him as family, in a strange way, and he seemed to claim her in turn. Perhaps because Elena and Jasper were his sole remaining link with his mother—a woman who had given the very last of her life energy in composition form to Elena's parents, allowing them to conceive when previously they could not. And two such remarkable children as they had used her compositions to produce!

The more I considered it, the more parallels there seemed to be between Declan's ability and what Amias described. Declan accessed his ability with regular, written compositions, but he could use it only for the healing transfer of energy. And he could not access power at all, being essentially born sealed, as it sounded like the Tarxi were also.

I leaned forward, as eager now as Matthis was suspicious.

"So you're saying you can take energy similar to what Elena does, but directly? You didn't answer Jocasta's question."

He grimaced. "Our abilities are not as simple as yours. You all work the same way, merely differing in strength and control. But among us there are greater differences. We all use written compositions to access our abilities, but we are much more limited than you—and not just because we are only able to manipulate energy. Each family passes down only a single type of ability, and that ability varies between families."

He met my eyes. "You know some can take energy, you've seen it with your own eyes—first in the foothills with our own man, and again just today. But that is a rare gift. The most common is the ability to give our own energy. That is what I can do."

I frowned at him. That sounded like Declan's ability, and I knew the heavy cost of that.

"And what does that energy do when you give it?" I asked, trying to think how to frame my questions without revealing anything of Declan's secrets.

"Do?" He looked at me in surprise. "It gives someone else extra energy, of course. It is not the most useful of gifts but can sometimes assist those with a serious illness to keep fighting. And I would often use it to help my younger sister when we roamed too far, and she grew tired."

I raised an eyebrow. "It seems an extravagant gift."

He shrugged. "I ended up less exhausted at the end of the day that way than if she collapsed from fatigue, and I had to carry her home."

"So this energy you give comes back to you?" Jasper asked slowly, clearly thinking of Declan just as I was. "It replenishes like normal?"

Amias's brow creased. "Of course."

Jasper and I exchanged another look. So Amias's ability differed from Declan's then. When he gave away a portion of his energy, it was gone for good. But it did far more than just replenish the reserves of the receiver. He used it to work impossible healings. If Amias was telling us the truth, then this must be a separate ability from within the grouping possessed by the Tarxi. Although from his confusion at our questions, I guessed that no one with this ability remained among his people. Perhaps Declan's family had been the only ones.

"The ability to take energy explains how you attacked Tabor so easily and why his shield did nothing against your composition," Jocasta said. "But it doesn't explain why our own compositions don't affect you."

"That's a different ability," Amias said. "Another rare one. But we have one so gifted among us. She can shield her own energy, or that of another, so it cannot be touched."

A momentary silence fell as we all tried to puzzle his words out in our minds.

"Fascinating," Jocasta breathed. "We cannot sense energy, and there is still so much we don't understand about it. If shielding your energy means our power has no effect on you, then you're saying that when we use power to control another person directly—to prevent their limbs from moving, or force their tongue to speak, for example—we are interacting with their life energy. I suppose it makes a sort of sense. The mage on your team must have been supplying you all with such compositions."

The fervent light in Jocasta's eyes gave a hint of the impact this new information would have back at the Academy and the University. I could already hear the echo of heated debates as academics explored every possible nuance of this discovery.

Amias nodded to her comment about being supplied with protective compositions but seemed distracted by something else.

"You can't sense energy?" He looked between us. "None of you?" Apparently we weren't the only ones discovering things today. "So then we could have—"

He cut himself off with the briefest glance at Matthis. For a moment suspicion reared itself inside me. What didn't he want to say? But I could hardly blame him for being on edge about his choice of words—not with the way Matthis had been glaring at him non-stop.

"Elena can sense energy," I offered.

Amias smiled. "So she is definitely like us a little, then. All Tarxi can sense energy from when we are very small."

"If you sense energy like Elena can," Jasper said slowly, "then our refraining from using compositions would have done nothing to hide our presence from you."

Amias nodded. "Not to cause offense, but here in the mountains you are like noisy giants, crashing around with no way to hide."

"This might all be of interest to academics," Matthis said, "but we had already worked out how to fight you, which is the only relevance this information has to me right now. You say your ancestors were driven out of our lands. I would like to know why. And I would like to know what these leaders of yours want with the princess."

Amias hesitated, a strange shadow coming over his face. But after the brief pause, he spoke again, and his voice remained steady. "It all comes back to our abilities. Once our ancestors lived throughout the peninsula as energy mages, alongside mages of your kind. But over time, many of the power mages became uneasy with the differences in how our abilities work. They began to claim we were not true mages and should not be composing. Our leaders say they were jealous." He shrugged, a guarded look in his eyes. "I suspect they were scared. Isn't it in our nature as people to fear what is different? Whatever the cause, they decided energy abilities were unnatural, and our ancestors were rounded up and banished."

"You're saying all of our kingdoms did this?" Alaric asked.

Amias nodded. "Apparently the rulers consulted with one another and acted in concert. No one wanted to risk being the kingdom that received all those fleeing the banishment of the others."

"And so you've lived in the mountains ever since," I murmured. "This must have been a long time ago."

"Many, many generations," Amias agreed. "And, as I said, some among my people would have liked to return among you in secret. But others have always believed that if we attempted to rejoin the flatlands, our abilities would be sensed, and we would face attack and punishment for daring to leave our mountain refuge."

"How do we know any of this is true?" Matthis asked. "You portray yourselves as the victims, but that is easy enough to do when you say it was so long ago no one has any memory of it."

"It's true I've never seen records of any such banishment," Jocasta said slowly. "But we have precedent to know that records can be lost or altered. And language changes over time. Some of the older records can be difficult to decipher, at least in their subtleties."

"Have you read something that would support this history, Jocasta?" I asked.

"Nothing outright," she said. "But we know that mages have long sought ways to use compositions to increase energy—or to share it—so that individual workings of greater strength and complexity could be achieved. Much of this study has been spurred on by a belief that has long existed in academic circles—a belief that the oldest records suggest it was once possible. The general theory has been that the knowledge of how to work such compositions was somehow lost and is waiting to be rediscovered. But it is entirely possible those ancient records actually refer to energy mages—or the Tarxi as they are now known."

"Most of us long for our families to enjoy an easier life on the flatlands," Amias said. "We want to live in peace with your people and with those you call commonborns. When the news came about the Spoken Mage, we realized a new world was being formed. And we dared to dream we might have a place in it, if we could find a way to make contact with you. When our leaders saw an opportunity to capture the imperial crown princess, we saw an opportunity for one of us to provide a service to your people that would win us the chance to be heard."

He shook his head. "Princess Kalani's trip to Ardann was the first such opportunity that had ever offered. And you can imagine their shock when they captured her and discovered she was sealed, and no longer the crown princess at all."

"Why come south then?" I asked.

He grimaced. "They thought to make use of her still by bringing her down into Ardann and stoking conflict between the emperor and the southern kingdoms. They thought they might still salvage some good from the situation if they could provoke your peoples into war."

"It seems like a poorly thought through plan," Jocasta said.

Amias shrugged. "Our top leaders did not come in person to place themselves at risk. Those they sent are powerful, but thinking on their feet is not their greatest strength. They hoped they could still win favor by turning the situation for good, but when they lost the princess the first time, they saw the error of their ways. Now they wish only to avoid returning to our leaders empty handed."

"And so you wish to assist us," Jasper said.

"I hope to win enough goodwill that I might broker a deal for our people to at last return from the mountains. When you were first captured, I tried to find an opportunity to speak to you and the princess in private, but it was impossible. The best I could do in the end was to help you escape and obfuscate your tracks enough that you were able to get away."

"You mentioned nothing of having any help," Matthis said to Jasper.

He looked uneasy. "That's because as far as I knew, we had no help. But I will admit it always seemed strange to me that once we escaped we managed to elude them for so long."

Amias nodded eagerly. "That was me. You would definitely have been recaptured otherwise. And I would have stayed to help the princess escape again, but I discovered that the others intended to abandon the two we had left behind rather than staying in the area to rescue them as they had claimed was the plan. I had to come to speak to you before we passed completely out of reach."

Jasper looked up at Matthis. "It's plausible, but I can't actually confirm it."

"I can still help you rescue the princess and the other girl," Amias said. "Will that prove my loyalties to you?"

"Or perhaps you'll lead us straight into a trap," Matthis said.

I stood and faced Matthis. "We have to try. They have the princess and Saffron."

He shook his head. "Our overconfidence has led us into enough trouble already. If this boy is telling the truth, then his people will not harm the princess if we take our time. And if he is lying, then we are better off not trusting a word he says."

I leaned in closer. "We can't just leave them!"

"We cannot act rashly." He turned away, ending the conversation, and issuing a stream of instructions instead. "Alaric, go and fetch Reese and Elias. Bring them here. And bring their prisoners as well. I will send a message to Their Majesties, and we will await their orders." He strode to the far side of the small space, pulling out a composition as he did so.

I stared after him in frustration. I couldn't just sit here while Saffron was in danger.

A quiet voice spoke at my side. "I agree with you."

I glanced at Jasper whose focus was on the captain. He turned to meet my eyes, his own troubled. "We can't just leave them and wait around doing nothing. And I don't think we would be the only two to feel that way."

I raised my brows. "You think perhaps we should send a message of our own?"

"I have no means to do so," Jasper said, "but, you, on the other hand…"

I nodded. "If anyone asks, tell them I need a minute to myself and some breathing space. I'll stay in sight so they don't think I've run off rashly."

I slipped away from the rest of the group, exiting onto the path in Alaric's wake. I needed to get out of voice range of the others before I could work my composition.

When I returned to the small clearing, Jasper looked furious and Amias resigned.

"Our orders are to wait for reinforcements," Jasper told me.

I stared at him, appalled. "But that will take days."

"Yes," he said. "It will. But those are our orders."

"In that case," I dropped my voice low, "perhaps it's a good thing that you and I have a bad track record when it comes to following orders."

CHAPTER 23

SAFFRON

*S*ips of water were held to our lips, but our captors made no offer of food. The youngest of them had left—possibly on some sort of scouting mission—but the reduction in their numbers did nothing to aid us. Bound hand and foot, without weapon or composition, we had no way to overpower one person, let alone three.

Darkness fell, and they rolled out mats for themselves, but there was no question of sleep for me. The man who had carried the princess took up watch, while the other two lay down and began to snore. The watch didn't look toward us but out into the darkness in the direction they had come. Someone was definitely still alive then because they feared pursuit.

Kalani began to wriggle, an abrupt departure from her previous stillness. I strained to see her, enough light from the moon filtering down that I could just make out her shape and something of her features.

"What are you doing?" I breathed, but she shook her head at me, so I fell silent again.

I watched her closely, however, and saw the moment her hands sprang apart. My eyes widened, and I angled my body to the side, doing my best to block her from view in case the Tarxi on watch glanced our way.

I held out my own hands, and she began to work on the knots that bound me. It took a long time, her fumbling fingers seeming clumsier than usual, probably because of their long captivity.

At long last the ropes fell away, however, and I had to hold back a sigh of relief. Moving slowly, so as not to attract attention, I massaged my wrists and fingers, trying to bring them back to life.

I nearly squeaked in shock when Kalani disappeared from beside me. She moved more stealthily than I would have thought possible, creeping away from our tree. She didn't move away from the camp, however, but toward our captors instead.

When she had nearly reached them, she looked back at me, her eyes flashing in the moonlight, and gestured for me to be silent. Everything in me wanted to scream at her to be careful, but I just nodded once and began to work on the rope around my ankles. Every few seconds I cast anxious glances at the man on watch, but the snores of the others covered any faint sounds Kalani made.

Out of the corner of my eye, I saw her ease open the pack that lay at the feet of the sleeping woman. Retrieving something from it, she crept back in my direction.

I had only just succeeded in releasing my feet when she reached me. Sitting back down, she positioned herself in such a way as to shield me mostly from view, hunching down as if still bound.

I looked at the two items she had dropped in my lap. Parchment and a pen. When I looked back up at her, she nodded significantly at me.

We had seen them burn our compositions the night before. Last time they had kept any workings they could use, but perhaps they had concluded that with forewarning, we would have keyed our compositions to be used only by us. Or perhaps they feared

Kalani and Jasper had somehow got their hands on them and used them in their escape. Whatever their reasoning, this time they had burned them and then gone to sleep, confident we were helpless.

But they had forgotten that they held me instead of Jasper. They had a non-sealed mage as a prisoner, and I didn't need my stored compositions when I could write a new one. But I hesitated.

My energy was already low, and I might only have the chance to write one. I needed to make it count.

I gripped the pen in trembling fingers. If I put in too much power, it would burn through my remaining energy, and I wouldn't have the strength left to run once I worked the composition. But if I put in too little, it might run out before we could get away, and then it would all be for nothing. I could think of only one solution.

I bent over and wrote furiously, my letters large and sloppy. All that mattered was speed. When I finished and looked up again, Kalani was watching me with wide eyes. She must have been reading over my shoulder.

I shrugged uncomfortably. My approach was risky, but it was also the only way to be sure.

I waited for one of the sleepers to begin a particularly loud snore and then ripped the parchment cleanly through. Mist rose from the ground around us, growing thicker and higher by the moment.

Kalani and I scrambled to our feet, our movement now hidden in the white fog. I nearly lost my footing, and Kalani clutched at me, steadying me.

"I'm all right," I whispered. "We have to go."

She didn't let go of my arm, tugging me forward and keeping us anchored to each other as we tried to give the simple camp a wide berth.

The mist must have reached the Tarxi on watch because he

gave a loud yell. The other two came awake with curses and exclamations, but their blankets wrapped around them, tripping them and slowing them down.

I didn't need to see it happening because I could feel the power streaming out of me to animate the lengths of material. It was a strange sensation, and it briefly crossed my mind that this connection to her working must be how Elena felt every time she did a verbal composition. For me, I had only ever felt the flow of power into parchment as I sat with pen in hand. Usually, by the time I actually worked it, it was no longer bound to me.

The Tarxi who was already on his feet began to stumble in our direction, his flailing arms driving the mist around in eddies. But a moment later I felt my power connect with him, and he gave a strangled yelp as his jacket wrapped itself around his neck.

Now that our captors were distracted, their arms entangled, rocks lifted themselves from the ground and pelted through the air toward them. They were small rocks, however, and without any precise aim. I hadn't dared write the composition more specifically, and I was glad of it now because even this minor effort was draining my energy alarmingly fast.

We had been strictly warned against using such open compositions by our instructors at the Academy, and I wouldn't have considered it in any less dire circumstances. Writing your composition so that it drew on further power from you once worked, instead of using only stored power, could have deadly consequences. I had retained enough sense to write in a signal by which I could cut off the working, but if I misjudged when I used it, I could still be in danger. And if one of them hit me with the sort of draining they had used on Kalani and Tabor, I was dead for sure. It didn't matter if I was unconscious, my working would continue to draw on my power, draining my energy in the process until I had nothing left.

The Tarxi were yelling and screaming now, too distracted by the material and rocks attacking them to try to find us in the mist. Unfortunately, the lack of visibility slowed us down as well, and their noise was dropping behind us at a slower rate than I would have liked.

And every second my attack kept up, more power flowed from me, and more of my energy dissipated.

I stumbled again, and Kalani only just caught me this time.

"You need to stop it," she said, "or you won't have any strength to run. If we're fortunate, at least one of them will have taken a rock to the head by now or lost their fight to keep their airways open."

I swallowed at her gruesome wish, but I couldn't deny that our chances for escape increased if we had fewer angry pursuers. More energy drained from me, and I nodded. Chopping my left hand down through the air, I made the signal to cut off the working.

The flow of power stopped abruptly, and I swayed. Fear gripped me. I had lost more energy than I realized.

But I couldn't stop now. Already the mist was growing thin and starting to disappear. Soon it would be completely gone. And I could no longer hear angry shouts and screams in the distance.

"Come on!" Kalani pulled at me, and I stumbled after her.

We had been carried uphill, so we aimed downward, but we had little hope of remembering the exact track. I let Kalani take the lead since it was all I could do to put one foot in front of the other and follow in her wake.

I was tired. So tired. My eyes drooped. I just wanted to lie down and sleep. I reminded myself if I did that I would be captured, but I couldn't seem to muster enough energy to care. Nothing else mattered but being horizontal.

"Saffron!" Kalani shook my arm violently, and my eyes sprang back open. When had they closed?

Something sounded from behind us. We were being pursued.

"In here," Kalani whispered, dragging me between two large boulders. The gap looked too small, but somehow we squeezed through. She pushed me down into a crouched ball, the crevice behind the rocks only just big enough for the two of us.

"Why aren't we running?" I asked.

"It's a dead end. We took a wrong turning." She hesitated. "And you can't run, Saffron. You can't even walk."

Tears slipped out of my eyes. I had gotten us away, but to what end? I had used too much energy, and now we would be recaptured.

"Leave me," I said. "You go on your own. See if you can find help."

She was a princess, she should know about necessary sacrifices. But to my surprise, she stubbornly shook her head.

"I had no chance to save my own people," she said. "I will not leave someone else behind to die."

"Who said anything about dying?" I said weakly, but it was true that she was the one they wanted. Without her, would I be valuable enough to keep alive? If they were angry enough at the damage my composition had done, they might decide I wasn't.

But then they might feel that way if we were both captured as well.

"Kalani…" I tried again, but she shushed me, pointing past the boulders, and I fell silent.

Two sets of footsteps and two voices approached our hiding place. Kalani had said it was a dead end, so they must know we were here. They could take their time looking for us—eventually they would find us. From the angry tone of the unfamiliar words, we wouldn't like what happened when they did.

CHAPTER 24

JULIAN

e had so many shields against physical attack cloaking the camp and everyone in it that there was no danger of anyone noticing the power being used by the invisibility composition shielding Jasper and me.

Matthis was on watch, and everyone else slept only fitfully, so it had been a necessary measure. Even with the extra help, it was difficult to navigate our way through the tight space without stepping on someone or making any loud noises.

No one had offered Amias a mat, although we had several spare, so he sat, his back propped against a boulder. His eyes were closed, but it was hard to believe he was truly sleeping in such a position. But since Matthis threw constant suspicious glances back in his direction, I could understand why he might wish to feign sleep, at least.

When I whispered his name in his ear, he didn't immediately respond, however, and I had to shake him slightly. He started, his eyes flying open, but I spoke quickly.

"Close your eyes. You won't be able to see us anyway."

He did so obediently, and I breathed a sigh of relief.

"This is Jasper, the brother of the Spoken Mage," Jasper whispered in his other ear. "We're going after the princess and our friend, despite our orders. You said you would help, but we can't take you with us. We'd never be able to sneak you out of here. But if you have any useful information you can give us, we'll report your assistance to both my sister and the Sekali princess."

"A rescue!" Amias's whisper sounded delighted. "Excellent!" He made a slight grimace before quickly smoothing his face again. "I'm not sure how much help I can be from here, however. They took them northwest, higher into the mountains, before making a camp. You may not need to go that far, though. You and the princess were very enterprising in the actual escape last time, so she might have managed it again. I was the one to tie her bonds, and I made sure to leave the ones around her hands loose."

"What are their abilities?" I hissed. "The three who have them?"

"One can shield energy—the woman—and one can take it," he said. "That one should be easy to recognize since he's huge. The other can only give."

I grimaced. Of course Saffron's captors would include both the one among them who could shield energy and one who could take it.

"Thank you," Jasper whispered. "If we find everything as you said, we'll speak up for you."

If we make it back alive, I thought but didn't say.

We began to move away, but Amias whispered again. "Are you still there?"

I hesitated, already two steps from him. I could barely make out his words.

He said something quickly that started with Jasper's name, but I couldn't catch the meaning of it. Reaching around blindly with my arm, I managed to clap Jasper on the shoulder.

"We need to get moving," I whispered.

He seemed to hesitate, but a moment later he was moving in my direction. I let my hand drop and resumed my passage around the sleeping people toward the exit from the tiny clearing.

Neither of us spoke until we had successfully made it clear and walked all the way back to our original camp site. My composition faded, the power exhausted, as we paused in the clearing, both of our eyes on Tabor's grave.

"What did Amias say?" I asked. "At the end there?"

Jasper frowned. "It wasn't very clear, and he was speaking quickly. But something about recognizing me? He said they recognized me when they attacked the delegation, and that's why they took me along with the princess. I had been assuming it was because I'm an ambassador, but now I don't know what to think."

"Unless he meant they had been watching the Sekali court and recognized you were an ambassador," I suggested doubtfully.

He ran a frustrated hand through his hair. "It didn't sound like that. And you remember earlier he seemed excited to hear I was Elena's brother, saying something about it explaining...something. Only Matthis cut him off."

"Matthis just lost one of the men under his command," I said, feeling unexpectedly defensive of the captain. "That takes a toll. He's a good commander, but none of us came out here prepared for new abilities and all the rules changing."

Jasper hadn't done a term at the front. He didn't have any experience of what it meant to lose people under your command.

He nodded, accepting my words. "I don't blame him. He's just trying to keep everyone safe. But I'm not going to sit around for days. I remember what it was like to be the one tied up, hungry and afraid."

I didn't offer my reasons for disobeying orders, but I suspected Jasper had already guessed them.

"It sounded more like he thought I was one of them," Jasper said, resuming the earlier topic. "But, of course, he doesn't know anything about my origins or Declan, or any of that..."

"Can you sense energy like Elena?" I asked, although I was fairly sure he would have mentioned it if he could.

He shook his head. "I've never sensed power or energy or anything. Even when they had me try composing, I didn't sense anything."

I remembered those experiments. It had been back when we had just discovered Elena's ability. Jasper was still studying at the University, and I was on assignment there from the Royal Guard. They had put up all sorts of shields around him and had a healer standing by and then made him try writing something. Even with all the precautions and shielding, I had heard he nearly died before the healer swooped in and patched him up.

Had he ever told Elena? I suspected not. She would have been beyond furious.

"Have you tried composing since you were sealed?" I asked, driven by curiosity.

He shot me a guilty look. "I might have tried once. I figured it couldn't do any harm. And it didn't." He sighed. "It didn't do anything at all, of course—that's the whole point of sealing. Just words on a page. Not that I'm complaining," he added quickly. "That's a whole lot more than I used to have."

"I'm sure I would have tried it, too," I said. "I bet everyone who's sealed has." I rubbed the back of my neck. "Perhaps they're just sensing some part of Declan's mother's energy in you? Whatever it is, I'm sure Jessamine will be happy to study you to your heart's content when we get back if you want to try to work out what he meant."

Jasper shuddered. "No, thank you. I've had enough of Duchess Jessamine's study to last a lifetime."

I pulled out a composition. "I wrote a couple more of the tracking compositions. I just hope it's enough."

"There's been a lot of activity around here," Jasper said. "Let's head northwest and upward a little way before you work it."

I nodded agreement, and we moved out in silence. When I

tore the composition, a bright glow lit up the night in front of us, the marks of a number of feet all heading in one direction, although they were rough and smudged in some places with an occasional footprint going the other way. Amias, presumably. We followed the path they laid out.

Eventually the glow faded, and I had to use the second composition. We continued on for some time, moving steadily upward, when Jasper suddenly gripped my arm and pointed off to one side.

"Is that another glow over there?" he asked.

The path we were following still continued upward in front of us, but there did seem to be another glow some distance away, just within the range of the composition. We would have missed it in daylight, but in the dim of the night, it caught the eye.

"Remember what he said about how they might have escaped." Jasper had dropped his voice almost to a whisper, as if he feared the Tarxi might be lurking close.

I matched his volume. "No harm in having a quick look, at least. We can always return to this track."

I led us sideways, picking an awkward path around several rocky ledges and a protruding spur of stone. When we reached the second glow, there was no doubt the power of my composition had caught another recent path. But there was no way to tell how recent, although it looked like a number of people had come back down this way.

The steps didn't have the tight, single file look that had characterized the other path. At least one set of prints seemed to sway wildly, their owner apparently staggering more than walking downhill.

"One of them might be injured," Jasper said quietly.

My throat closed over at the image my mind supplied, and I quickly thrust it away. My feet moved of their own accord, leaping downward at a dangerous pace, following the new tracks. Jasper kept close behind me, making no protest at my speed.

The steps veered to one side, following the path of least resistance, but my heart sank as we entered what looked like a shallow gully. If they had gone down here and hit an impassable slope, they would be trapped.

Voices sounded ahead, and I froze. Reaching into my jacket, I pulled out one of my precious shields against physical attack.

"Stay close," I whispered to Jasper before continuing my forward progress.

A short way further in, I turned a slight bend in the gully and caught sight of a man and a woman. The man appeared to be leaning between two boulders, pulling at something that offered him resistance while he kept up a constant stream of unfamiliar sounding curses.

When he yelled and pulled back, holding his hand out to the woman to display clear tooth marks, she pushed him aside with a disgusted sound. Any doubt as to the situation evaporated, and I leaped forward with a battle cry.

The two Tarxi spun, too distracted by their quarry to have heard us coming. They both looked disheveled, half-dressed, and their visible skin covered in scrapes. A swelling of pride filled me. They hadn't found Kalani and Saffron easy prisoners.

Whatever the two girls had done, they had managed to send the Tarxi chasing after them without even taking the time to buckle on their swords. A fortunate circumstance for me and the longevity of my shield.

I drew my own weapon and positioned myself in front of the gap in the boulders, my shield pushing the Tarxi away as I edged around them. Once I was in place, I called over my shoulder.

"You can come out. As long as you stay close to me, you'll be shielded."

Kalani's face appeared in the gap, looking drawn but as composed as ever. "It's Saffron. She's totally out of energy. She did a composition to get us out of there, but she made it an open one."

"What?" I barked, drawing a steadying breath with difficulty. "She could have killed herself."

"I know. And now she doesn't have the strength to get out from behind these boulders let alone down the mountain."

The Tarxi had worked out I was using the type of shield they couldn't just walk through and had started picking up rocks from the ravine floor to throw at me. The shield repelled the missiles, but with every blow it must be weakening a little. I already had another shield in my hand, ready to tear the moment this one failed, but it meant I could only give half my attention to the conversation with Kalani. And eventually I would run out of shields.

The woman stopped throwing rocks and started rummaging in her damaged clothing. Eventually she found what she was looking for—a crumpled piece of parchment and a half-broken pen. She thrust them toward the man, saying something in words we couldn't understand.

"Amias said it was the woman who shields energy," Jasper said, sounding nervous. "And that the huge man was the one who takes it. Well, he looks pretty large to me."

I eyed the man who was a good head taller than me. "It has to be him. And apparently it's finally occurred to them that my physical shield will do nothing to stop him from draining our energy. They might not have any of his draining compositions on them, but that won't stop him writing a fresh one—or four."

"So what do we do?" Jasper asked.

"I try to write an entirely new type of shield," I said grimly. "And then we hope it works."

I pulled out pen and parchment of my own and crouched down on the ground. I hadn't prepared a shield to protect against energy attacks before we came, concerned about my energy levels after a long day and already needing to complete the two tracking compositions. It had been too long since I had a good sleep.

I had been hoping we could sneak in and get the girls out before the Tarxi realized we were there—a foolish dream, but it had seemed a better plan than collapsing halfway up the mountain because I'd written a composition I might not need. And one that might not even work. But I had to try composing it now.

I wrote fast, ripping the parchment only moments before the Tarxi ripped his. I held my breath as I waited. Could power hold back an attack of pure energy if it was crafted to do so? As far as I knew, no one had ever tried—not for centuries, anyway.

Another breath passed, and another, and I stayed on my feet.

I let out a sigh. "It worked."

The woman rummaged around and produced a second parchment.

"For now," I added.

I had been too distracted to keep track of what was happening with the others, but movement behind me attracted my attention. I turned in time to see Kalani emerge from the gap, dragging a half-conscious Saffron behind her. Jasper had half-clambered up one of the boulders so he could lean down and help ease Saffron through the narrow gap.

As soon as she was through, she dropped to the ground, lying flat. I fell to my knees beside her and took her hand.

"You are not allowed to die," I told her fiercely. "I absolutely forbid it."

Her eyes fluttered open, and she smiled at me.

"I'm not dying," she said, and my heart started to beat again.

"I'm just not walking anywhere either," she added, and it stuttered once more.

I glanced at the Tarxi in time to see him release the composition he had just written on the second piece of parchment. How much strength was he putting into them? And how much power did my shield need to use to repel each one? I had no way to know the answer to either question.

For the moment, however, my shield still held. But when the

woman picked up another rock and threw it at us, it sailed through the air and nearly caught Jasper in the shoulder. My physical shield had just failed.

The woman gave a shout, but I had already ripped the composition still gripped in my hand from earlier.

I met Jasper's eyes. "I don't know how long my shield against energy attacks will hold. And I don't think we want to let that one fail. I have to go on the attack, but all my shields are keyed to me. I can't give you one, and if I move away from you all, you'll be unshielded."

"What about attack compositions?" Jasper asked.

I winced. "I went through everything I have, and it turns out I favor the sort of attacks that work directly on the body. If I'd known we would encounter someone able to block such attacks, I would have made sure to have a wider range of compositions at my disposal. I can assure you I'll be rectifying that gap as soon as we get back to Corrin."

"Which doesn't help us now," Jasper said.

He glanced down at Kalani and then at the couple of pieces of blank parchment I had discarded on the ground in my haste.

"I wonder..." He stepped forward and took my place, crouching down to write. "It can't hurt to try."

I leaned forward, trying to see what he was writing, but I wasn't willing to let go of Saffron's hand, so I couldn't quite make out the words.

"What are you doing?" I asked.

"Amias seemed to think I was one of them," Jasper said. "And he said the most common ability is being able to give energy. It can't hurt to try. Amias said it was just a matter of using the right words..."

Kalani looked back and forth between us in confusion, but neither of us stopped to explain it to her.

"I thought you said you already tried composing," I said.

"The normal type, yes," Jasper said. "But that was never going to work. My access to power is blocked now, and before that, it was uncontrolled. But now I'm not trying to access my power— I'm trying to access my energy directly. Not like Elena does, like Amias and Declan do."

"Hopefully more like Amias than Declan," I muttered.

He didn't pause in his writing. "Hopefully."

"What are you doing?" Saffron tried to struggle upward into a sitting position, but she was too weak to manage it.

"Trying something desperate," I said.

The Tarxi man tore another composition, and I bent myself over Saffron, protecting her with my body in case my shield failed.

It held, but it couldn't have much power left. I felt light-headed from the amount I had poured in when I was composing it, but my reserves had already been so low.

"I need to compose another shield," I said.

"Let me try this first," Jasper said. "I can't carry Saffron all the way down the mountain, and I sure as anything can't carry you if you overdo it as well." He looked at Kalani and Saffron. "If this works, we all stick close to Julian as he launches an offensive. Got it?"

Kalani nodded, but Saffron just looked at him with confused eyes. "If what works?"

"If this composition I've just written succeeds in giving you some of my energy."

CHAPTER 25

SAFFRON

My foggy brain couldn't possibly have understood his words right. Jasper couldn't compose, and no one could give someone else energy.

He ripped the parchment cleanly in half and immediately gasped.

"Well?" Julian asked, his grip on my hand tight, tension visible in every line of his body.

"It's doing something," Jasper said. "I hope I worded it right."

A moment later something hit me, and my whole body spasmed. Julian's grip grew somehow even tighter, his face concerned as he leaned over me.

I gasped at the sweet sensation of energy flooding back into me. Impossible, beautiful, life-giving energy. I felt like I could bound down the mountain, so great was the contrast with how I had felt a moment earlier.

I contented myself with sitting up instead.

"That felt...amazing!" I shook myself and jumped to my feet. "I have energy again."

Julian swept me into an embrace, as if unable to help himself, and I lost myself in the feel of his arms around me, a sensation even sweeter than the energy I had just received. But the angry screams of the Tarxi reminded me where we were, and I pulled back.

"You didn't give me too much, did you, Jasper?" I asked. "I feel amazing."

He shrugged. "Let's hope not. I gave you half."

"Half!" I gasped. "You shouldn't have given me so much."

"Well, now we're even." He smiled at me. "I must say you look a lot more energetic than I feel. Maybe it's a side effect of receiving it. Be ready for it to wear off because you're definitely not at full reserves from what I just gave you."

I shook my head. "I'm not even going to ask how you did that."

"Good," Kalani said, "because there's no time for that." She gave Julian a pointed look. "Shouldn't you be attacking someone?"

Somewhere along the way he had discarded his sword, but at her words he started and snatched it back up off the ground.

"You all have to stay close," he warned. "Really close."

We shuffled into position behind him. It wasn't going to be easy for us to keep up with his movement, or for him to fight with us pressed so close. But we would have to do the best we could.

He lunged toward the man, who was just accepting yet another sheet of parchment from the woman, but the Tarxi stumbled back out of reach. Both his pen and parchment had been abandoned, however, and as Julian lunged again, I bent over and scooped them up. The man and the compositions he was writing to drain our energy had been the real threat. Without pen or parchment, that advantage was gone.

"Go!" I yelled at Julian. "We'll defend ourselves."

I flung out my arms to catch Jasper and Kalani, holding them back. Julian didn't hesitate, and his trust in me buoyed me almost as much as the fresh energy had done.

He pulled a parchment out of his jacket and ripped it. The power around him instantly crumpled. He had cut off his shield. It would no longer hold the Tarxi back, but that also meant he could get closer to them himself. Unarmed, they didn't stand a chance against Julian's training.

The man still fought well. He was the giant who had carried me up the mountain, and he actually managed to land a blow despite not being armed. But Julian dodged at the last minute, the fist hitting his shoulder, not his head. His blade flashed sideways, and the man went down, the muscles in both his legs cut. He howled in pain as we all ran past him.

The woman had fled while Julian fought the man, not willing to face the three of us when she didn't have a weapon. For a moment I thought our way was clear, and we would be able to run straight out of the gully, Julian leading the way. But a flash of motion above us made me scream a warning, just as a stone flew toward his head.

He flung himself to the side, avoiding it, and Kalani leaped forward. Her hand could just reach the crevice where the Tarxi woman had wedged herself, a supply of rocks at her side. The princess caught hold of one of the woman's feet and pulled with all her weight.

With a scream, the woman fell, landing hard on the ground and not getting up. Kalani brushed her hands together briskly before looking toward us.

"I think it is time to be gone from here," she said.

I fervently nodded my agreement, and we all took off at a trot. We had soon made it out of the gully, and Julian led us a short way across the mountainside to where another set of tracks glowed faintly in the distance.

"This is the way down," he said.

"We were so close," Kalani murmured.

"I should have written a tracking element into my composition," I said.

"Don't be foolish." Julian spoke sharply. "You almost died, remember. You did as much as you could with the energy you had, and it was enough."

A strange whistling sound behind us made us all pull up, looking back over our shoulders.

"Was that an arrow?" Jasper asked, just as a bright light split the night sky.

Another arrow arced toward us, but this one burned brightly, its tip alight with flames. In the light it cast I got a glimpse of the missing Tarxi, a bow in his hand and a quiver at his feet. He had been the one on watch back at the camp, and from the brief glimpse I'd seen of his exposed skin, it looked like he'd borne the brunt of my composition.

"Apparently you didn't kill him back at their camp after all, Saffron," Kalani said. "A pity."

"It's time to run," Julian said abruptly, and we all complied, half-running, half-sliding down the slope.

Another arrow came after us and another, although they seemed very poorly aimed. When a fourth flaming arrow hit a dry pine in front of us, I realized my mistake. The Tarxi had never been aiming for us at all.

The tree went up with terrifying speed, the fire jumping to the one beside it. Whereas before it had been dim, the moon and the bright light of the tracking composition providing the only light, now it was bright—too bright.

A breeze blew in my direction, and I coughed violently on a lungful of smoke. A warm, strong hand found mine, and I didn't have to see Julian's face to know whose it was.

"Run," he repeated, and we all picked up our pace.

It was hard to move so fast with my hand attached to Julian's, but I didn't let go, and twice he pulled me up when I nearly lost my balance. The fire was spreading, racing much faster than we possibly could, and the air had already grown uncomfortably warm.

We tried to keep sight of the glow of the trail, but it was hard in the burning glare of the flames. Jasper led the way, but he came to a halt when the fire leaped from crown to crown of a series of trees, jumping ahead of us and cutting off our route.

"What do we do?" he asked.

We looked at each other. We had just seen what happened when you tried to find your way through these mountains without a trail to follow. If we ended up in a dead end gully again, but with a fire at our backs, we'd all be dead this time.

"We have to go through," Kalani said, but her voice lacked its usual assurance.

Jasper looked at Julian. "I don't suppose you have…"

He shook his head. "That would be Elias's specialty. I had no idea we'd be encountering so much fire on this trip."

Now that I knew him better, I could recognize the tension behind his light words. I squeezed his hand, but the look he gave me in response was tortured. He had saved us back in the gully, but he couldn't see a way out of this. And I could tell it wasn't his own safety that worried him.

"We'll find a way," I whispered, glad that my voice stayed steady.

"Jasper?! Is that you?" A familiar but unexpected voice sounded over the crackling of the fire, sounding from impossibly high in the air.

"Elena?" Jasper's answering shout sounded half-strangled, as if he couldn't believe his ears. I certainly couldn't believe mine.

"Douse!" came her ringing voice, and water condensed from the air all around us, pouring down on the fire until nothing was left but wet ash and smoldering trees.

I looked down the trail we had been following, but it was movement above us that caught my eye. I looked up in time to see Elena float down from the air to join us. Her eyes were on her brother.

"Please tell me the princess is with you, because if not, we're going to have a real—oh, good," she said as her eyes swung over the rest of us, landing on Kalani. "I was hoping one of those veiled people was you."

"Elena can sense people," I whispered to Kalani. "And anyone who's sealed feels veiled."

"How fascinating." She examined Elena as she embraced her brother.

"But how are you here?" I asked my friend. "I don't understand anything."

"I got Julian's message," Elena said, "so naturally I came straight away. The king was assembling a team to ride straight for the mountains, but I wasn't going to wait for them. And it looks like it was a good thing I didn't. Although that fire was actually helpful in leading me to you. I've been roaming the mountains trying to pick up on any spots of energy, but the fire served as an enormous beacon and led me straight here."

Julian made a choking noise. "But Elena, I sent you that message earlier today. How are you here already?"

She looked uncomfortable, her eyes darting between us. "Do you all promise not to tell? There are quite enough ridiculous legends about me circulating already." She took a breath. "I flew."

"Flew? Like...a bird? All the way from Corrin?" I knew my mouth was hanging open, but it wasn't obeying my instructions to close.

"You all know the composition," she said. "The one where you make a platform of solid power beneath you and then direct it where you want to go. Well, I just modified it a little and told it to go fast. Very fast." She bit her lip. "And I skimmed energy from everyone I passed. Just the tiniest bit so they wouldn't feel it. But I passed a lot of people."

"I'll bet." Julian shook his head. "Only half of eastern Ardann."

"You've practiced that before, haven't you?" I said accusingly.

She laughed. "Maybe. I admit nothing."

I thought about it for a moment more. "And I bet you could make that platform big enough to fit someone else."

She eyed me warily. "If you say anything to Finnian about this, I will disown you, Saffron. There's a reason I've sworn you all to secrecy."

"I don't remember swearing anything," Julian said, all innocence.

She narrowed her eyes at him before her gaze suddenly dropped to our entwined fingers.

"Yes!" she crowed. "I *told* Coralie—"

"I knew you were going to try to claim credit," Julian muttered darkly.

I flushed and tried to drop Julian's hand, but he only held on tighter.

"But where are my manners?" Elena said abruptly. She directed a shallow bow toward Kalani. "Your Highness, it is a pleasure to find you unharmed. I believe there are a number of people nearby who are currently looking for you."

"Those would be my father's people," Kalani said calmly.

"Yes, it looked as such," Elena said dryly. "An entire delegation of them, wandering around the mountains." She didn't mention the Sekalis were encroaching on Ardannian soil, but I picked up from her expression that it wasn't an expedition that had been sanctioned by the Ardannian crown.

"I sent for them before we left Corrin," Kalani said. "Ambassador Chen was most helpful with the matter."

"I'll bet he was," Elena muttered.

I eyed Kalani, shaking my head. No wonder she had made no attempt to take control of our team earlier. She had known the whole time that she had her own people on their way to back her up. No doubt she had always intended to take charge of the situation once the Tarxi were apprehended.

"I'm glad to know that even without your valued assistance,

help was close by," the princess said to Elena in the polite tones of a diplomat.

And I had to admit, I agreed. We hadn't been as alone on the mountain as we thought we were. We had called, and our friends had answered—from both sides of the border. Knowing you had support when you needed it was what it meant to be one part of a loyal family—this was why it was worth finding that difficult balance between growing to your full potential and serving the ones you loved.

The warm hand still gripping mine reminded me that we had both birth family and the family we found. And I was more sure than ever that I wanted Julian to be part of my family forever—even if he was the son of someone I disliked as much as General Griffith. The Callinos part of my family might be surprised—even disapproving—of my decision, but they would soon see that I could be my best self with Julian at my side. I could become the kind of person who would always make them proud.

Turning, I looked up into Julian's eyes. The expression he was directing down at me made me flush, but I held my ground.

"Julian of Devoras," I said. "I love—"

I didn't get to finish my declaration because he swept me up against him and pressed his lips down hard over mine.

CHAPTER 26

JULIAN

Saffron's lips tasted just as sweet as I had dreamed. And her words still burned through me, lighting every nerve on fire. When I felt my breath growing short, I pulled back and panted out, "I love you, too," before capturing her mouth again.

Someone nearby, possibly Jasper, cleared their throat loudly. With a groan, I drew back, tucking Saffron against my chest.

"Could everyone please go away?" I said.

Elena just laughed at me. "We're actually about to get more company. So unless you want the Sekali contingent to see this charming display…"

I groaned again but stepped back a little from Saffron, my fingers finding hers and weaving through them. When I looked down at her, she was flushing so beautifully, I nearly lost all self-control and started kissing her again.

But a shouted hail brought me back to my senses. Kalani moved forward, waving regally at the full squad of robed Sekalis and their accompanying honor guard. Even here on the mountain slopes, the commonborn guards carried long wooden poles with sharp spearheads half hidden by small yellow flags.

A number of the mages broke off and trotted up the slope toward us.

"Remember," Elena muttered to us all, "no mention of the flying."

"Why did you send a message to Elena?" Saffron whispered to me as the Sekalis approached closer.

"We were dealing with mages who manipulated energy," I said. "And she's the only one in Ardann who has experience with that. Plus you were missing and in danger. We needed her here."

"That's very sweet." She stood on tiptoe to brush a gentle kiss against my rough cheek. I shivered at her touch.

The Sekalis arrived and bowed low to their princess.

"Your Highness." One of them stepped forward and bowed again. "Your imperial father will be most relieved to hear of your safety. As am I."

She inclined her head toward him. "Your well-wishes are gratefully received. You may send troops to scour the slopes above us. If he has not roasted in his own flames, you will find a Tarxi. Apprehend him. And you may also send troops in that direction." She pointed back the way we had come. "There is a gully with two more wounded Tarxi. I don't know if they yet live, but if they do, you may have them healed. They may yet be convinced to provide information and assistance to the Empire."

The man bowed low again and then issued a stream of orders that were instantly obeyed. The princess turned to us.

"Now that our enemies are taken care of, I believe there is much still to be discussed and explained between us."

She nodded at a soldier who had been lurking nearby, and he sprang forward. Removing something strapped to his back, he unfolded a small bamboo stool. Another soldier followed close behind and another, and the five of us were soon all seated in a small circle.

The sky was still dark with night, although the moon had cleared the last of the clouds and now illuminated the scene strongly. The air around us still steamed and smoldered from the extinguished fire, and a loose ring of Sekali soldiers stood just out of earshot, facing outward into the night, their spears poised and ready. It was by far the strangest meeting I had ever attended.

I looked at Jasper. "You'd better tell them about the Tarxi. No doubt you can remember what Amias said word for word."

Jasper explained briefly to Elena about our initial encounters with the Tarxi, and then gave a detailed recounting of our interaction with Amias. I could see in both Saffron and Elena's faces that they instantly made the connection with Declan, although neither of them mentioned him in front of the princess. No doubt we would discuss later the fact that apparently the Kallorwegian kings had deemed one family of energy mages too valuable to be banished with all the others.

I admitted Jasper's and my direct defiance of orders, and then Saffron jumped in to explain what had happened to them. Elena gave her a stern look when she heard about the open composition, but she was soon distracted when Saffron got to our rescue.

Her eyes flew to Jasper, and for a moment she couldn't seem to find words.

"You're a mage, too?" she finally whispered.

"Well, not a regular one," he said. "I'm still sealed, so I can't access power—a good thing, since I could never control it. But… yes, I guess I'm one of this new type of energy mage."

Elena beamed at him. "But that's amazing!" She hesitated. "And you get your energy back?"

"I think so." He glanced at Kalani. "That's how Amias described it."

Elena didn't look entirely relieved, but neither could she keep a grin from periodically spreading across her face. Did she feel less alone now to know that it wasn't just her and Declan who could manipulate energy? Did she feel less of a curiosity? She had confided once that she felt out of place sometimes, even in her own family. But now her brother was a commonborn mage as well.

Of course, as Spoken Mage, Elena was still utterly unique. She didn't access energy the way the rest of the energy mages did, which meant she could use her abilities for so much more. But she knew another piece of her background, at least. That had been significant to her in the past.

We quickly caught her up on how we had ended in the middle of a raging fire, and then I paused before looking from her to Kalani.

"It appears so far that everything Amias told us is true. And he obviously did loosen your ties before he ever came to us, Your Highness, that's how you escaped. Jasper and I assured him we'd put in a good word for his people with both of you. I think we at least need to meet with them. Now that we understand their abilities a little better, it should be easy enough to use a truth composition to be sure that those who want to come back really are peaceful. They're not immune to our compositions unless they're specifically shielded."

Elena's eyes glowed with interest. "I wonder what that feels like," she said. "When you sense someone who's shielded that way, I mean. Will it be like the veiling for those who are sealed?"

"I didn't want to say anything before," Jasper said hesitantly, "but I think I can sense energy now too. It's the strangest thing. But it's like I can tell all four of you are sitting right there, even if I close my eyes."

Elena grinned at him. "That's how it happened for me too. I couldn't sense energy until after I did a composition with it for the first time."

Kalani looked thoughtful, not seeming to pay attention to their conversation.

"Will you take their request to your father?" I asked her. "Do you think the Empire will help them?"

She considered for a moment. "Twice now this Amias has

assisted me, although I didn't realize it on either occasion. I am honor-bound to carry his request for him. And if they are truly our cousins, outcast all this time, then I think they will be welcomed home."

It was a pretty answer that glossed over the more complicated aspects of the situation. But then the emperor had been ready to claim Elena and Jasper as Sekalis due to distant ancestry when he had decided they would be of use to his empire. It was entirely possible Kalani was right, and the same would apply here.

I glanced at Elena, who gave a fleeting grimace. "Obviously I'll make their case to King Stellan, but I couldn't guess as to how he'll react. There's a lot going on in Ardann right now already."

"All we promised is that we would speak on his behalf," Jasper said. "But I hope we can find a place for them somewhere."

He exchanged a loaded look with his sister. It was no longer an abstraction for them. Jasper's discovery about his own ability had proven that in some twisted way, the Tarxi were their people, too, through Declan.

Kalani stood. "I must consult with my mages. You may tell Captain Matthis that we will be ready to meet with him and the Spoken Mage in the morning." She gave a respectful bow to Elena.

Turning toward me and Jasper, she gave another half-bow. "Thank you Ambassador Jasper and Julian of Devoras for your assistance. My family will not forget your efforts on my behalf."

We all scrambled to our feet and returned her bows.

She looked at Saffron last of all. "And you, Saffron of Callinos. I will not forget you."

"And I won't forget that you wouldn't leave me, Your Highness," Saffron replied. "I mean to keep my word and come visit your lands as soon as I can."

"We will be ready to welcome you..." She looked from Saffron to me. "Both of you, perhaps."

I bowed again, and she swept away to where her people were waiting, three tired and dirty Tarxi in tow.

"You have my blessing, of course," Elena said to Saffron and me in a grand voice as soldiers appeared to retrieve their stools.

The four of us from Ardann all started down the track which was somehow still glowing faintly.

Jasper snorted. "I don't think they need *your* blessing, Elena."

"Ah, but you're forgetting." Her eyes twinkled at us. "As of Midsummer, I'm now officially the highest-ranking member of the Devoras family. Julian, you can be sure I'll let your father know that I've already given the family approval to the match."

Saffron let out a sound that was half-squeak, half-stifled snort.

"Thank you, sister," I said. "Your approval is most gratefully received. Now if you'll give me a moment, I might actually get the chance to talk to Saffron about whether I have *her* approval."

"What?" Elena stared at me reproachfully. "You mean you haven't done that yet?"

I cleared my throat significantly and glared at her, and she giggled. Grabbing Jasper's arm, she dragged him ahead of us down the mountain, giving us a small cushion of space.

I glanced down at Saffron who looked shyly away.

"I'm sorry about all of that," I said. "That's not how I was going to talk to you."

She bit her lip. "I was the one to basically throw myself at you back there, remember. And in front of everyone, too. I don't know what came over me. I don't want you to feel obligated just because everyone…"

I held up a hand to halt her flow of words.

"I'm going to have to stop you right there. There's no question of obligation whatsoever. And I certainly hope you don't feel any such thing. I love you, Saffron of Callinos, and I want to spend the rest of my life with you. I'm rather hoping, given the way you kissed me back, that you might feel the same way."

I grinned down at her, and her embarrassed look returned.

"If you're not sure," I said, "we could try it again, and you could see what you think a second time."

She swatted at my arm. "I think I've made it perfectly clear how I feel, and any more such displays can wait until we have a moment in private."

She gave me a warning look, and I subsided with a chuckle. I only hoped such a moment came very soon.

"But, yes," she said in a more serious tone. "If that was a proposal, I accept."

"It was," I said swiftly. "Although apparently I'm bad at them." I looked down at her. "Did you mean it back there with the princess? You'd like to go to the Empire? Because you know I've already been assigned to do a posting as an ambassador at their court. But I know how you feel about your family…"

"I love my family," she said. "And I wouldn't want to be away from them forever. But I think it's time I stretched my wings a little. I would love to travel to the Sekali capital as the wife of an ambassador."

She looked at me with a trace of nervousness in her eyes. "But when your posting is over, I might want to join the growers. Would you object?"

"Of course not," I said promptly. "If you're willing to travel all the way to the Empire for me, I can hardly object to spending half the year traipsing through the muddy fields of Ardann for you."

She giggled. "I'm sure it's not that bad."

"That's true. You'll be sister-in-law to a princess, you know. You can probably arrange for a prime position assigned to the palace gardens."

She bit her lip. "Is it bad that I would actually like that?"

"Not at all." I stopped so I could pull her into my arms. "You'll have all the gardens your heart can desire. In fact, you're going to love the gardens in the Empire."

Her eyes brightened. "Maybe there's some way I could join the growers before we go, even. I used to think I could never aspire to a position at the palace, but you heard what Jocasta said —and even Amias said something similar. This is a new world we're building, and it's not purely about strength anymore. The crown sought out a Seeker from a minor family, and a discipline head gave a senior position to a minor mage. And now there are energy mages. I've always worried so much about disgracing my family because I'm weaker than the rest of them, but maybe that doesn't matter so much anymore. If I stop worrying and holding myself back, who knows what I might end up achieving. I could learn so much in the Empire and bring it back to Duchess Annika. I could earn that position at the palace garden instead of being handed it by Elena."

"An excellent idea," I said. "And that will be Aunt Annika to you soon enough."

She squeaked and buried her head in my chest. "Are you related to everyone?"

"Not at all. Just Elena and every single Devoras. But some of them very distantly."

When she showed no sign of re-emerging, I gently eased her head back and looked down into her eyes.

"You will be an excellent grower, Saffron. And a brilliant Callinos. And an outstanding Devoras. And I'm sure you'll make an even better wife."

I pressed my lips down against hers, gently this time, savoring every moment. She responded, and I pulled her closer, the kiss deepening. But I could feel myself slipping under, so I broke the connection with a groan.

"We're standing on the middle of a mountainside in the early hours of the morning," I said. "And my adopted sister is somewhere ahead of us, probably looking back up here and taking credit for everything right now."

Saffron laughed. "You know she once offered to set me up with Calix."

I growled and tightened my arms around her. "Calix can keep his hands off you."

She giggled and wrinkled her nose. "As if I would ever have been interested in Calix!"

I loosened my hold and grinned down at her. "I'm very glad to hear it. I don't mind my brother competing with me for our father's approval, but I have no interest in him attempting to compete with me for the girl I love."

"There's no fear of that," she said. "And anyway, I'm perfectly ready to tell anyone who asks that I'm yours."

"I like the sound of that," I said, a bit of the growl still in my voice. I lowered my lips to hers again, but she pulled back.

"We really do need to get back to the others." She gave a little sigh which I tucked away to savor later.

"Very well, then," I said. "Let's go and shock our sleeping camp. Can you imagine what they're going to say when we stroll back in with you and Elena in tow?"

I tugged her along, picking up speed. "Come on. We don't want to miss out on the fun."

SAFFRON

To say our arrival back at camp caused surprise was putting it mildly. I could tell Captain Matthis wanted to reprimand Julian and Jasper for disobeying orders, but he didn't dare do it with Elena there. Especially not when they'd successfully rescued the princess and restored her to her people.

The presence of the Sekalis in our mountains obviously caused him some consternation, however, and he disappeared for some time to send a message back to the capital.

"Does the king actually know you're here, Elena?" I asked her.

"I'm sure he does now," she said. "I told Lucas what I was doing, of course."

I shook my head. "King Stellan told you not to come with us! I heard him myself."

"That was different. We had no idea what was going on back then, and we even feared it might be some sort of Sekali diversion. The messages from Matthis and Julian changed everything."

I raised an eyebrow. "Let's hope the king sees it that way." I hesitated. "You really do approve of Julian and me?"

"Of course!" Her face held nothing but delight. "I've been planning it for months."

"Months?"

"Well," she amended. "It might only have been weeks. Certainly since graduation."

I shook my head. Elena had always been incorrigible.

"How long ago graduation seems," I murmured. "Will things ever stop changing?"

She sighed. "It would seem not."

The four of us managed to grab a few hours of sleep before we were roused from our mats to go join the Sekalis. Elena sidled up to Jasper as soon as we started moving to tell him his energy levels looked normal enough given our terrible night's sleep.

"They're certainly not as low as last night—and more than half."

She didn't explain the significance of that, but I understood her meaning as well as Jasper did. He hadn't permanently given me half his energy, as Declan would have in the same situation.

I think I felt as relieved by that as Jasper did. I wasn't sure I could have lived with the burden of knowing I had taken something so essential from him.

We stopped at our previous camp site on the way past, and both Kalani and I paid our respects to Tabor's grave. The princess's mask, which had seemed to loosen a little the longer we traveled, was back in full force, but I thought I detected true sorrow in her eyes.

It took us some time to get all the way back down into the foothills. The two groups traveled together, but remained separate, the Sekalis keeping hold of their three prisoners, and Matthis keeping a close eye on our two, as well as on Amias who he had reluctantly allowed his freedom.

I was reminded of my certainty that Kalani had always meant to take charge of the Tarxi. With Elena here, she made no attempt to claim Captain Matthis's two prisoners, but we were equally unable to claim the three held by the Sekali mages.

Amias stuck close to Jasper and Elena as we traveled,

peppering them with questions, and explaining to Jasper more about how his ability worked.

"It might not operate exactly like yours," Elena warned. "We're an odd pair. My ability is certainly not like anyone else's."

Amias showed great interest in Elena and Jasper's family and their lack of ability, but the two kept their lips firmly shut on the matter of Declan and their strange history. I suspected they wanted a chance to talk to Declan before they told Amias or his people about the Kallorwegian's existence.

Mostly I listened, but occasionally I asked some questions of my own about Amias's ability in particular. A thought had taken root in my mind, and while I didn't want to encourage myself to indulge in false hope, the idea continued to grow. Traditional mages—power mages, as the Tarxi called us—could do nothing to help my mother because they couldn't replenish someone's energy. Even Elena couldn't do that.

But Amias could. And apparently many of his people could as well. And they did it without the permanent sacrifice of Declan. That didn't mean they could heal energy sickness, of course. My mother didn't need a short-term gift of someone else's energy. But there was potential there. And if the energy mages settled in Ardann, perhaps some of them might find their way to my uncle's estate to work and study with the healers. It was no guarantee, but it was more hope for my mother than I had ever had before.

The mutual fascination between the Tarxi and the rest of us made the journey go quickly, although I was starting to long for a proper bed with far more passion than seemed reasonable.

When we finally reached Julian's estate, we found it was already half-full, with two entire platoons of soldiers camped among the buildings. The Sekali soldiers pitched tents as well, while the mages and our own group of travelers were accommodated inside the main mansion.

I hadn't expected to meet my future father-in-law again quite so soon, but he awaited us inside the entranceway. And when we saw who stood at his side, it explained both his presence and that of the eighty soldiers. King Stellan himself had come to visit the general's home, his son with him.

Elena rushed straight into Lucas's arms, and the two conferred quietly, heads bent together. The king gave her a somewhat disapproving look but spoke only his welcome. Apparently if there were to be reprimands, they would be done in private. Understandable, I supposed, now that she was part of the family.

Princess Kalani and her mage contingent were greeted formally, although the king unbent and warmed significantly when the head mage delivered a long greeting from his own ruler. The emperor's message was full of gratitude for the care Ardann had shown to his daughter and apologies for sending his people into Stellan's lands so precipitously.

Once the various greetings had all been exchanged, the Devoras servants streamed forward to lead everyone to their rooms. We would reconvene over the evening meal, apparently, in the great Devoras banquet hall.

King Stellan waved Matthis over, however, gesturing for him to join him wherever the king had set up headquarters in the mansion. No doubt he was eager for a full debriefing. Lucas and Elena trailed behind them, still talking quietly, and I trusted that between Matthis and Elena, the royals would learn everything they needed to know about the situation and the Tarxi.

With everyone dispersing, I thought I had escaped any immediate introduction, but Elena paused just before she left the entranceway, looking back with a wicked glint in her eyes.

"Oh, Father, I nearly forgot."

General Griffith eyed her with something like wariness in his eyes. Elena didn't call him father often or without a point.

"Joyous news," she continued. "Julian is betrothed. I have

given them official Devoras approval, but I'm sure you will wish to bestow a father's blessing as well."

"Julian?" The general swung around to stare at his son. "Betrothed?" His eyes latched on to me at Julian's side, and I called on every bit of my Callinos pride and duty to stand tall and unflinching beneath his scrutiny.

Julian gave Elena an exasperated look before stepping forward. "Yes, Father. I intend to marry Saffron of Callinos."

Griffith glanced back at Elena, now disappearing from view with Lucas, and then at the two of us.

"Saffron of Callinos," he repeated, saying the words slowly as if testing out how they sounded. "I see."

I could feel Julian holding his breath, and I wished I could tell him not to worry. I was strong enough to withstand anything his family might say about me or our match. I had changed up in the mountains, and I no longer thought of myself as the weak Callinos. I was a Callinos, and that was what mattered. My family loved me, and they would have reason to be proud of me as well. As would my new family.

But the general made no derogatory remarks. He merely looked me over again and gave a single nod.

"Tell me, Saffron, did you have a chance to join a discipline before the interruption to our Midsummer festivities?" he asked.

"I didn't," I said. "But I intend to join the growers at the first opportunity."

"The growers?" He looked pleased at that news. "An excellent choice. Annika is Julian's aunt, you know."

I nodded, pleased that my selection of a Devoras-led discipline had made such a favorable impression. It certainly hadn't been in my mind when I decided that I enjoyed helping new life sprout and grow.

"It's been a tiring trip," Julian said. "I should show Saffron to her room."

"Yes, of course," the general said, and then as an afterthought, "congratulations to you both."

I murmured my thanks and hurried away as quickly as politeness allowed.

"I underestimated her," Julian said, awe in his voice. "What brilliant wisdom my father showed in adopting Elena into our family! What foolishness on my part to oppose the plan. Why, it might be the most excellent decision my father ever made."

I laughed, all my overwrought emotions spilling out in the chuckles until my eyes ran with tears. When I recovered enough to talk, I patted his arm.

"I can take a bit of criticism, you know. I won't wilt."

"I know you won't. I just hate to think of my family not appreciating you."

"They will have to learn to do so," I said firmly. "As my family will have to learn to accept a Devoras."

"Oh ho! So my introduction to the Callinos clan will not be all smooth-sailing?" He seemed to relish the idea. "Shall we send Elena in first to prepare the way?"

"Don't!" I held up a hand to stop him. "Or I'll start laughing again. I really do need a chance to freshen up before dinner, you know."

"Very well, then." He slipped his arms around my waist and stole a kiss. "But I don't care how many important people we have at the table, I'm having you next to me."

I let him steal another kiss before disentangling myself and escaping into my room. Leaning my back against the closed door, I took several long, deep breaths. It seemed I was to be accepted into the Devoras family with minimal fuss after all. My previous worries, so consuming at the time, seemed insignificant and hard to understand now.

I would join the growers and learn to nurture green life. I would travel and see the Sekali Empire and bring back new knowledge for my discipline. I would make my family proud, regardless of my strength. And I would do it all with the man I loved at my side.

EPILOGUE

ELENA

The Grayback Summit, as it later came to be called, took most of us by surprise. Amias presented his people's case to both Princess Kalani and Ambassador Chen—who had also been waiting for us at the estate—and to King Stellan. Both took several days to consult with their advisors—or in Kalani's case with her father, through Chen.

Amias had willingly submitted himself to both a Sekali and Ardannian truth composition, and both rulers had accepted that the Tarxi were divided into two groups. The peaceful majority wished to escape their leaders' dreams of vengeance in favor of improving their families' lives, while the violent minority wished conflict and vengeance on the people of the flatlands—despite the current generations having lived their entire lives without knowledge of the existence of the Tarxi.

At the end of the three days, the Sekalis and the Ardannians presented their offers. The emperor offered to accept every Tarxi who would swear under a truth composition that they intended no harm to the Empire or its people. But they would be separated, the various family groupings scattered throughout the Empire's vast populace.

Amias had spent much of the three days with Jasper and me. As well as training Jasper, he and I had studied each other's ability with equal interest. He was a good-natured young man, quick to laugh and smile and full of stories of his younger sister. I liked him, and I knew Jasper did too. He had come to feel like some long-lost cousin, and when I heard the offer made by the Empire, I felt certain he and his people would choose Ardann.

King Stellan offered that in exchange for oaths of loyalty to his crown—made under bindings of power—he would carve them out a small territory of their own, a protectorate within the borders of Ardann where they might live together in peace and largely govern themselves.

I had expected Amias to defer his answer until he had an opportunity to return to his people and consult with them, but he assured us that he had been empowered to make a decision on their behalf. He didn't deliberate long before he publicly accepted the Sekali offer.

I watched him, shocked, as he profusely thanked King Stellan for his generosity and assured him of his desire that the Tarxi remain in close kinship with Ardann despite their new life as children of the Empire. When Chen asked if he needed to return immediately to his people to take them the news, he said it wasn't necessary.

"They have been secretly packed and ready since the moment I left them," he explained. "I sent a message as soon as the princess was rescued the second time. My people are already on their way out of the mountains. I will travel back to the Empire with you and then north to meet them at the base of the Graybacks."

"How did you send a message so far?" I asked, still fascinated by the various uses they had found for their limited abilities.

"It was a pre-arranged signal," he said. "I sent some of my energy to my sister. She is so familiar, that I can do it across any distance. When she felt my energy hit her, she knew I was telling my people we had found a safe haven, and they should descend from the mountains. We do not want to waste any time."

Later I confronted him in private, though. "I had hoped to have you and your people closer," I admitted. "So we might continue to learn from each other."

He had agreed, most readily, but said the safety of his family had to come first.

"Those we leave behind in the mountains have been so twisted by their anger and bitterness that they cannot accept any path forward but that of hate," he said. "They will turn their backs on the promise of change and a better life so they can continue to nurse their dreams of violence and power. And that small group will see the rest of us as traitors. As much as we would love to stay together, in a land of our own, free to interact and trade with the whole flatlands, such a situation would make us a target. Spread throughout the Empire, we have a better chance of staying safe. I know this is what my people would choose if they were here."

I promised him my support, if he should find himself in need of it, and he did the same. While I might regret his decision, I could understand it. I knew what it felt like to know your family was in danger and to be desperate to see them safe again.

In private I asked Lucas if his father was greatly disappointed by the Tarxi decision. Whatever threat our distant ancestors had felt the Tarxi posed seemed inconsequential when weighed against the value of mages who could pool their energy. I knew firsthand what feats could be accomplished by a mage who had access to more than a single person's reserve of energy. And soon, with the help of the Tarxi, other mages with much greater technical knowledge and skill than me would be able to begin experimenting with the same thing.

But they would not be Ardannian mages, as I had hoped.

"It's complicated," Lucas said, which seemed to be the answer to everything when you were a royal. "On the one hand, their ability could bring great advantages, and many in our kingdom would love the chance to explore it further."

I rolled my eyes. "You mean Lorcan and Jessamine are positively desperate to study it."

He grinned at me. "Of course I do."

"But that wasn't enough."

He sighed. "No. Our kingdom is already undergoing great social turmoil—that's the reason my father couldn't offer them a place within our populace. Our society is splintering and remaking itself, and placing any more strain on that process might cause the whole thing to collapse. We cannot ask the people to accept a new, and possibly dangerous, ability among them when they are already stretching their capacity to accept new and different."

He reached forward and pulled me against him. "Besides, we already have you. And now Jasper. We are not entirely without mages who can manipulate energy."

I wrapped my arms around his neck while frowning at his words. "But we're only two people."

"Two of the most powerful, though. You aren't Tarxi, remember."

I sighed, accepting his words. "I hope Declan won't be too disappointed. I haven't even had a chance to get a message to him about it all yet."

"He can always travel to the Empire to meet them. All our borders are open now." Lucas ran his fingers softly down my cheek, only half focused on his words. "The Empire was already stronger than us, and the Tarxi are few in number. This won't change the balance of things enough to put Ardann in danger."

"That's good," I murmured, distracted by his touch and forgetting what I was replying to. I leaned into him and gave a soft groan. "Remind me again why we have to wait until Midwinter for the wedding?"

"Because that is the way of royalty. I don't like it any more than you do. I am more than ready to call you my wife, Elena."

~

His words echoed in my mind now that the day had finally, finally arrived.

I stood outside the double doors of the ballroom, waiting for the moment of my entry. We had chosen to be married in the ballroom instead of the throne room, and I had to admit that the deep red and gold looked stunning for a winter wedding. I had crept in earlier, before any of the guests arrived, to take in the decorations. I suspected I would be too distracted to properly enjoy them when the doors opened for the ceremony.

Impossible white and gold flowers draped everything, lending a fresh look to the red velvet runner and curtains and the floating gold chandeliers. The blooms were no doubt created with power and would wilt and die within a day, but for now they filled the room with beauty and a gentle fragrance.

The same white and gold blossoms, mixed with striking red roses, made up my bouquet, which draped so low it brushed softly against the ground when I held it. I would have thought it extravagant at any normal occasion, but it fit the moment.

My attendants were arrayed behind me, ready to adjust the enormous train of my white lace dress as needed. They all wore deep red and carried posies of white and gold. My eyes lingered on Clemmy. Her eyes were enormous, seeming to consume half her face as she tried to take in every second, but she looked so grown up alongside the older girls. She was no longer a child, though my mind kept forgetting it.

She clung close to Coralie who looked radiant, as did Saffron. Free from the constraint of royal tradition, Coralie had been the first of us to marry—with both Saffron and me as attendants. But

Saffron hadn't been far behind. She had looked gorgeous, everything about her glowing as she walked down her own aisle to stand at Julian's side. It hadn't been a state occasion, as my own wedding was, but the guest list had been illustrious enough with both bride and groom coming from the household of a discipline head.

I had watched all the Devoras attendees closely, but nothing had occurred to cast the slightest shade on the happy day. I suspected Saffron had been the last person to realize she was someone of significance in the new Ardann.

Seeing the joy on Julian's face, and the way he couldn't take his eyes from his bride, had filled my heart to bursting. I still had no more than a truce with Natalya, my first adoptive sister, but I had been delighted to embrace Saffron after her wedding ceremony concluded and call her sister. Back when I signed the official papers, I had never dreamed that becoming a Devoras would bring me family members I could love.

Both the new brides kept giving me soft looks and little happy sighs. They had already assured me many times that I would have a wonderful day and adore being married. They certainly did.

Finnian had taken a little convincing where Julian was concerned, but Saffron had found a new layer of strength and confidence up in the mountains, and she soon had her cousin brought into line. In fact, I suspected the two men were growing to actually like one another, and when Saffron and Julian were in Ardann, the two couples spent an increasing amount of time together.

Sometimes I envied their freedom a little. But whenever I looked at Lucas, I remembered that no sacrifice was too much. And with every begrudging step our kingdom took toward change, I remembered who I served and why they were worthy of the struggle. I regretted nothing about this day.

And, in truth, I wasn't the only one with responsibilities. Finnian and Coralie were resident at his father's estate, training to be healers, and Saffron and Julian had already taken up their posting at the Sekali court. My soon to be father-in-law had intervened on Saffron's behalf, since she had gone to the mountains at the request of the crown. An exception had been made to the usual rules around joining a discipline, and Saffron was now officially a grower, on assignment to the Sekali Empire.

Privately I knew she was doubly excited to spend time at the imperial court because Amias and his family were there. Together they were working with the imperial healers in their spare time, studying what effect the Tarxi might be able to have on energy sickness—a blight on the Empire just as it was on the southern kingdoms.

Saffron and Julian had traveled here especially for my wedding, bringing Kalani along as part of the delegation. The Sekali princess was another of my attendants, positioned beside a young girl a similar age to Clemmy. The slightly terrified looking girl was the younger sister of Kallorway's new queen, and she had barely said a word in my presence since we were first introduced. But it didn't matter if she liked me or not. She was here to represent that the war was over and that our two kingdoms had a future together, and it was a message I embraced whole-heartedly. There had been enough bloodshed for many lifetimes. It was time to sow peace.

I had fought for my final three attendants, but I was the bride —and the Spoken Mage beside—and I had prevailed. Araminta, Leila, and Dariela would also walk with me down the aisle. As my officials, they had all dedicated themselves to both me and Ardann, and they deserved to be at my side now.

With all eight of them, every part of me was represented fully: Ardann, the Empire, and Kallorway—each owning a piece of my history—and commonborn and mageborn of every type—great families, minor families, and the sealed from all corners of society. All of them had pieces of my affection, and all of them had a place in the future I was helping to forge. I wanted everyone to recognize that fact today as I both joined with the love of my life and was crowned a princess of Ardann.

But when the doors opened, all such thoughts fell away. Chairs lined the long room in neat rows, leaving only the aisle in front of me clear. The throng all leaned forward, straining for a glimpse of me, but my awareness of them faded as my gaze locked on Lucas.

Even across the distance, I could feel the fire of his gaze and the depths of love beneath the flames. I had put a great deal of thought into the politics of the day, but now I could let all that disappear and be a bride like any other.

I caught a glimpse of the smiling faces of my family, tears running down both my mother's and Clara's cheeks, but I couldn't focus on anything but Lucas for long. He drew my eyes back to him over and over, their magnetic pull sucking me deeper and deeper.

Our wait was over. We would finally be joined together, and I dared anyone to try separating us again.

I reached the end of the aisle, unsure if I had walked or floated down its length.

"You are almost too beautiful to endure," Lucas whispered.

The official conducting the ceremony began to speak, and all too soon we were exchanging our vows. When it was over, the crowd screamed and cheered, yelling for a kiss, and Lucas obliged, his touch soft and full of promised fire at the same time.

"I will always love you, Elena," he murmured, for my ears alone. "My wife."

"And I will always love you." I smiled up at him, trying to put my heart into my eyes. "You have made me too happy for words."

Thank you for continuing to explore the world of Ardann with me. I hope you've enjoyed getting to know some of Elena's friends and family a little better. To discover what happens when Elena's daughter is sent to the Kallorwegian Academy, and to explore the rediscovery of energy mages, read my Hidden Mage series, starting with Crown of Secrets.

To be informed of future releases, as well as Spoken Mage

bonus shorts, please sign up to my mailing list at www.melaniecellier.com. You'll find an exclusive bonus chapter of Voice of Power—retold from Lucas's point of view—in the welcome email, as well as several other bonus chapters freely available on my website, including one from Saffron's perspective.

And if you enjoyed my Spoken Mage series, please spread the word and help other readers find it! You could start by leaving a review on Amazon or Goodreads or Facebook or any other social media site. Your review would be very much appreciated and would make a big difference!

Sekali Empire
Greyback Mts.
Torcos
Ardann
Kallorway
Brenton
Corrin
River Aresta
Kingsley
Kallmon
River Chekov
Alakira

ACKNOWLEDGMENTS

I didn't initially intend to write a companion novel for the Spoken Mage books, but once Elena suggested Saffron and Julian might be a good match, the idea began to worm its way into my head. Power of Pen and Voice has also been something of an experiment for me—my first time writing a book where the hero and heroine alternate points-of-view. I enjoyed trying something new, although I'm undecided as to whether it's a format I would do again. Pen and Voice is also the first book I completed after an extended period of severe illness, so it feels like a triumph of creativity to find myself productive again.

I'm so grateful to my family who saw me through both the illness and the intensive writing that followed it. Marc, Adeline, and Sebastian, all my books belong to you as well.

My team of beta readers have all—for various different reasons—been unusually busy, so I'm especially grateful to Katie, Rachel, Greg, and Ber, who still found time to provide feedback. And, of course, my developmental editor, Mary, who had to show even more flexibility for my timeline than usual.

The same thanks are due to my copyeditor and proofreader who went beyond expectation on this occasion. And thank you to Karri, my cover designer, for making my first cover that includes both members of the couple on the front. I love that it looks unique while still incorporating elements of the other Spoken Mage covers.

I wonder what we will think when we look back on 2020 from the future? It certainly won't be one of those unremarkable years that blends into the tapestry of our history and becomes hard to separate out in memory. All I know is that in the midst of so much uncertainty and change, I am grateful to be able to cling to an unchanging God, as I am grateful that he continues to fuel my creativity, despite everything.

ABOUT THE AUTHOR

Melanie Cellier grew up on a staple diet of books, books and more books. And although she got older, she never stopped loving children's and young adult novels.

She always wanted to write one herself, but it took three careers and three different continents before she actually managed it.

She now feels incredibly fortunate to spend her time writing from her home in Adelaide, Australia where she keeps an eye out for koalas in her backyard. Her staple diet hasn't changed much, although she's added choc mint Rooibos tea and Chicken Crimpies to the list.

She writes young adult fantasy including books in her *Spoken Mage* world, her *Mage's Influence* world, and her various *Four Kingdoms* and *Kingdoms of Legacy* series that are made up of linked stand-alone stories that retell classic fairy tales.